POLLYWO⬦ **S0-AQP-671**

3 MINE STREET

FLEMINGTON, NEW JERSEY 08822

(201) 782-6500

NO PLACE TO HIDE . . .

Dizziness threatened to overwhelm him, and Ben felt an unexpected fear of falling. The floor had sunk away an inconceivable distance. He seemed to be perched on a tiny platform twelve feet in diameter and at least a hundred feet above the base. Suddenly, he noticed something strange was happening.

The air mysteriously thickened. The room about him darkened and disappeared. In the now-dense air above the platform, shapes like the three-dimensional images of the Gray-fur's pictures were struggling to be born.

The four beams still reached out to touch Ben's skull. Fear, then terror—then panic was being stimulated in him by the beam. Ben found himself crouching, turning to look for a place to hide. But there was no place, no place at all . . .

He had come to an alien planet to conquer—now all he wanted to do was survive!

PUBLISHER'S NOTE: This novel was originally published in 1965. In the intervening years the author has found portions of the novel which he believed could be improved; and so, he has rewritten these sections for this edition.

Also by Gordon R. Dickson
Published by Ballantine Books:

THE DRAGON AND THE GEORGE

MISSION TO UNIVERSE

Gordon R. Dickson

A Del Rey Book

BALLANTINE BOOKS • NEW YORK

A Del Rey Book
Published by Ballantine Books

Copyright © 1965, 1977 by Gordon R. Dickson

All rights reserved under International and Pan-American
Copyright Conventions. Published in the United States by
Ballantine Books, a division of Random House, Inc., New
York, and simultaneously in Canada by Ballantine Books of
Canada, Ltd., Toronto, Canada.

Library of Congress Catalog Card Number: 76-56760

ISBN 0-345-30654-6

Manufactured in the United States of America

First Edition: March 1977
Second Printing: October 1982

Cover art by Rick Sternbach

To Lester del Rey,
Craftmaster in the Mystery of Story-smithing.

MISSION
TO
UNIVERSE

□ CHAPTER 1 □

BEN SHORE WOKE——and the long interior of the barracks-like building around him was still, moonlit dark. For a moment on waking he could not remember where he was. He lay motionless, waiting for memory to come back to him.

He had come awake suddenly, automatically, and ready for action, as was his habit. Now for a moment he hung halfway between sleep and wakefulness, waiting for everything he had forgotten to catch up with his abruptly roused body.

It came back, all at once, with the solid, body-blow impact of remembering a crime, planned, but yet to be committed; and he stiffened on his cot as if one of the men sleeping around him had jumped up without warning to shout accusingly at him.

Then the first shock passed, leaving behind it only the steady feeling of emptiness, bleakness, and determination he had felt first after the decision two days ago. It was settled and done. With the muscle of will power built up over the eight years now since he had first made up his mind that the phase ship must be built, he shoved the present emptiness and the rest of it into the corner of his thoughts, out from under foot. He turned his attention to the coming day. There were only hours left, and everything still to be done.

He rolled over on his side and picked up the small alarm clock from the pale new wood of the floor. In the moonlight, the sharp black hands pointed like daggers at sixteen minutes to four. He pushed in the unnecessary alarm button before it went off, as he had set it, at fifteen minutes to the hour. He got up on one elbow, looking down the room.

The double row of cots running along it were filled with sleeping men, all the way to the dark end that was the wall of the latrine. In the long wall opposite him, the cold, distant full moon shone brilliantly as a spotlight through the bare, glass panes of the windows over the row of cots opposite him. The moon's rays passed above those cots and the dark center aisle to paint at last false windows of light, half on the upper half of the cots on his side, half on the wall behind him. Above these false windows, the wall at Ben's back and the windows in it were dark. The night coldness of these northern latitudes in September struck through the thin wooden shell of the uninsulated wall. But the air bathing Ben's face and neck and hands was hot.

Just over his cot, a muted, heated roar came steadily from the blower like a giant's continuous outbreathing in an endless rushing breath exhaling toward infinity. For a second, his half-awake state moved in Ben to give birth to the wild idea that it was the unstoppable breath of time itself, breathing on them all, blowing the whole tense, overarmed world forward to nuclear self-destruction. He jerked his mind back from that notion and looked down the double row of cots to the far dark wall at the end. It was pierced by a rectangle, the fine-as-if-pen-drawn line of yellow light outlining the door to the latrine. At right angles to that was the inset block of darkness in the opposite long wall that was the door to the unborn day outside, waiting for him. Ben threw back the blankets and sat up on the edge of the cot.

The floor was cold to the bare soles of his feet. For a moment, sitting up, he had felt a little dizziness, a light-headedness from lack of sleep. That was not right. It had been only yesterday—no, he corrected himself—it had been the day before yesterday, that he had ordered everyone up here from the underground site fifteen miles away. In that forty-eight hours or so until now, he had only had the three hours of sleep just past. So the dizziness was justified. All the same, he could not afford it. Later, he would have all the time in the universe

to sleep. Now—he reached into the dark wooden stand
by his cot, fumbled out his kitbag of toilet articles and
towel, and got up, heading for the latrine door.

The old, hastily laid floorplanks creaked slightly under his feet as he moved down the center aisle between
the sleeping men. Guilt flooded back into him without
warning. He had a sudden self-image of himself creeping between their unsuspecting bodies like a traitorous
captain. Once more he stiff-armed the feeling from him.
With fifty nations standing armed and ready at each
other's throats, it was no time to play at self-reproach.
But it had wakened another ancient doubt and worry to
plague him. He was determined to go through with it.
But, how would they—these men he thought he knew
well, and the women, too—how would they react to it
when it was too late to change anything?

Quietly, unobtrusively, over the past six months, he
had tried to weed out the nervous ones, the fearful, the
unreliable among both the men and women. For that
matter he had tried to weed out the women entirely, but
that had not worked. He thought those that were left
now could be counted on. But was he right?

He looked at the faces not hidden by darkness—the
faces of the men on his left, caught in the pattern of the
moonlight, as he passed them. Now, on this last morning, even if they didn't know what was coming, if there
was a weakness in any of them, certainly, keyed-up as
he was, he should be able to see it. He stared at the
lean, high-schoolish face of Ralph Egan. It was young
but serene in the moonlight. He moved on, to the dark,
unyielding black face of Matt Duncan. Matt, he knew
he could count on. He moved on . . . Kirk Walish,
half-bald in the moonlight. Hans Clogh, his plump face
relaxed, his clever mathematician's gaze hooded in
sleep. Julian Tyree, his Jamaican face as dark as Matt's,
but smaller-boned, more secret and withdrawn. . . .
These three were all older men. Physically, they should
be all right, but there was a certain hardening of attitude that came with age, a loss of the ability to adjust . . .

Cooper Malson, sprawled out on his stomach, the
long length of him with his brown hair tumbled in his

eyes. The youngest among the men. But his reflexes of body and brain were unmatched. He could adapt, but would he have the stability that a few more years would have given him? Ben came at last to the two final cots in the row touched by the moonlight, and paused.

These, who would be his seconds-in-command, he must at least be able to count on. And certainly he could, after the years of knowing each of them. If he knew anyone, he should know these two. And still . . . this final morning the moonlight fell on their sleeping faces and seemed to mock him, challenging him to recognize them in the pattern of cold light and lightless shadow.

Ben's own shadow fell black between the two cots and touched both of them. The moonlight passed through all the distance of space and night and through the windows to slide over his shoulders and illuminate the sleeping men. Lee Ruiz was on Ben's left. Walter Bone on his right. The moonlight fell on both their faces and showed them with a difference.

Their upper bodies and faces were revealed by the light. Their lower parts were in darkness. The small personal elements of their faces were stripped away, leaving only light and shadow.

In these cold abstract patterns of black and white, Ben looked without success for the men he had known—Lee for eight years, Walt since high school. These two, Lee and Walt, were the ones who had actually created the phase ship—Lee, the technical master, Walt, the theoretical genius and originator of the field of phase physics he himself had developed. Ben had only imagined the ship, had forced it into being, had directed its making. After four years of the three of them working together, though, certainly Ben should recognize them—even in the moonlight!

But he could not be sure now. The pattern of light and dark seemed to have aged Lee, on Ben's left. Lee was made old and savage. All his good looks were drawn down to the skeleton shape of his skull, as if by prolonged suffering, and the platinum chain holding the crucifix around his neck looked like the burnt-in black halter scar of some ancient slavery.

Beside Lee, Walt Bone seemed no longer even living. His massive-boned, sleeping face, topping the giant's body under the covers and the darkness, stared straight up from the pillow, motionless as the face of a stone god. The illumination fell white on the broad bones of his brow and cheeks and powerful, jutting jaw. It left darkness pooled in the deep sockets of his eyes, in the grim cleft of his chin, and along the straight line between his closed lips. The shape shown by the moonlight looked no more mortal flesh than the metal of the Nobel Prize medal, contemptuously pierced and fitted with a chain to serve as vest-pocket counterweight to the eighteen hundred dollar pocket watch lying beside it among the small change atop Walt's cot-side stand.

All the thoughtfulness and searching of the man Ben had known on and off these long years was wiped out by the light from space. What was left was the carved, closed mask of some ancient tyrant or prophet.

Mask and mask, the two men slept side by side. Slave and tyrant—and Ben knew neither of them. Walt, least of all. The coldness of the floor against his bare feet ran suddenly up his legs in a shiver, up his spine, and spread out in a band of tight coldness across his shoulders. Suddenly he was certain that, alone among all the men and women of the phase ship crew, Walt had known all along what Ben was planning to do.

Ben shook it off. He turned to the latrine door. He went across the few feet of dark-floor still remaining and through it, leaving only a furtive flash of light into the dark sleeping chamber behind him. Three steps down and his bare feet touched the even greater coldness of cement floor. Light dazzled at him from the white enamel of the wash basins and stools, the wall-long mirror above the basins.

Ben put his toilet bag on the shelf below the mirror and above the last wash basin next to the showers. To his own eyes, under the fluorescent lights over the mirror, his own square face looked back at him, brutal in appearance and incapable of weaknesses. Once he had hated it for refusing to mirror the questioning and doubts he felt inside himself. Now, he was grateful for that failure. Without needing moonlight, he wore a mask.

When he stripped off the tee shirt and shorts in which he had slept, his lean, tall, still hard-muscled body looked pale in the mirror from the two years spent mostly underground. He walked naked into the shower area and turned on the hot and cold taps of the first shower together. When the spray was warm enough, he stepped under the showerhead. What had felt lukewarm to his hand felt hot to his sleep-cold body. As soon as he began to revive, he turned the water up, warmer. With the heat that was soon sending steam smoking about the galvanized metal walls of the shower stall, the ghosts of strangers and doubts withdrew and he began to come alive.

The ordered needs of the day now starting pushed aside his lightheadedness from the lack of sleep and moved like disciplined soldiers into the forefront of his mind. His thoughts ran ahead to the meeting with Marsh Otam, the Washington liaison man, and to the daylight, and began planning the order in which the necessary things would have to be accomplished. His problem-solving mental machinery, which had come floating free out of the endless universe of sleep, now touched earth once more, put on its armor, and took up its tools of battle. He faced the coming day and left the shower.

Five minutes later, shaved and dressed in work slacks, shirt, and worn brown leather jacket, he stepped out into the chill, still-dark morning. The wind blew cold against his fresh-shaven cheeks and chin.

The sky was paling slightly. The sun would be up soon, but for now the camouflaged buildings of the surface installation and the distant hillock that was the phase ship itself, in disguise, were blocks and lumps of darkness. He stood looking about at them for a moment, then turned and walked across the short distance of gravel, pounded flat by the tractors and trucks, and went softly up the five steep, narrow wooden steps to the door of the women's barracks. He opened the door and stepped quietly inside.

The women's barracks was an older building and there was a phone just inside the door, against the wall. He lifted down the handpiece and dialed the message center, back at the underground installation. While he waited for the message center to answer, he looked around at this other, long sleeping room.

Here, it was exactly as it had been in the men's barracks, except that half the long room was empty. The blower was on here, too, and the warm air felt harshly hot on his face and hands after the coldness of his brief walk outside. In the shadow of the closed door, holding the phone and waiting, he looked at the women of the phase-ship crew. They slept more quietly than the men, those he could see in the moonlight, and they were smaller under the blankets.

But the moonlight, mixed with the creeping dawn, marked them also. In the moonlight, farthest off of those who were visible, Polly Neigh's face looked small under its dark hair against the pillow. One bed closer, Tessie Sorenson slept, relaxed and younger than he had ever seen her. Closest, Nora Taller's strong beautiful features under her black hair looked strangely lonely in the stillness. Ben felt his own loneliness echo inside him at the sight of hers.

The phone buzzed. A small voice spoke from it.

"Message Center. Waller speaking."

Ben put the handpiece to his mouth.

"Ben Shore," he said softly. "Any sign of Marsh Otam's plane on the radar yet?"

"Just a few miles out. Coming in for a landing now," said the voice.

"Good. Tell him to take the rail car through the tunnel to the Surface Installation here, as soon as he lands. Say I'll be waiting for him—he'll know where."

"Right."

"Oh," said Ben. A thought had occurred to him. "If his plane's pilot wants to take off again right away, ask him please to wait."

"Right."

"That's all then." Ben hung up the phone. He looked at the sleeping women for a second more, turned, and went softly out of the door and down the steps. On the gravel he paused. The moon was fading in the face of the brightening horizon opposite. Still, it was not yet day. It would be ten minutes or more before Marsh could get here.

He turned away from both barracks and walked slowly up a little slope toward the camouflaged phase ship and the end of the Installation.

Small, hooded lights gleamed at the corners of the buildings he passed. A row of windows was alight at the back of the mess hall and in the infirmary. The combined Installations' two doctors would be getting ready to give the phase-ship crew the medical examinations he had ordered for them before breakfast. Under the combination of faded moonlight and brightening sky, Ben glanced at his watch again. Its black hands stood squarely on ten minutes past four. He walked on until he came out at last between two large buildings, stopping above a field of late wheat and only some forty yards from the hillock that was the camouflage dome over the phase ship.

From this came a few stray twinkles of yellow light, the sound of voices and of heavy objects being shifted on surfaces of cement or metal. Loading should be nearly complete.

He looked away, out over the field of wheat. At first glance it was only a vaguely moving carpet of darkness, but as he stood watching and the minutes ran slowly away, the dawn brightened until he could see just the ripe heads of the grain making up the texture of its surface.

The cold breeze of morning moved across that surface. He could trace the wind's passage in the small extra darkness here and there where the graintops bent before the invisible pressure of the moving air. He felt the breeze himself on his hands and face and throat, filling his lungs coldly, outlining the heat of his clothed body with its chill; and suddenly he imagined all the moving ocean of air above the world.

A deep and desperate feeling moved in him. He imagined the stony metallic bones of the earth under his feet, the depths of the oceans, light and dark, river and lake, season shifting into season, all the life of this planet on which he had been born and of whose substance he was made, flesh and bone, molecule and atom. The feeling moved deeply in him. The muscles of his shoulders ached and he reached down suddenly, in between the gravel that came to its end with the edge of the Installation, here, and took up a handful of plain dirt. He clenched it in his fist with all the muscle of his arm and held it there. For a moment he felt rooted in the world himself, like a stone, or tree.

"—Ben?" said a harsh, and somewhat breathless voice behind him.

He turned, letting the dirt fall. A shadow came at him from out of the shadow between the two buildings behind him and stepped out into the growing daylight to show itself to be Marsh Otam, back from Washington on schedule. As Marsh came close, the pale light left darkness in the lines of his middle-aged, heavy-boned face so that he looked older by ten years or more than his forty-eight years. He was no more than average height, half a head shorter than Ben, and shrunken further by weight and fatigue.

"Yes," said Ben.

Marsh halted before him, holding a package in his hand.

"Don't know why you wanted me to meet you here," he said. His breathing was heavy in the stillness. The suit he wore bulked out of press and rumpled.

"There may be some highly secret orders in what you're carrying," said Ben.

"There isn't." Marsh handed the package over and wiped his forehead with the back of his hand as Ben broke the seals on the package. "Save yourself time, Ben. I know what's in there. Oh, you got the military ranks you asked for. Everybody's commissioned in the

Air Force. Copies of the order in there for all of them. You'll have two captains, Bone and Ruiz. You're a Brigadier General, yourself. The gap's so you can promote now and then to give the illusion things are still happening."

Ben sorted through the orders and extracted a long envelope, also sealed. It was addressed to Brigadier General Benjamin Allen Shore and was of some light shade impossible to make out in the dawn light, not white but close to white, and of heavy, rich paper. Seals were impressive on it.

"Look if you want, now," said Marsh. His voice was harsh and throaty. It seemed to be always on the verge of breaking out into angry argument. "Just something to keep everyone happy."

"You've read it?" Ben said. "You know what's in it?"

"I don't have to," said Marsh. "You expect too much of the man, Ben. He's President of the United States, not God. Four billion people in the world now, and they all want to live. So we've got fifty nations with gigaton bombs and all ready to shoot the first time anyone sends up a toy Fourth of July rocket. It's not his fault."

"Someone has to make a move," said Ben, breaking the seals on the envelope.

"No," said Marsh. "It's no use, I tell you. Everybody's under the ax, and everybody wants to live. So, it's a world gone paranoiac as the psychologists say. Saying it doesn't change it. Nobody dares disarm, nobody dares attack. We all sit waiting for the accident— for the pin to drop. Test-flying this phase ship would be the pin, Ben."

"No," said Ben. "Radar can't see us if we make one big jump to orbit position. We don't go from here to there. We stop being here and appear there." He was unfolding the pages inside the envelope. "I tell you, Marsh, it's a matter of breaking a stalemate. Just let us loose to find one livable planet—."

"Ben! Ben, will you stop it!" said Marsh, harshly and wearily. "How many times have you told me? How many times have I told them down in Washington? It's no good. Eight years ago you had me convinced, and I thought it was good. But it's no good now. It's eight years worse. The people want to live, Congress wants to live—even the President wants to live. Oh, he'd give you the order if it were just his own neck, but in one week word would leak, the country would blow up, and then the world would blow up!"

He stopped. Ben, who was reading the pages, could not see the older man's face.

"Face it, will you, Ben?" Marsh's voice said. "It's too late. All your bright ideas about the world coming to its sense when it finds out the phase ship's in space, the idea we can find new worlds—it's all a dream. It never was anything but a dream, and it never would have stopped the way things are anyway—"

He broke off. Ben, now done reading, looked up, refolded the sheets, and put them back into the envelope with exaggerated care.

"What is it?" Marsh's voice was suddenly sharp.

"It seems you're wrong," said Ben. He was making a great effort to speak calmly, but inside him his heart was thudding with steady, slow blows in his chest. "I've been ordered to take independent military command of both Installations here and test the phase ship."

Marsh stood absolutely motionless, looking at him. The light had brightened, and the lines on his face no longer caught darkness. Instead his whole face looked washed-out, gray, and old.

"Ben—" he said. "Ben—"

Ben put the envelope into an inside pocket of his leather jacket.

"If you'll wait a few hours before heading back to Washington," he said, "I'll have something to send back with you." He took a step away from where he was standing, but Marsh flung out a hand and caught hold of a leather-jacketed arm to stop him.

"Ben," said Marsh, hoarsely, "that message didn't say anything like that."

Ben pulled his arm loose.

"I'm sorry, Marsh," he said. "It did. I've got to go now, there's a lot to do."

He took another step away and Marsh's voice stopped him.

"Ben!" The voice rattled. "Ben, let me see that message!"

"I'm sorry, Marsh," said Ben, without turning around. "It comes under the regulations of military security now. I can't show it to you."

He turned and walked away, leaving Marsh behind him. He came to the camouflage of the hillock hiding the phase ship and lifted a flap of canvas to go through it.

Inside, in a shallow concrete well, was the seventy-five-foot long egg-shape of the phase ship. Workers were still busy loading cartons of freeze-dried rations aboard it. He went down the concrete steps to the floor of the well, across to the loading ramp, and up through the entry airlock to the inside of the ship. Inside, he walked down the short, echoing, close-walled metal corridor to the Crew Chief's quarters in the center of the shop.

There he sat down at a desk in the office half of the quarters and pushed the call button on his desk phone. The screen above it came alight with a lean, tired face under close-trimmed hair.

"Message Center. Waller speaking," said the face. "Oh, Ben."

"Jim," said Ben. "This is an official call. Both Installations as of now constitute a single military Command under authority delegated to me by the Congress and the President. I've just now got the orders. My rank is Brigadier General, and other ranks will be given later. But as of now this Command by my order to you is put in a condition of strictest security. No planes and no personnel, including the plane on which Mr. Otam just arrived, are to be allowed to leave. No outgoing calls will be allowed. All incoming calls to be taken and handled under conditions of strictest secrecy concerning the change of these Installations from civilian to military authority. You're to act as if we were still under ordinary conditions and civilian control."

He paused.

"You understand?" he said, looking keenly at Waller. A week since, he had arranged things so that it would be Waller who would be on duty at this hour—now he counted on the intelligence and perceptivity of the man. Waller's slightly sunken blue eyes stared at him from the screen for a second.

"Just one question," said Waller, slowly, after a moment. "Ben—I mean, General. Am *I* in the military and under your orders, now?"

"That's right, Jim," said Ben. "I'll tell you about your rank later." —It was an innocent lie though the commissions were only for the crew of the phase ship. "And we'll publish the orders. Meanwhile—."

"All right," said Waller. "All right—General. I'll handle things the way you say. Is that all?"

"That's all," said Ben. He punched off the phone, then punched it swiftly on again. "One more thing. This office I'm calling from, here on the phase ship, will be my headquarters for the moment."

Waller nodded. Ben punched off again. He looked up and was suddenly aware of one of the loading crew standing in the doorway of his office, staring at him.

"Mr. Otam's at the airlock," said the man. "I told him no one was allowed in—"

"That was right," said Ben. He looked narrowly at the man. "You heard what I was saying on the phone just now?"

The man nodded.

"Then you understand the new situation here," said Ben, evenly. "What about Mr. Otam?"

"He wants to see you. Can he come in and see you?"

"No," said Ben. "No, he can't see me." He looked again at the crew member. "I'm going to give you an order," he said. "Find someone else on the loading crew, and the two of you take Mr. Otam to one of the empty staterooms on the ship here and keep him there until you get further orders from me.—Can you do that?"

The man hesitated.

"Yes," he said.

"Don't worry," said Ben. "Mr. Otam won't give you

any trouble. That's why I said take two of you. Go ahead, then."

The man turned and left. Ben sighed and leaned for a moment on the desk with his elbows and rubbed his forehead. He was mildly surprised to find, when he took his fingers away, that they were damp. He felt shaky inside and in need of coffee.

He reached out and switched on the screen's connection to the receptors outside the camouflage dome. He wanted one more last look at the wheatfield and the unbroken horizon stretching toward the dawn. It came on the screen. The sun was not yet up, but a bright band of daylight stretched above the wheatfield. Far off, black against it, a V-shaped flight of gray Canadian geese headed south like trailing dots of movement.

The sight of them raised his spirits. He was reminded that they made the trip every year, putting their individual lives at stake, but they had to make it—or else the race of geese would not go on. He felt the urge to wash his hands and get down to work. He looked down at them on the table. The fingers of the right hand were still damp from his forehead. The fingers of his left were still stained with dirt.

□ CHAPTER 2 □

"EXCUSE ME, BEN," said Lee Ruiz, then checked himself "—or should I be saying *sir*?"

It was a seriously put question, Ben saw, as he looked up from his desk to see Lee in the doorway of the crew chief's office. Lee, like the rest, had been informed of his new commission and captain's rank, directly after the early morning medical inspection and before breakfast. Like the rest, Ben saw, Lee had been made self-conscious by it. Ben was tempted to grin at his friend of eight years, to put him at ease, but stopped himself in time. His grinning days, he thought soberly, were over. In charge of the phase ship now, his authority was linked to his impartiality and isolation from the others.

"Not yet," he said, unsmiling, grateful again for the hard mask of his face. "What is it?"

"Well . . . the ship's team . . . I mean the crew," said Lee. Two weeks back Ben had ordered the change of title for the group that would move and handle the phase ship, but old habits stuck. "There's a lot going on. That is, a sort of rumor that this isn't just another simulated, full-dress takeoff—but a real one. Can I ask. . . . is it only another simulated takeoff?"

Ben, out of the loneliness of his new authority about to say no, checked himself just in time. Plainly—he looked at the tanned, pleasant piratical face of Lee—some of the crew had put Lee up to asking this. He would not have been so demanding on his own. Lee, Ben remembered now, was the man he had picked to be his pipeline to the crew—it could not be Walt, with his computer-like self-sufficiency. To use a pipeline, you had to keep it working.

15

"It isn't," said Ben. He watched as Lee's face lit up and added, "We're taking her up into orbit in a single jump."

He saw Lee gazing at him, teetering on the edge of a temptation to ask what would come once they were in orbit, and deliberately kept his own gaze forbidding and uncommunicative to block the question.

"Thanks," said Lee, turning away. "Everybody's going to be glad to know we're moving at last."

He was going out the door when Ben remembered something.

"Oh, Lee," he said. "Will you see if someone can find me a pair of scissors?"

Lee looked back over his shoulder, puzzled.

"Scissors?" Lee said.

"Scissors."

"I'll—I'll see," said Lee, and went off, still plainly trying to fit scissors, somehow, into the fact that they were finally going to test the ship.

Left alone, Ben remembered to look at his clock on the desk. It was almost 8:00 A.M. He thought again of coffee, which he had never got around to having—or breakfast. The crew would be on board the ship, now, and somebody could bring him some—he suddenly remembered that he had also forgotten to send the imprisoned Marsh Otam, to say nothing of the men who were guarding him, any breakfast. He was reaching for the phone button when Nora appeared in the doorway, holding a pair of scissors.

"Lee said you wanted these." She brought them to his desk. Ben realized that, since Nora was the Stores Officer, as Lee was Equipment Officer and Walt was Navigation Officer, he should have asked Nora for the scissors in the first place.

"Thanks," he said, taking them. He looked up into her calm face, curious to rediscover the traces of loneliness he had seen on it, or thought he had seen on it, when she had been sleeping earlier this morning during his phone call from the women's barracks. But he saw no signs of it now.

"Oh, Nora," he added, "I seem to be asking for things

from all the wrong people this morning—but Marsh Otam is locked up in one of the staterooms with a couple of the loading crew standing guard. —No, don't ask me why, please. But, would you see if you can find him and have the guards turned loose and Marsh sent in to me here?"

She took it calmly.

"Right away," she said. She went out. Like all the crew members, she was wearing the white coveralls that were their uniforms aboard the spaceship—somehow, thought Ben, watching her back as she left the office, she looked smaller in them than he usually thought of her as being.

He picked up the scissors and took up the envelope containing the pages he had read before telling Marsh that the ship was ordered on a test flight. The second page was a duplicate. The first was signed by Walter Eugene, President of the United States, Commander in Chief of the Armed Forces of the United States of America.

He read it through again:

To: Brigadier General Benjamin Allen Shore and officers of Phase Ship Mark III:

You are hereby ordered to hold yourself in readiness to take off on any training flight that later may be ordered. It is hoped that before long you may one day leave the surface of our Earth and even the vicinity of our solar system to find and claim a world habitable by the human race. Indeed it is hoped that the day may soon come on which there may be no misunderstanding as to the aim and purpose of such a flight and on which the latitude and freedom of your search may be unlimited. This is the earnest hope of this nation and, I know, of all peoples of the world.

Meanwhile, pending that day, you are hereby ordered to prosecute your work upon the phase ship itself until it may be capable of a safe search, if necessary to such ultimate limits of space and time as the outermost reaches of the physical universe and for a voyage of forever and a day. For I promise you that the time is coming in which we will so search all systems within reasonable range of our own before accounting the search a failure and returning with such a new home for our human race unfound.

Walter Eugene

PRESIDENT OF THE UNITED STATES OF AMERICA

Ben laid the second sheet aside and spread the first out before him. Taking a pencil from the desk, he began going through the lines of print before him, crossing out sections of it. When he was done, he read it through again and then picked up the scissors and took a sheet of blank typewriting paper from a drawer of his desk.

He cut narrow strips of white paper from the blank sheet and fastened them with transparent tape over the sections of the page he had lined out with pencil. Then he ran the censored message through a copier on his desk, making two copies. The copies showed a mutilated, but understandable, text. He was just putting the copies away in his desk when the loading crew guard ushered in Marsh.

"Thank you," said Ben to the guard. "That's all. You can leave the ship now. Close the door, will you?"

The man went out, closing the door. Marsh dropped heavily into a chair facing Ben's desk. He looked shambled and broken.

"I'm sorry you didn't get any breakfast—" began Ben. Marsh's hand, lifted and dropped, showed what he cared for breakfast. He sat slumped in the chair, hardly looking at Ben.

Ben reached for an official envelope and a desktop sealing machine. He put one of the duplicates of the censored message into the envelope and began using the sealer on it, actually heatbonding the special paper of the envelope together under the large blue seals affixed by the machine.

"Ben," Marsh's voice was hoarse but steady. "Let me see that message."

"I'm sorry. No," said Ben. "But I'm sending a copy of it back with you."

He passed the now blue-sealed envelope across the desk into Marsh's hands. Marsh sat turning it over and staring at it.

"Ben," he said. "Don't go."

There were two patches of red, like stage makeup standing out against the gray skin surrounding Marsh's cheekbones. Watching this man, whom he also had known for eight years now, Ben felt his inner self, his bowels of compassion they would have said with biblical flavor two hundred years ago, twist with pity and a little disgust. Then the disgust evaporated, and he was only sorry for Marsh.

"Marsh," he said, as gently as he could, "the world isn't going to blow up."

"It's not *that* I'm afraid of," said Marsh. "I'm not afraid of dying—even if I'm still a young man." He raised his eyes suddenly to meet Ben's. "Did you realize that, Ben? As politics goes, I'm a young man. I've got twenty more years to aim for one of the top jobs."

But he would never make it, thought Ben, watching him. He had been close enough to politics these last eight years to see that it was no different from other professions. In the end, the top positions went to the men who had proved themselves unstoppable. Walt, with a Nobel Prize for science in his twenties, was such a man. It made no difference that Walt had won that prize before he was thirty. If somehow he had not won it then, he would have won it before he was forty—or fifty—eventually. It was the men only death could stop that ended up in the top positions. Marsh's twenty years would do him no good.

"What is it you're afraid of then?" Ben asked.

"You know." Marsh's eyes were red and rimmed with creases, staring at Ben. "I'm afraid of what you'll find, out there."

Ben stared at him. "You've been seeing too many monster movies."

"Yes, but this isn't movies!" Marsh's voice went up and he leaned forward, putting a thick-fingered hand on the outer edge of Ben's desk. "Ben, a hundred trillion stars, a hundred trillion suns in the galaxy. A billion of

them maybe with planetary systems—there has to be
something out there, alive, out of all those possible
worlds where life could be, that can do something to us
worse than we ever imagined. —If we let it find out
we're here."

"Yes," said Ben. He sat still behind his desk.

"Then . . . don't go."

"Wild geese have hunters waiting for them too," said
Ben.

Marsh stared at him.

"I don't understand . . .?" Marsh said.

"The wild geese and other migratory birds have to fly
south regardless, Marsh!" said Ben, letting his voice
sharpen, as the other man opened his mouth to speak
again. "You'll have to go now. We're about to take off.
—I've phoned the message center to give clearance to
your plane and pilot."

Marsh's fingers loosened, lost their grip on the desk-
edge. He slumped back in his chair, then slowly heaved
himself up out of it, clutching the blue-sealed envelope.
He turned and walked toward that door of the office
leading to the women's side, the corridor, and the airlock.

"Goodby, Marsh," said Ben.

Marsh did not answer. Opening the door, he went
out.

Ben cleared his desk and got to his feet. As he did so,
there was a buzz and the red-colored one of four different colored lights on his desk lit up. He paused to reach
over and press the "receive" switch on his desk intercom.

"Ship sealed for takeoff," said Walt's deep voice.

"Thank you," said Ben. He let go of the switch,
which flipped back up into "off" position, and went out
through the side door at the right of his desk into the
curving corridor on the men's side of the ship. He
walked down past the corridor with the series of doors
to eighteen roomette-type "staterooms" on his right and
the wall of the Control, Computer, and Observation
Sections beyond it on his left. The doors of some of the
staterooms were open, but no one was in them. Follow-

ing the curve of the corridor around, he came to the Lounge-Dining room at the front of the ship and saw most of the off-duty people there.

He nodded at them, followed his casual tour of inspection around and down the other side of the ship, with the women's staterooms this time on his right-hand side and the wall of the Operating Sections on his left. There were only ten staterooms on the women's side, which accounted for that number of women in proportion to the eighteen men in the crew. Not that the designers of the phase craft had intended any such thing— or Ben, himself, in the beginning, four years before. The present crew, or team, as they should rightly be called, had never been intended actually to take the phase ship far into space. Their job was merely to work the bugs out of the individual jobs aboard her as the ship was developed, and then give place to an all-male crew of trained astronauts.

Remembering this, Ben came to the end of the women's staterooms, passed the corridor leading to the airlock by which he had entered the ship four hours earlier, and came up against the wall of the topside storage room. All other storage, together with the phase drive units and the recycling equipment, was in the lower half of the ship, which was divided horizontally by its single main deck, above which were all the rooms he had just been inspecting.

Having completed his tour, Ben turned back up the corridor, walked back around to the front, or Lounge point of the ship, and turning his back on that single large room, entered the door to the Observation Section.

"What's going on—some kind of game?" he snapped. Kirk Walish and his second, Jay Tremple, were out of the seats before their comparison-scopes, and standing in the doorway to the Computer Section. It was true that here on Earth, jumping to a fixed and many-times previously calculated position in orbit about the world, and with even the shutters closed on the large observation port over their head, there was nothing for them to do. But they were on duty, as the first of four teams that would hold down this Section around the clock in space, and now was as good a time as any to start cracking down.

They ducked back to their seats, and Ben walked on through the now unobstructed doorway into the Computer Section. The three here were all in their seats, though at this moment only one of them had anything to do—and that was to be alert for the moment of shift. But then, that one was Matt Duncan, team chief of the first computer team. He looked up at Ben from his traveling tapes, giving the shifting position of this point on Earth's surface relative to the theoretical centerpoint of the galaxy, second by second.

"Holding," he said.

"Thanks, Matt," said Ben, and stepped on through into the final, Control Section.

This tiny room held Cooper Malson, at his single control instrument, keeping Matt's figures reconciled with the equally, but normally more predictable shifting point of their destination. Standing behind Coop, looming expressionlessly even above Ben in the tiny room, was the overalled figure of Walt, as Duty Officer of the first two teams in all Sections.

"Holding," he said briefly to Ben.

"Computer told me. Thanks," said Ben. "Clear outside?"

Out of the corner of his eye, he could see the row of small white lights announcing that the area around the phase ship's hull was clear of people or impediments to takeoff. But this was something that fell in the province of the Duty Officer.

"All clear," said Walt. "Ready to shift, then?"

"Go ahead. Prepare to shift," said Ben.

"Prepare to shift," said Walt to Coop.

"Report," Coop said into the phone grille before him.

"Match," said the voice of Kirk Walish, announcing the agreement of Observation with the shift.

"Match," said the voice of Matt from Computer, reporting that Coop's progressive figures were agreeing with the figures his Section was producing on the computer before him.

"Match," agreed Coop.

"Sir," said Walt, oddly and formally but somehow not ridiculously, to Ben. "Ready to make the shift."

"Shift, then," said Ben, looking above Coop's head at the TV screen that now showed only the canvas underside of the camouflage dome over the phase ship.

"Shift," echoed Coop. His finger came down on a single red key mounted in the middle of the shelf below his instrument.

There was a momentary, indefinable sensation, like a faint nausea that came and went too quickly to be really unpleasant. Then it disappeared as the artificial gravity of the phase field oscillations took over. Ben looked into the TV screen.

It showed only the blackness of space, a field of stars, and the giant curve of the Earth occluding the lower third of the screen.

Ben's ears rang to the sound of sudden cheering and excitement. The metal walls of the three small Sections threw the uproar back and forth between themselves until it sounded as if the whole ship was vibrating. In the Lounge up front, Ben thought, the off-duty crew members would be cheering, too. And indeed it was a great moment. For the first time the phase ship had proved Walt's mathematics and Lee's technical inventiveness by reducing the normal distance between two points—one on the surface of the Earth, one five hundred miles above it—to practical nonexistence.

Ben let them cheer for several minutes, then he turned to Walt.

"Shift completed without incident, sir," said Walt, unmoved as the Colossus of Rhodes might have been at this success that was more his than any man's. The cheering died suddenly, and Ben was aware of the personnel of all Sections waiting to hear his next words. He made them wait a few seconds, then spoke as dryly as he could.

"Very well done," he said. "Please begin observation

and computation on the next shift, which will be to the orbit of Saturn, in opposition to the Sun."

"Orbit of Saturn, in opposition to the Sun. Yes sir," said Walt.

"I'll be in my quarters. Call me when the shift is ready," said Ben. He turned and took the back door of the Control Section that led him directly back into his office, leaving Walt to silence the second outburst of cheering that began almost immediately.

He heard Walt doing just that through the door as he closed it behind him. The noise died. Somehow, though Walt had never been known to show anger—or much emotion of any sort—he got much more instant obedience from everyone than did Lee, whom everybody liked. Starting to ponder this for the most recent of uncounted times, Ben suddenly found the mental effort involved was too much for him. He was numb-brained and half-blind from fatigue. Almost stumbling, he stumped across the office, through its back door into the combination bedroom-sitting room that was the other half of his quarters, and literally fell onto the bed there.

Immediately, it seemed, someone was shaking his shoulder.

"Yes . . ." he mumbled, and pushed himself up into a sitting position on the edge of the bed.

"Saturn," said Walt, towering over him. "Ready to shift."

"Thank you," croaked Ben. He forced himself reflexively to his feet and followed Walt, as the other man led the way back into the Control Room.

He felt chilled to the bone. On the verge of opening his mouth to ask Walt about the internal temperature of the ship, he had the sense to realize that the chill was the result of his own exhaustion rather than any coolness in the ship's atmosphere—the temperature, pressure, content, humidity, and even ionization of which was automatically controlled. He felt he must look like a walking corpse, and made a special effort to stand straight and stride purposefully. His sleep-chilled face shaped itself most easily into a scowl, so he scowled.

"All right," he said to Walt, as soon as they were both in the Control Section together, standing over a waiting Coop, "prepare to shift."

The customary chant of report and counter-report went off smoothly, and the ship shifted. This time, however, there was a slight pause before Walt reported "shift completed without incident" and Ben had to grope mentally for a moment before he remembered the reason for it. Observation would be taking a picture of the stellar scene and computer-comparing it with a slide made up beforehand to show the stars as they should be seen from their point of destination.

"Observation reporting," spoke the phone grille. "Destination point achieved."

"Shift completed without incident," said Walt to him.

"Thank you," said Ben, groggily. He made himself pause for the minimum time necessary to make the order seem thoughtful and unhurried. "The next shift will be to an orbit—the equivalent distance of the present position of Venus, with respect to our Sun—around the star Alpha Centauri."

"Orbit at Venus-distance around the star Alpha Centauri," Walt acknowledged, unmoved.

"I'll be in my quarters," croaked Ben. He turned and went out, walking as indifferently as he was able until the door between his office and the Control Section was closed behind him. Behind him, this time, he heard no cheering.

He had managed to exceed their greatest expectations. A test-flight into Earth orbit was something for which they had all hoped. A further jump to the orbit of Saturn was the capping of the wildest dreams on the part of their most optimistic members. A further shift, immediately following to Alpha Centauri, the nearest Sun-like star to the solar system—over twenty-five trillion miles from Earth—that had awed them into silence.

But right now, Ben did not care. All he wanted was to get back to his bed. It would take more than four hours, even with known data to aid Observation, to calculate the shift to Alpha Centauri. Now he could really sleep.

He fell once more on the bed. This time he had the sense to drag the bedspread loose and wrap it around him before sleep sucked him down into unconsciousness like a mayfly in a whirlpool.

This time again he came awake by himself, with the automatic self-timing to which he was accustomed. Without looking at his watch, he knew that four hours had passed—and he felt surprisingly refreshed and alert, not tired at all.

It was a false feeling, he knew. Two more hours and he would have awakened sodden with the slumber that came from tapping a deeper well of tiredness than he had let himself touch in a short four hours of rest. But for the several hours of alertness now required of him, the short rest would do. He sat up, scrubbed a chin that somehow seemed to need shaving again—that was an illusion, he would settle for washing his face—and thought this time with some purpose of coffee and food.

He decided this once to take advantage of his rank and position and send for what he wanted, instead of going himself to the Lounge, where he was sure to be met with questions—questions that he would not want to answer at this time. He got up and spoke to Lee, who had now taken over as Duty Officer in the Control Room—the second teams in all Sections having just completed their four-hour stints to end the first half of the sixteen-hour shipboard "day."

Fifteen minutes later, seated in the office at his desk with a tray on it, he was hungrily making inroads on a pot of coffee and a large plate of reconstituted bacon and eggs from Stores. He was just finishing off his third cup of coffee and thinking how unusually good it tasted, when there was a knock on the door leading to the Control Section and Lee came in.

"Ready to shift, sir," said Lee, smiling and obviously delighted—with the possibility of such a shift, with the hearty breakfast he could see Ben had made, with the very formalism of military reporting.

"Already?" Ben said, putting down his cup cheer-fully—and instantly regretting the lapse into the famil-iar habit of friendliness built up over the past eight years. The life of everyone aboard, he told himself sav-agely, might well depend on the measure of discipline he was able to instill in them—and how could he expect it in them if he could not produce it in himself? To cover up his mistake, he got up hastily from the table and walked quickly to the door as if impatient with the delay consequent on calling him.

Lee stood aside. Ben stepped into the Control Room. Tessie Sorenson was at the Control desk. She looked up and threw him a smile as he came in, and he was caught between the embarrassment of refusing to return it and his renewed determination to establish discipline on the ship. He produced a fit of coughing as his ex-cuse.

"Prepare to shift," he said, turning to Lee in relief.

Lee repeated the command. As the responses came back from the other two Sections, Ben thought he was aware of a difference this time. Accustomed as nearly four years had made them to the fact that in phase shift-ing, movement from one end of the universe to the other was theoretically no different than a transfer across the width of a room, the crew could not help seeing, like an ominous ghost hovering in the air before them, the figure 23, followed by twelve zeros and the word "miles."

Nor could Ben himself ignore it. The distance was too vast, too great for the mind to capture. He became aware all at once that the sequence of responses was completed. Lee was waiting for him to give the order.

"To Alpha Centauri," he found himself saying, unor-thodoxly, "shift, then!"

"Shift!" echoed the voice of Tessie Sorenson—and in the fraction of a second of faint nausea that followed they seemed to feel the universe change position under their feet.

Ben, Lee, Tessie, stared up into the TV screen. A star, larger than the Sun as seen from Earth, burned almost in the center of it. Like a voice from some unimaginable distance came the voice of Hans Clogh. "Observation reporting. Destination point achieved."

"Shift completed without incident," said the voice of Lee.

Ben leaned forward over Tessie's shoulder and pressed the key on the phone that would let him speak to the whole ship at once.

"All Sections," he heard his own voice saying, "put your instruments on *Hold*. Everybody report to the Lounge for a small celebration. Nora, if you'll come to my office, there's some special supplies I'd like to have you break out of Stores for the celebration."

He turned and went back into his office, hearing the first sound of the jubilation break out behind him. He walked around to sit down at his desk, sat down, and rubbed the heels of both hands hard against his forehead. The door from the corridor on the women's side of the ship opened and Nora Taller came in.

"Oh, Nora . . ." he said. "If you'll look in Special Stores you'll find a good-sized crate with a 'Secret' seal on it, and the letters A C stamped on its top. If you'll break it open, you'll find some food and wine I had put aboard for just this occasion. Maybe you'd better take the crate down to the Lounge and break it open there—get some of the men to carry it for you."

"All right." She turned away toward the door and then stopped to look back and smile at him. "Aren't you coming?"

"In—in a little while," he said hastily. "I've got some things to do here."

He watched the door close behind her. The excuse he had things to do here was the poorest sort of lie, but he did not think she had suspected his subterfuge. —Only it was beyond mortal man or beyond mortal conscience. He could not go down to the Lounge and eat and drink with them there, knowing all the time what he was going to do to them. And even if he could have, he was not, he told himself, that good an actor.

He fished out the second dry-copy of the censored message with the President's signature at the bottom of it. He also found four thumbtacks in his desk. After that, there was nothing to do but kill time. He drank the remaining coffee in the pot and thought about what he would do once he had spoken to them all. He had gone over what he would do many times, but once more might suggest an improvement in his plans . . . the important thing would be to get them all busy at something right away . . .

He came alert to the alarm of his inner clock, warning him that sixty minutes were up. Getting to his feet, and remembering to stand and walk straight, he took the dry-copy and thumbtacks and went down through the deserted Sections and out the far door of the Observation Section near the front of the ship. He crossed the corridor without being noticed and stepped into a lounge full of noisy people slightly intoxicated with the champagne he had brought aboard in the sealed and insulated cold pack case.

There was a small rostrum at one end of the lounge, opposite the dining area, and he made his way hardly noticed through the crowd and onto the rostrum before many were aware he was among them. He faced them all. Slowly, heads turned, and the room fell into silence.

When the silence was so complete as to be nearly painful, he began. His voice sounded unnaturally harsh against the walls.

"I'm standing here to speak to you," he said, "not as Ben Shore, whom you all know, and who feels as happy about being here off Alpha Centauri as you do—but as Brigadier General Shore, Commander of this ship by authority of the Congress and the President of your country."

He paused. They still stared at him, perplexed, but still in silence.

"I should be saying something congratulatory about our being here," he said, "but as it happens I don't think this is the time for it, in view of what I have to tell you now."

He lifted the copy so that those in the room could see it.

"This is a copy of an order," he said, "signed by the

President of the United States. I've had to censor out certain references to secret matters, but the message is still readable. As soon as I finish talking here, I'll thumbtack it on the bulletin board on the wall, there, and you can read it for yourselves. Briefly—" he took a deep breath, "what it does is order us all to search for a habitable world, as proof that the phase ship can find new worlds for our human race to populate—and not to come back until we find it."

He paused a moment to let that sink in. Watching, he could not tell if the silence meant it had done so—or only that they were all in shock.

"I realize," he said, "as the President himself undoubtedly did, that drafting you into this duty is unfair by any standard. None of you had any inkling of this when you were asked to apply for commissions in the Air Force, which made you subject to such orders, nor even when you came aboard this morning. But the critically tense situation in the world will have to serve as an excuse."

He paused again. They still were silent and motionless.

"We're here. We're going to fulfill our mission," he said, "and we're going to make the best of it. You'd all better start figuring what special and personal supplies you'll need from Stores for extending living aboard the ship. And I'll see Captains Lee Ruiz and Walter Bone and First Lieutenant Nora Taller in my office in five minutes for a conference."

Amid a silence that still continued, he got down from the rostrum, picked his way through the crowd to the bulletin board, and thumbtacked there the sheet with the copy of the message. He ran his eye over it, though he knew it by heart now. It read:

To: Brigadier General Benjamin Allen Shore and officers of Phase Ship Mark III:
You are hereby ordered to
take off

leave the

surface of our Earth and   the vicinity of our solar
system to find and claim a world habitable by the
human race.

              that   there
may be no misunderstanding as to the aim and purpose of such a flight

                            you are hereby ordered to
prosecute
              a   search,   to such ulti-
mate limits of space and time as the outermost
reaches of the physical universe and for a voyage of
forever and a day.

              before accounting the search a failure and
returning with such a new home for our human race
unfound.

Walter Eugene
*PRESIDENT OF THE UNITED STATES OF
AMERICA*

Ben turned and walked out of the Lounge and slowly
back through the empty Sections to his own office. He
sat down at his desk, and for a moment he merely sat
there with his hands resting flat on the desk top.

Then he breathed out a deep, harsh, and determined
breath, and reached down to take from the drawer of
his desk the original order and its duplicate. Rising, he
walked across to the walk-in safe in one wall of his office, opened it, and stepped inside to file the envelope
containing the order and its duplicate. He locked the
safe again, returned, and sat down at his desk.

Lee, Walt, and Nora would be here in a minute or so.
Meanwhile . . . he snapped on the small outside TV
screen set in one side of his desk at a slant with the
surface and looked both down and out into a wilderness
of unfamiliar stars. Staring, his eye seemed to plunge on
and on into immensity, until it felt as if he would be lost
forever. This was the unknown territory into which they
would now venture— He tore his eyes away suddenly,
snapped off the set, and sat upright at his desk.

A suit of icy armor seemed to enclose all his body and limbs.

He, too, was afraid. He admitted it to himself squarely at last. But in this flight of wild geese, he held the point of the v-formation and was flock leader. The rest must never know he shared the weakness of fear. They would not know, he promised it now, silently, to himself.

He put his palms flat on the desk and waited for the coming of his Captains.

□ CHAPTER 3 □

"WHAT I WANT," said Ben slowly, "is the following: First, to establish aboard here the military kind of discipline that'll be the only thing to hold us together in the long run, crammed together as we shall be in a small space for months or possibly even years."

He paused to let them consider that first point. They were in conference in his office, around the symbol of that activity: a coffeepot and four cups on his desk top. Ben occupied his normal position behind the desk, Nora was on his right, Walt across from him, and Lee on his left. It was the usual arrangement—although in the past it had been around some other desk—and its familiarity had a tendency to soften the impact of Ben's speech, just minutes past, in the Lounge.

"Second," Ben went on, "to set up the training of people in jobs besides the ones they know now. Lee, it's most important that you train someone right away to replace you as technical officer, and you, Nora, that you train at least one substitute nurse."

This last was the weakest point of all Ben's undercover planning for this moment. His own checkered college years had seen him wander from engineering through psychology and into history in his attempt to find some understanding and place among this human race of half-angels, half-devils into which he had been born. On the way, one part of his studies had been a full schedule of premedical courses and a year in medical school before his inner self-doubts caused him to withdraw. This last year he had supplemented that first small taste of medical information with as much private reading and studying as he had time for. His brain, with its usual flypaper retentiveness, had managed to pack itself with academic knowledge about the practice of medicine. His ears, eyes, nose—and above all his hands—remained ignorant. Nora, however, had actually worked as a registered nurse. She was their real insurance, thought Ben, against sickness or accident aboard.

"Tessie," said Nora, immediately, "and maybe Polly."

"Julian," said Lee. Julian Tyree, Ben remembered had already been working with Lee in the matter of the recycler, in the lower half of the ship, that reprocessed their air, water, and wastes to make the ship a closed universe. Ben recalled a week ago seeing the two of them bent over a torn-down section of the recycler and wondering that they should find each other so congenial to work with. Julian was gentlemanly to the point of being stiff—an attitude his softly British accent underscored. Lee was as informal as his own buccaneering appearance indicated. Apparently, however, they made a natural team.

"Walt," Ben went on, "I'm assuming almost anyone could take over as Navigation Officer, after a fashion, and that beyond that point there'd be no hope of your trying to train them on short notice like this, anyway. Am I right?"

"You're right," said Walt. He made a simple statement of it, without apology. In a sense, they were all navigators aboard the phase ship. Over and above that, was Walt's special appreciation of the universe in terms of the phase physics that only he fully understood.

"Well, then," said Ben. "Third, I want to set up occupations for the off-duty people beside their training in other jobs. Not only a regular program of physical exercise, as the Lounge is set up for, but recreational and study occupations. One of the things that occurred to me was to have everyone aboard keep a personal log with entries once every ship's period each time they come off duty. If we clear the drug lockers in the top-deck Special Stores room, everyone aboard can have a private, locked compartment in which to keep his or her logbook—"

He broke off. There was a knocking at the door on the men's side of the ship.

"What is it?" Ben called, annoyed—not so much at the interruption as at the lack of discipline the interruption implied.

"Kirk—Walish, General," came the voice of Kirk from beyond the metal panels of the door. "We've got a stowaway."

"Stowaway!" said Lee. They had all sat up at once. Ben remembered just in time to maintain his new, distant formality of attitude.

"All right," he said, evenly, "bring him in."

"Him or her—we don't know which," Kirk said, opening the door and walking in. He was grinning and carrying a brown and yellow brindled object that Ben to his astonishment recognized as a half-grown cat. Its fur stuck out roughly and untidily, and, held to Kirk's chest as it was by one hand under its stomach, it looked uneasy and antagonistic. It did not fight against Kirk's grasp, but it kept its four legs stuck out stiff, as if it were a much younger kitten, fearing to be dropped without warning; and it opened its mouth to hiss silently at them all as Kirk brought it forward and set it down in the center of Ben's desk in their midst.

"Found it down in the Food Stores Section of the main storeroom below, just now," said Kirk. "It was my turn to go down and get fresh supplies for the automat in the Lounge. I heard something, and there it was."

A corner of Ben's mind made a note of the fact that the automat, so-called, that automatically cooked and produced the foods punched for in the dining area of the Lounge, should not be needing resupplying this soon. But, before he could go further with that thought, he found his attention claimed by the cat, which was acting unpussylike, to say the least. "Undomesticated," Ben thought might be a better word.

The cat had not moved when it was set down. It had, however, immediately adopted a half-crouch on the desk top, tail-tip twitching and jaws agape in unfriendly fashion.

"There weren't any cats around the Surface Installation, were there?" asked Nora. "Or even back at Underground?"

"It acts wild," Lee said, staring sympathetically at the animal.

"That's not a wild cat!" said Nora.

"No—I mean, gone wild," said Lee. Now that the creature was close, Ben could see burrs matted in its fur—that explained the untidy look—and a look of skin-and-bones under the fur. "It might have been some farmer's cat gone wild. It acts like it's not used to seeing people at all."

This was about the only possible explanation for the cat's appearance, Ben had to admit to himself. From the moment the Surface Installation had been decided on, Secret Service agents had bought up and occupied the surrounding farms, which they continued to farm, to support the camouflaged, farm-buildings appearance of the Surface Installation itself. A cat left behind by the original owner of one of those farms might easily have ranged as far as the neighboring Installation. But an animal this young could not possibly be such a beast, forgotten four years ago.

"It was probably born wild," said Kirk, "from a mother who'd gone wild. It acts as if it expects to be eaten alive at any minute."

This was only too true. The cat's head was turned toward Ben at the moment. He looked directly into the needle teeth and the pink interior of the silently snarling jaws. Motionless except for the twitching tail-tip, the cat still managed to give the impression that it might fly with claws extended on all four feet into Ben's face at the first suspicious move. There was something about this attitude that reminded a corner of Ben's mind uncomfortably about their own position in the phase ship, surrounded by the unknown dangers and devils of which the galaxy must be supposed to be equipped.

"How could a little kitten grow up out in the wild?" Nora was asking.

"Like the young of any of the wild cats, I suppose," said Lee. "The mother hunts for them to start with and then takes them out and shows them how. Gets them—what's the word?"

"Blooded," supplied Kirk.

Ben winced internally—not so much from the word as from the train of thought that sprang instantly to mind from it. He had suddenly become aware of something he should have thought of before; and immediately his unsentimental, calculative mental machinery was developing it to its logical conclusion. Filled with a sudden self-hatred for having this facility, he turned roughly on Kirk.

"All right," he said. "We've seen it. Now take the animal out of here and see if some of those burrs can't be cut out of its hair. I'll make you responsible for it."

"I was intending to be," said Kirk, a little sharply. Ben stared at him until he saw the balding man's gaze bend before him.

"From now on," snarled Ben, in the uncomfortable stillness of the office, "we'll have the word 'sir' used to all superior officers unless they specifically say *not* to use it. And, from now on, when I'm in conference with my assistant officers, we won't be disturbed for anything that can be put off until the conference is over."

"Sir—" said Kirk, grudgingly. But his eyes flashed up under his black eyebrows to meet Ben's for a second, and Ben caught a fractional glance of pure outrage and fury.

"All right then," said Ben, evenly. "You can go."

Kirk picked up the cat and left. The closing of the door behind him left an uncomfortable silence pooled around the desk, to which only Walt in his immobility seemed indifferent.

"Ben—Sir," said Lee, hesitatingly, "These people aren't the kind that take to regimenting easily. And particularly the older ones, like Kirk—"

Ben stared at Lee—almost as hard as he had stared at Kirk. "That's the way it's going to have to be. Without a framework of authority and discipline, this ship will fall apart in two months. We can't live here the way we lived as research and development people back on the surface of Earth. Sooner or later, we're going to run into a situation where only everyone's immediate and automatic obedience to the necessary orders will keep us alive and going. Now, if you don't see that, any of you—" his gaze moved around to Walt and Nora, "I want you to take my word for it. And if you can't do that and act as if you were convinced of it yourself, I want you to tell me—now."

He waited. None of the three spoke up.

"Yes sir," said Lee, at last.

"Good." Ben cracked the hard held lines of his face in a smile. "Because you three are going to have to demand obedience as well as give it. Now—" He reached for a star projection chart on the desk and pulled it out where they could all have equally good views of it. "I think the wisest step is to begin our search with the nearer stars, even when they don't resemble a Go type star like our Sun. When we get farther from home, we can begin to be more choosy and pick only Sol-like stars to investigate. Now—" he pointed at the chart, "Sirius and Procyon seem to be the immediate close-in candidates for examination, followed by Altair, Vega, Arcturus, and so forth. Now what order suggests itself to you, individually, in which to make our hops to these stars and their possible systems?"

"Sirius first, don't you think?" said Lee. "And Procyon second . . ." The talk became technical and therefore impersonal, Walt's deep voice taking over more and more of the conversation. They had left the human problem and entered the abstract one of phaseship movement. Ben suspected that, after the emotion of the past hour or more, it was a relief to all of them. He knew it was to him.

In the six weeks that followed, as they calculated their position relative to the galaxy's theoretical centerpoint, the comparable position of their destination, shifted, and then began the calculations all over again, Ben watched the awareness of their situation sink like some dark dye into the unconscious minds of all those aboard and be as resolutely denied by their conscious minds. He was finding himself generally left alone by the crew members aside from the three senior officers—he had promoted Nora to Captain, immediately following the first day's conference in his office.

It had always puzzled Ben that people believed that the great creative minds that moved the race forward went *through* the technical barriers in the road of human progress. The fact was just the contrary. They went *around* them. They looked away from the impassable barrier before them to find an alternate solution elsewhere. Man had not solved the problem of ocean crossings by learning to walk upon water, but by building ships. He had not taken to the air by flapping wings attached to his arms, but by building planes heavier than air. Certainly, thought Ben, it should have seemed the most obvious consequence in the world that, faced with the limiting speed of light at a hundred and eighty-six thousand miles per second, far too slow to permit reasonable exploration of even the nearer stars, men should look outside the problem for an alternate solution to crossing the vast galactic distances in practical periods of time.

If distance divided by a fixed speed limit gave an impractical answer to star travel and the speed limit could not be changed—then how about changing the distance factor? Specifically, was it not possible to look at the universe in terms that assumed that the distance between points in the universe did not exist?

Walt's mathematics had found that the way, using the Heisenberg Uncertainty Principle as a departure point—that declaration by Werner Heisenberg in 1927 that stated it was impossible to specify or determine simultaneously the position and velocity of a particle as accurately as wished. The determiner could be precise about position only at the expense of being uncertain about velocity—and vice versa.

Assume therefore that velocity could be absolutely determined—this was the proposition that had fascinated Walt, even when Ben had first known him in the twelfth grade in Rockford, Illinois. Then, theoretically, the position of the particle would be ubiquitous—it would have all points in the physical universe as its position. Starting with this desired end, Walt had begun by mathematically speculating that phase shifts in keeping with the wave theories of quantum mechanics indicated a requirement for an exceedingly small, but calculable, "timeless" interval. This interval—of "no-time" as it was more correctly called—would require an absolute fixing of velocity and an absolute universality (or ubiquity) of position of a particle.

From this came the mathematics of his phase physics. From the mathematics of phase physics, with Lee as translator, had come first the theory, then the actuality, of the phase ship.

In the pure sense of the word, thought Ben now, this phase ship about him never moved. It merely oscillated between two conditions—one, during the so-called phase shift, in which it existed everywhere in the universe at once, and another in which, as now, it existed with maximum determination at some particular point in that universe.

Practically speaking, the phase ship "moved" by going from maximum probabilities of existence at one position in the universe, through universality, to maximum probabilities of existence at another position.

Since all points in the universe were the same to it in universal condition, there was therefore no theoretical reason why the phase shift could not cross the width of the galaxy as easily as going from Earth's surface to Earth orbit. But that was only theoretically. In practice, the more there was of ordinary physical distance separating the point of departure and the point of destination, the more involved and extended was the calculation required to make the move with precision.

This could be somewhat offset by making longer jumps to less precise destinations—to larger and larger general areas, rather than exact points. But even this became impractical eventually. A jump of three hundred light years with the hope of landing anywhere within a sphere forty light years in diameter took several days to calculate. A jump twice that distance with the same factor of uncertainty took as many weeks in calculation. It reached a point where probable error began to equal, then exceed, probable distance shifted.

So, it was not the distances outside the walls of the phase ship that concerned her crew, but the time spent calculating within those walls. And this circumstance was allowing them to shut their minds to the vastness of the interstellar space about them, now. They were able to maintain an emotional illusion that they were inhabiting at most a remote and slightly detached bit of their own native Earth. And that brought Ben back to the inexorable train of thought originally suggested by the sight of the stowaway cat.

Ben got up restlessly from his desk and began to pace the short distance of the office floor back and forth several times before he became aware of what he was doing. Catching himself up short, guiltily, he was returning to his desk when there was a knock on the door leading to the Control Section.

He went to the door and opened it. Lee stood there. "Ready to shift to Achernar at Saturn-equivalent distance," said Lee, briefly.

"Oh, yes," said Ben, stepping into Control Section. He paused, sniffing at the air, suddenly aware of something that had been nagging at his olfactory nerves for some time. "Does something smell?" The odor was flat and heavy, if barely perceptible, like the odor of machine oil.

"It's in the recycled air," said Lee apologetically. "I've been working on it. I'll get back on it as soon as we change shifts and Walt takes over as DO, after this shift to Achernar orbit."

"I'll come have a look at it with you," said Ben. The recycler had proved to be a fallible piece of equipment. Kirk's remark the first day about resupplying the automat had led Ben to investigate. He had discovered, as he had suspected, that the shortage was all in foods taken from the freeze-dried supplies brought aboard, and none in recycled food. However, he had also discovered that it was not merely an emotional squeamishness that was involved in the crew's avoidance of the recycled foods. Those foods actually left an odd, unnatural, and unpleasant aftertaste in the mouth.

—A little, he suddenly recognized, like the flat, oily odor in the air now. Yet, tests of the food had found it safely edible—he put the matter out of his mind with a sudden effort. It was time now to order the shift, and there was a particular reason to be interested in this one jump. Observation Section believed they had evidence that in Achernar they had finally discovered a star with at least one planet.

"Ready to shift," Lee was repeating now.

"Shift then," Ben said . . . and the routine went off in regular fashion. He felt the wave of nausea and stared hopefully with Lee and Coop at the overhead TV screen.

It showed only stars.

"Too much to expect we'd land right on top of it," said Lee, framing the thought aloud that must be that moment in the minds of everyone aboard. There had been a general, unconscious, emotional deterioration of the crew these last two weeks. They were, Ben had thought, a little stir-crazy.

"Never mind," said Ben. "Search for it—" he broke off as Walt stepped in through the entrance from the Calculation Section.

"I relieve you, Captain," said Walt, emotionlessly to Lee.

"Thank you, Captain," said Lee, with equal formality—formality, however, that, Ben's ear was pleased to recognize, was acquiring the un-self-consciousness of habit. "Present orders are to search for the satellite of Achernar."

"Search for the satellite of Achernar," repeated Walt. "Very well."

Lee stepped across to a shelf against the wall on which rested the Control logbook, and entered in it the time of his relief and the passing on of his orders.

"Good," said Ben, as Lee signed the logbook and turned away. "Let's have a look at that recycler—you can write up your personal logbook later, Captain."

Forty minutes later, on the lower deck, Ben was as wringing wet as if he had been trapped in a swamp.

Condensation moisture dripped from all surfaces in the fifteen-feet-square recylcer room, and the atmosphere was moist to the point of fogging. Lee, stripped to the waist and thoroughly soaked, turned from the section of the recycler he had partially dismantled. They were both now so plunged in the odor he ignored it.

"No good," Lee said to Ben, wiping his forehead and his beaded eyebrows with an only slightly less damp forearm. "I'll have to shut down before I dismantle any further."

"Shut down?" said Ben. "The emergency tanks only hold enough air for twelve hours."

"I can get it apart and together again in twelve hours," said Lee. "That's not what's worrying me." He gestured at the recycler. "The problem is where to lay out the parts as I dismantle. There isn't enough room down here to work—even if we shifted stores to the top deck to open up the storerooms."

"What's wrong with the recycler?" asked Ben. It was in the odds that there would turn out to be at least one bug in the ship's machinery—he had not expected it to be the recycler.

"I don't know," said Lee, frowning. "It's too complicated for one thing. Something in there's not working right—and it's bolixing up the rest of the machinery. I won't be able to tell until I get it apart. If the recycler won't work, we're done for."

"Yes," said Ben. He thought, scowling. "Maybe we could rig up a pressurized addition to the ship, out beyond the airlock . . ." he became thoughtful again.

"There's the pressure domes," suggested Lee. "But they're designed for housing under atmosphere on a planet's surface. I don't know if they'd take the exposure to vacuum."

Ben nodded.

"Well," said Lee, smiling a little crookedly. "Maybe Achernar will turn out to have a fine, Earth-like planet for us to set down on."

"Maybe," said Ben.

The worsening of the smell in the air and the taste in the food was gradual, but noticeable, in the hours that followed. Ben was in his office with Nora, Lee, and Walt, making plans to attach one of the pressurized buildings to the airlock as a work area to permit the tearing down of the recycler. The rest of the off-duty personnel were clearing the main storeroom below deck, which would be used in any case.

"The point is," Nora was saying, "we're a hundred light-years from home here. If we had to make it back in twelve hours—if the recycler couldn't be put back together once it was torn down—we couldn't make it in a minimum of three calculations and jumps in that time."

"If I take it apart, I can put it back at least as good as it was," said Lee. "Only . . ."

"Only," said Walt, calmly, "if a part gets lost or damaged because of the working conditions, we're out of luck, is that it?"

Lee nodded.

"The point is—" he was beginning, when there was a knock on the door to Control Section.

"Come in!" snapped Ben.

The door burst open. Kirk Walish stood framed in the opening. His eyes glittered on Ben.

"We've found it!" he said—and for a moment not even Ben noticed the omission of the "sir."

"Found? —Achernar's planet?" snapped Ben.

"Yes," said Kirk, almost glaring at him in triumph. "Just the other side of Achernar, itself. We can calculate the shift to orbit the planet in fifteen minutes!"

Ben throttled down the excitement within him. He forced himself to a glacial, almost ponderous calm.

"Captain Bone," he said, turning to Walt. "You're Duty Officer."

"Yes sir," said Walt, getting to his feet.

"Please make the next shift as soon as possible to orbit this satellite of Achernar."

"Yes sir," said Walt. He went out, his bulk herding Kirk before him back into the Control Section, and the door closed behind them both.

"Now," said Ben, icily, seeing Lee and Nora alight with the same excitement he now had under control within himself. "shall we get back to the immediate and more important problem? —In spite of all objections," he said, turning to Nora, "I think we can use a pressurized dome attached to the airlock. Tell-tales can be set up to warn us of any loss of air pressure—and whatever cracking occurs isn't going to be bad enough so that we'll be losing parts into space."

He looked at Lee.

"Don't you agree?" he said.

"Yes . . . I guess so," said Lee, reluctantly. "Of course, if there's a chance that this planet of Achernar's could turn out to have a surface where we could set the ship down for repair—"

"Suppositions are a little beside the point right now," said Ben harshly, "don't you think? For now suppose we stick to what we know is possible, out here in space."

"Yes . . . of course," said Lee. He looked crestfallen. Ben sympathized with him but dared not show it. Behind the harsh mask of his face, his mind was wrestling mightily with the same possibility Lee had mentioned. But Lee and the others had not spent the last few years envisioning all the things that could go wrong in a set-down on an alien world. If there was an accident—if for some reason the ship became trapped down there—in dealing with the unknown, anything was possible. Also the others had not yet grasped that the phase ship was essentially a creature of space and really safe only as long as it stayed in space. The most attractive and Earth-like planet could harbor traps for them, and Achernar's satellite, under a blue-hot star like Achernar, was not likely to be Earth-like.

"All right, then," said Ben, "you'll need gravity, and the ship's artificial gravity won't apply to the pressure dome . . ." They continued discussing their problems until Walt reentered the room.

"Ready to shift," announced Walt.

"Thank you," said Ben rising. "Come along. There's room in the control Section for all of us to watch."

He led the way into the Control Section.

"Perpare to shift," he told Walt. Walt turned away to give orders.

"Match! . . . Match! . . . Match!" came the voices of the different Sections. "Ready to shift," announced Walt.

"Shift, then," said Ben.

They shifted. Everyone in the Control Section stared up at the screen.

On it, Achernar—brightest star of the constellation Eridanus—was a blue-hot pinprick of light casting as much light from the black sky of space as the sun of Earth, seen from Venus-orbit. In its harsh and pitiless light the barren planet they all now saw centered on the screen looked like a coin punched from a single piece of slagged and brutalized metal.

"Captain," said Ben to Walt, "have Observation find out as much as possible about surface conditions on that world. Then join us in my office again while we work out means for repairing the recycler."

He led the way back into his office and both Lee and Nora followed him. Some fifteen minutes later the teams changed, and with the coming on duty of the third team, Lee took over as Duty Officer and left the office temporarily, being replaced by Walt.

Shortly thereafter, Lee came back in from the Control Section with a piece of paper that he put on the desk in front of Ben.

"Surface Conditions on the world—Achernar One, we're calling it—" said Lee, as Ben ran his eye down the paper. "Gravity's only a little more than Earth's and the temperature at the equator's not bad at all, up to twenty degrees Centigrade, practically sixty degrees Fahrenheit. And there's an atmosphere of sorts, even if it's not breathable—mostly nitrogen."

There was a running undercurrent of excitement in Lee's voice as he reeled this off.

"I see," said Ben. Well, he had come to the decision at last. Repair of the recycler in space, even with the pressure dome, would be a risky and extremely difficult procedure. Down on the planetary surface Lee had described, it ought to be little more different than doing the job back on the surface of Earth. —In the face of this argument, there was only the excitement to be felt in Lee and the others, the excitement over the prospect of actually setting down on a different world, which could lead to foolish actions and danger. That, and his own fears of the unknown.

But—it had to be faced sometime. What was it Kirk had said about the stowaway cat? As a kitten it had needed to be blooded, brought face to face with the hunt and the kill by which it would learn to survive. As a crew he and the others aboard would have to be blooded, sooner or later, on some strange world. It might as well be now.

"All right," said Ben. He turned to Walt. "Prepare a shift to a working area on the surface of the planet below us."

"Right away," said Walt.

There was a glint of excitement even in Walt's normally emotionless face. Lee was smiling happily—and so was Nora. Looking out from behind the mask of his features with a coolness of despair inside him, for the first time Ben felt the loneliness of his command settle upon him in its full weight and measure.

☐ CHAPTER 4 ☐

HALF AN HOUR later they shifted down to within fifty feet of the equatorial surface of Achernar One and settled the rest of the way in a continuing series of automatically shortening shifts as the ship approached the ground. Ben felt the curious, faint sensation of the ship finally settling imperceptibly under its own weight to the gravity of Achernar One.

That ground, seen in the TV of Ben's desk, was mainly a whitish sand, here and there blown clear of the underlying rock. The distant blue-white light of Achernar gave the hilly surrounding landscape a ghastly look, like a surrealistic scene illuminated by glaring fluorescent lights. He leaned over to the intercom—he was once more alone in the office—and keyed to Lee down in the recycler room.

"All right, Captain Ruiz," he said. "You can start your teams attaching the pressure dome outside the ship and dismantling the recycler."

"Yes sir," replied the voice of Lee.

Ben let the lever under his fingers fly back up into "off" position. He got up and went out into the corridor on the women's side of the ship, from which the hatchway to the lower deck had it's most direct connection to the corridor of the airlock. Looking down the corridor, he could see spacesuited bodies manhandling the deflated dome into position to put it out the airlock as soon as the inner lock, which was now closing before Ben's gaze, should be securely shut.

Ben turned and went down to the lower deck.

Lee's crew of workers had already been busy tearing down the recycler while the ship was being brought down to surface. Now, individuals began to carry parts up, ready to be transferred to the dome, which was swelling like a balloon, just outside the hatch.

The work went quickly. The parts of the recycler were almost all made of the new—and exceedingly expensive—magnesium alloy that made up so much of the phase ship. The loads of those carrying parts upstairs to the attached dome were therefore bulky, but light. In the narrow corridors and stairs, there were more than enough hands to do the work. Still, it gave Ben a mild attack of conscience to be standing about idle when everyone else was so busy.

He went back upstairs to his office, so that at least his idleness would be less apparent. He had laid on himself the task of keeping a personal log as well as the official log of the phase ship, and he was working at this at the table set up for that purpose in the now deserted Special Supply room, when there was the sound of knuckles on the half-open door. He looked up to see Jay Tremple, Kirk Walish's teammate on the first Observation Team, standing in the doorway.

"Permission to go ashore, sir," said Jay, with a grin on his lean face under the red hair.

"What?" Ben stared forbiddingly at him. It did not seem to bother the lean Observation Section man.

"They don't need us to carry," said Jay. He produced what seemed to be a roll of colored cloth from behind his back and shook it out. Ben found himself staring at a homemade flag, about the size of a pillowcase. Looking more intently at it, Ben saw that it was in fact a pillowcase—with the stars and stripes painted upon it. "Matt Duncan and I thought as long as no one needed us we'd step outside in spacesuits and claim this world by planting a flag on the hill out there." He gestured in the direction of the airlock and the rocky upthrust beyond that Ben had seen on his desk TV screen.

"Matt?" said Ben, astonished. For Matt was one of the most level-headed among the crew.

"Matt and I," said Jay Tremple a little impatiently. "It's all right, isn't it?" He was actually, Ben saw, standing on one foot ready to go.

"No! It's not all right!" snapped Ben, gathering his wits once again. "There's only twenty-four of us on this phase ship and that means nobody to spare. I'm not going to risk a single life, let alone two, on anything dangerous unless it's necessary to keep the ship going and everybody else alive."

"There's no danger out there," Jay scowled.

"That's your assumption," said Ben. "At any rate you aren't going. You, Matt, or anyone else. Now, get down to the reycler room and tell Lee I said to find you something to do, to keep you out of trouble."

He glared as Jay turned about and went off. Then he returned to his logbook, dismissing the matter.

The personal logbook was his one confidant on this ship in which he had determined to hold himself separate and aloof. He kept the ship's official log in the barest of factual, impersonal styles. That official logbook would loom large in any judgment he would face, back on Earth. He did not expect it to excuse him—after all he had stolen (there was no other word for it) the phase ship and kidnaped (no other word for that either) the phase-ship crew, with his eyes open.

It was something that he had believed had to be done. Therefore he had done it—

His pen leaped suddenly, trailing a streak of blue across the pages of his personal logbook, as a sharp shock rocked the ship, followed by another. By the time the third shook the vessel, he was on his feet, had thrown the personal logbook into its drug compartment and locked the door upon it, and was striding down the hall toward Observation Section.

He burst into Observation. The Sections had been emptied of their regular teams since the ship was down on the surface, but he found Walt already there before him and a stiff-featured, white-faced Kirk Walish in one of the Section's two seats before comparison-scopes. The other seat was empty.

"Where's Jay?" snapped Ben.

"I don't know," said Kirk—but he did not meet Ben's eye. However, there was no time to go into that now. Ben swung on Walt, and Walt answered without waiting for the question.

"Earthquake," he said. "Evidently, there's volcanic activity within a few miles of here; and most of the surface here at the equator is unstable. Observation evidently noted this but didn't want to make a point of it in their report to Lee—and you."

Ben looked at Kirk, who met the gaze rather defiantly. Ben remembered that Kirk had not been part of the team on duty under Lee, when the decision to go down to surface had been made.

"It's going to continue? Get worse?" Ben demanded, swinging back to face Walt.

"No way of telling," said the physicist. "I suppose we ought to expect the worst."

"Yes," said Ben. "Get all Sections back to work in here on calculations and preparations for lift. I'll go see how close Lee is to having the recycler fixed and back aboard." He left, without waiting for Walt's answer.

Ben found Lee in the inflated dome beyond the airlock, laying out the order in which the parts were to be returned to the recycler room. Already parts were being carried back downstairs.

"Thought we'd get things back inside as soon as possible." Lee said to Ben. "I found the trouble. A filter unit supposed to sort out unrecyclable particles from the fluid of the nutrient bath. Somebody put it in backwards, back on Earth. It silted up, stopped, and nutrient production automatically stopped, backing up the whole chain of process."

"It's fixed then?" said Ben. He almost had to shout the words. There was a hissing against the dome surrouding him. The place was gloomy as a tent at night with the portable lights strung under the dark material of which it was made. The hissing increased abruptly, and the whole structure rocked.

"Will be as soon as I've got the cycler together again," said Lee. "Oh, that's the sand blown by the wind you hear. Getting windier outside, evidently. —What're you looking for?"

Ben had been staring around the dome.

"Have you seen Jay Tremple?" he said. "I sent him to you and they need him back in Sections."

"Jay? No, I haven't seen him," Lee was beginning, when a woman's voice interrupted.

"Jay?" Ben turned to see small Polly Neigh, almost invisible under the section of mental paneling she was carrying. "He and Matt went outside."

"Outside?"

"Why, yes—" Polly stared back. "Jay said he had your permission. Matt didn't think it was a very smart thing to do, just to plant a flag on a hill—but he said Jay ought to have someone with him in case of accidents—" she broke off, staring past Ben, and Ben turned to see that the big figure of Walt had come silently up behind him.

"Ben," said Walt, "as near as we can observe, there's been some large crustal subsidence in this planet's surface not far from here. There'll probably be secondary shocks, and there's a windstorm heading this way with winds probably over a hundred miles an hour. We'd better lift as soon as we can."

"I'll have all this back inside in half an hour," said Lee. "We can't leave before then."

"Then," said Walt, "I'll go after those two—Matt and Jay. If I don't find them in fifteen minutes, I'll head back. All right, Ben? —They're part of my team. It's my job."

Ben opened his mouth to refuse, faced the hard facts of the situation, and saw he could not say no.

"All right," he said. "But don't take chances. I don't want to throw a third life after two that're lost already."

"Don't worry, Ben," said Walt, deeply. "I've got things to do; and to do them, I have to stay alive. —I'll go suit up."

He turned and left. As if in a mild daze produced by the lulling hiss of wind-blown sand against the outer plastic shell of the dome, Ben heard Lee arguing with Polly.

" . . . that's too big for you, that piece. Take something smaller!"

"No," said Polly stubbornly, and Ben turned to see her avoiding Lee's attempt to take the panel from her, "we're short-handed with the Sections manned again. I can carry it." She went off with it.

"What do I carry, Lee?" asked Ben, turning to the other man.

Loaded with a couple of pieces of recycler, he joined the procession carrying other parts in reverse order back into the ship and stacking them as near to the already-filled recycler room as possible. On his third trip, he found Lee stopping everybody in the airlock and making them put on respirators. The dome had cracked and the alien suffocating gases of Achernar One were leaking in.

"—Not much longer!" Lee shouted—it was now necessary to shout—with his lips at Ben's ear in the dome. "That wind'll tear this apparatus right off the airlock in a few minutes. Lucky—we're almost through—"

Ben felt a hand tugging at his sleeve. He turned to face a respirator-anonymous face.

"Observation wants you—sir!" shouted the anonymous face in the British accents of Julian Tyree.

Ben nodded, turned about, and plunged back through the airlock. Ripping the respirator from his own face as he passed through the air-curtain guarding the inner entrance of the lock, he strode down the corridor and into the Observation Section.

Kirk Walish was there, alone in his seat. Standing over him was the lean young figure of Coop—who, Ben suddenly remembered, would be in charge here, now that Walt was gone.

"Ben—sir," said Coop. "Look at the screen. No, not the TV screen, the radar—we've picked up someone coming in through the sand. It's too thick to see on the TV screen, but it lookes to us like Walt, carrying somebody, by its shape and size. He's about fifty yards away."

Ben looked at the radar. There was a noticable blip, all right, but he was not experienced enough with it to deduce from that blip the shape of a man carrying someone else. A sudden, hollow sound like an explosion jerked his head around. He turned and stepped swiftly out into the corridor to hear the shout of voices and the sound of running feet.

Julian burst out of the corridor leading to the airlock, saw him, and came running up.

"Dome blew off—" gasped Julian. "Polly Neigh was thrown against the edge of the airlock door. Her leg— they're taking her to the dispensary. Nora says you must come—"

"All right," said Ben. "In a moment. Get on back down to that airlock. Tell them Walt's coming in carrying someone. I'll be there myself in a moment."

He turned and stepped back into Observation.

"Coop!" he snapped. "The minute you see the outer airlock door is closed, lift this ship into orbit. You hear me? Into orbit!"

"Yes sir." Coop turned and ran for the Control Section. Ben hesitated for a single glance at the TV screen. Through the swirling haze of sand and dust, he could now see dimly a spacesuited figure plodding forward, half bent over, with another figure across its shoulders. For a second the unbelievability of it numbed Ben's mind. For one man in a clumsy, heavy spacesuit to carry another was unbelievable enough—to do so in the greater gravity of Achernar One, in this dust storm, was legendary.

Walt must be almost to the lock. Ben turned and went out through the door into the corridor and ran for the lock, himself.

When he got there, Walt was already inside. Even as he reached the standing spacesuited figure, he felt the slight nauseous wave of feeling that told him the phase ship had lifted. Then the headpiece came off Walt's suit, urged by several pairs of hands, and Walt's face, pale and gaunt, streaming with perspiration, was revealed to him. Walt's eyes focused on Ben.

"All I could find—" he gasped, and then the eyes shuttered and the big body fell, almost pulling the others down with it.

Ben knelt beside Walt. There seemed to be nothing wrong with him except exhaustion from his superhuman effort. Ben turned to the other spacesuited figure. The headpiece had been taken off that, too, and the features revealed were those of Matt dead of suffocation.

"There's a rip in the back of his headpiece that long," said Hans Clogh, who was kneeling beside the body. His round face puckered. He added, in a strained voice, "Matt must have been dead even before Walt tried to carry him back."

All that way, thought Ben, looking at the dead man—all that way through the storm for nothing. A wall intercom buzzed. Somebody answered.

"—Yes, right away." Ben turned to look. "Sir, you're wanted in the dispensary."

Polly Neigh. Suddenly remembering, Ben turned and went back fast through the corridor from the airlock and turned right toward the door of the dispensary. When he stepped through the door, he saw a form under white covers on the table and the electrode leads from the electric anesthetizer attached to its head. Nora and a pale-faced Tessie Sorenson stood there, wearing white assistant's gowns.

Ben stared. Nora reached out and lifted the covering from the right leg of the figure of Polly Neigh on the table. Ben tightened inside at what he saw.

"Yes," he said, "you're right. It'll have to come off." He looked at the tourniquet above the crushed and mangled leg, which looked as if blunt pincers had closed upon it just below the knee. "Help me get ready, Nora."

She followed him into the adjoining room. Surprisingly, he was moving coolly and certainly now, washing up, getting into his own gown. But he could sense the danger of slowing down for a minute, of letting himself think that this was something he was not trained to do—something he had never done before.

To avoid that danger, he threw his mind back to that first year of medical school. He had never amputated a human limb in his life, but he had put a knife to a cadaver in roughly the same area. —It would be wisest to make the amputation as far down as possible, so that later on, someday, a real physician could redo it properly. He headed back into the other room.

The skin flap would need to be ample, to cover the stump . . . Nora was uncovering the leg again. . . . Then tie off the large blood vessels . . . suture the muscles to the bone . . .

Then Nora was handing him the heavy, cold shape of the electric knife, and suddenly time and space moved off into a different place than this room, and everything was crystal clear. . . .

Somehow it was over. Tessie had fainted. Somehow he and Nora had done it alone. Polly was sleeping under the electric impulses flowing through the electrodes into her brain—now set at sedation level. Washed up, free of his gown, he stumbled into his own quarters, into his office, and dropped into the chair behind his desk, almost too weary to move.

Murderer and butcher! If he had not kidnaped this ship and these people, two men would not be dead and young Polly would not be crippled. He rested his head in his hands, elbows on the desk. Easy enough to plead the survival of the whole human race as the necessity for what he did—hard to set the conscience within him at rest by such pleading.

It was that remark of Kirk's—the word "blooded" that had brought all this about. The mother cat in the wild brought its kittens face to face with the facts of life—the need to hunt and kill to survive. That word, that understanding, had forced it on him. Sooner or later, he had been forced to admit to himself, would come the time when the crew must come face to face with the realities of their situation, alone, in this ship, in a wilderness of stars and space that did not care whether they lived or died or got back home again.

Like the kitten, they had inevitably to be "blooded" for their own survival's sake. He looked down at his hands. They had been scrubbed palely white—but that made no difference to Ben, either.

The crew were not the only ones who had been blooded.

□ CHAPTER 5 □

"Ben!—Sir!"

Ben lifted his head with a start. Somehow, he had managed to doze off with his head in his hands and his elbows on the desk. He looked up and saw the round face of Hans Clogh in the doorway on the men's side of the ship.

"Walt," said Hans. "He's coming to—or waking up. Maybe you'd better come."

"Yes," said Ben. He pulled himself to his feet, feeling a sharp self-reproach. In his own moment of self-pity, he had forgotten that he had not one, but two patients. He followed Hans, who led him to the stateroom-compartment that was Walt's.

Nora was there by the bed, but she stood aside. Walt was muttering to himself, eyes closed. The others drew back. Ben reached under the covers for Walt's wrist. The pulse was slow and steady. Counting as he held it, Ben glanced around the orderly clutter of the room. Walt's watch and chain and medal lay on the desk, with a penknife, some change.

Walt opened his eyes. For a moment he seemed to have trouble focusing them.

"Ben?" he said.

"It's all right," said Ben. "You're back on the ship."

"Matt?" Walt's eyes widened. "How's Matt?"

"I'm afraid he didn't make it."

"He's dead?" Shock dulled Walt's eyes. "He was one of the ones I was counting on." The eyes closed. Slowly the face relaxed. Ben frowned down at the massive features. It had been an odd thing for Walt to say. But there was no chance to ask him about it now. His face and closed eyes were smoothed out once more in sleep. Ben put the wide, lax wrist gently back under the covers and turned to the doorway.

"He'll sleep. We'll just leave him alone."

"Yes," answered Nora. As he went out through the doorway, he felt her hand unexpectedly on his arm and turned sharply to look at her.

"You better get some rest, too, Ben."

"Rest?" he was suddenly horribly embarrassed. "Yes. Yes, of course I will!" Stiff and self-conscious, he tore himself out of her grasp and went down the corridor into his own quarters.

—But she was right, he acknowledged with the wave of weakness that overtook him as he shut the door of his office behind him. It was not a physical exhaustion he was feeling, but an emotional shock like that which Walt had evidently suffered. Ben headed for his bedroom and bed. Suddenly it seemed the most desirable place in the universe.

It was a matter of some weeks following the landing on Acherner One before Lee had the recycler properly working again. The air-recycling system had been put back to work immediately, but the food-base producing part could not be made operative for some time, and in that time twenty healthy appetites had caused the supply of freeze-dried sorted foods aboard to dwindle alarmingly.

The solar system of Earth lay a good two-thirds of the way out from the center of the spiral galaxy to which it belonged, out where stars were few and far between. The phase ship might dodge about from sun to sun out here for the lifetime of its crew and still never find a habitable world. But toward the center of the galaxy, the stellar population became many times more dense. Halfway in toward the center, fifteen thousand light-years from here, the phase ship would find the odds working in her favor instead of against her.

Ben had made this preliminary survey of the stars close to Earth because he had known his crew was not yet ready to face the larger voyage. Now, the crew was seasoned.

But the stored provisions were intended to make up only twenty percent of the ship's diet—the rest being supplied from the foods made of the food base produced by the recycler. The recycler was a chemical factory that reproduced the cycle found in primitive areas of Earth itself, those basic agricultural areas where human wastes were used to fertilize the soil in which were grown the crops that fed the humans who produced the wastes. As such, the recycler was about eighty percent efficient, with the lack being supplied from the stored foods of which the ship had possessed, on leaving Earth, a twelve-month supply. Aboard, they were now, thanks to the recycler's failure, down to little more than one month's supply—and with that the ship could not venture fifteen thousand light-years from home.

Somehow, thought Ben, grimly rubbing his forehead, that empty space in the food Stores Room below his office must be refilled. And without returning to Earth.

But the immediate prospects were not hopeful. Algol, when they shifted within observation distance of it, was planetless. The star Alcyone had two planets—but they were as bare and lifeless as the moon of Earth. After that there were hopes of Betelgeuse, then of Antares, but both proved fruitless. They shifted to Polaris, the Pole Star watched by the navigators of Earth's seagoing ships, and Observation began searching the neighborhood of the super-giant yellow star. Forty minutes later, Ben, working in his office, heard a knock at the door to the Control Section.

"Come in," he said, and looked up to see Lee smiling broadly in the doorway.

"A green planet?" said Ben before Lee could speak. Lee's grin slipped and he stared in astonishment. He could not guess that Ben was used now to reading the expressions of almost everyone aboard. "I'll come," added Ben, getting up and following Lee back into the Control Section.

"Prepare to shift," he ordered as the door closed behind him. The chant and procedure of shifting ran its course around him. They shifted—and every eye in the room came up.

Full on the TV screen on the wall there was a world the color of vegetation—lacking any large oceans, but with well-defined cold masses sliding at good altitudes above its surface.

Everyone was cheering.

"All right," said Ben, with deliberate flatness of tone. "Begin an intensive survey of this planet from orbit, Captain Ruiz." He turned and went back into the office.

It took two ship's days of sixteen hours each to make a complete examination of the newly found world from orbit. When it was completed, Ben called a conference and Lee brought the full report of Observation Section to it.

Ben sat reading the report, while Lee, Nora, and Walt waited in chairs around his desk.

"Well," said Ben, putting the report down at last, "the planet's clearly not habitable. Not in our sense. Not enough oxygen."

"It's not an impossible world, though," said Lee, diffidently. "Almost park-like. No oceans or any large lakes, you notice, not even any mountain ranges. Just that moss-like ground cover, the local herbivores grazing on it, and those clumps of big vines spreading out in the sun." He smiled at Ben almost shyly. "Almost a rest camp. And the surface temperature and gravity are only a little less than Earth's."

"A rest camp for all of us aboard this ship, is that it?" said Ben, ironically.

"We could wear oxygen packs and masks," said Lee eagerly. "And we could take precautions—"

"The way we did Achernar One," Ben said harshly. Lee looked crestfallen, and Ben felt a tinge of sympathy for him—but Lee was stuck with his role as spokesman for the crew as Ben was stuck with his as iron-willed commander of the ship.

"I'd like to make it perfectly plain," said Ben, tapping with a forefinger hard on the desk top before him, "that any unknown factor or area represents an unknown danger as far as this ship is concerned, and we aren't going to run into any unknown dangers just to give those of us aboard a chance to stretch our legs."

"Of course not," said Lee. "But there's the matter of the shortage in the food stores."

Ben looked at him.

"You're not thinking of slaughtering those animals down there for meat?" Ben said. "We couldn't risk eating alien flesh."

"No," there was a suspicion of a grin at the corners of Lee's mouth. "But whatever those giant vines are, that ground cover down there is chlorophyllous vegetation. There's a stage of the recycler we can use to engage in some chemical cookery. We ought to be able to reduce that vegetation to a solution and treat it with a process of hydrolysis to get glucose."

Ben blinked.

"You're sure of that?"

"Well—actually I'd have to try a sample," said Lee. "But I don't see why not." Ben looked from Lee to Walt and Nora. It was clear they had already had the scheme broached to them by Lee.

"All right," said Ben, abruptly. "But we'll build a wall around the ship the minute we touch down—and stay inside it."

"A wall?" asked Walt. "Against hervibores no bigger than dogs?"

"Big dogs," said Ben grimly. "But also in any case against what we don't know is down there—and because it's our duty to stay alive until we've found the world we're after."

This time they went down slowly and with the caution of a wild animal approaching the area of a possible trap. And as soon as they were down, Ben had armed guards out around the ship and they proceeded to fortify themselves.

The spot Walt had chosen for the landing was a shallow basin of open ground ringed with hummocks too low to be called hills. This open area was about a mile by half a mile in extent, and the tough, half-moss, halfsawgrass ground cover was everywhere except where the tangles of monster vines, eighty to a hundred yards across, dotted the slopes of the hummocks.

Under the ground cover an explosive charge echo-sounding, fired before the phase ship touched down, had revealed half a foot of gravelly earth and under that a bed of gray limestone. It was this bed that the phase-ship crew attacked with oxygen packs on their backs and protective antisunburn cream on all exposed areas of skin.

With ultra-high-temperature cutting torches, the exposed limestone was quarried up into blocks from a trench encircling the ship. Then, using a power-lift operated on electric current running through a cable from the drive unit inside the ship, the blocks were fitted and raised into a ten-foot-high wall along the inside edge of the ditch and banked by a slope of earth on the wall's inner side. Before night fell six hours later, there was about the ship a small open area some sixty feet from wall to wall, then a slope to the top of the ten-foot barrier of quarried stone, and a six-foot-deep, twelve-foot-wide trench beyond the sheer outer face of the wall.

With the sinking of Polaris, yellow and small as a lemon against the hummocked horizon, Ben had powerful lights mounted to illuminate not only the enclosure, but a good distance beyond the walls.

These burned throughout the night, while a team of four people stood guard at all times, armed with the new Weyerlander half-gun with which the phase-ship had been supplied. This was a rifle-pistol with adjustable stock, convertible to full automatic fire, with a hundred and forty grain bullet in what was known as a half-cartridge, in a clip of fifty. It was a trifle cumbersome as a hand weapon and had little accuracy over ranges beyond a couple of hundred hards, but Ben had chosen it as ideal for close-up defense by amateur shooters against unknown inimical elements. There were light and heavy long-range hunting rifles aboard, as well, for those who might know how to use them.

The rising of Polaris the next morning after all these preparations was almost an anticlimax. The early rays of that star showed the grazing herbivores, the vine clumps, the ground cover of the little area as peaceful as it had the night before.

"Just like a park," said Lee, with mild triumph to Ben, as they mounted the wall the following morning.

"Too much like a park," growled Ben. It could be that he was merely obeying a human impulse to defend himself, he thought, sweeping the area outside the fort with wide-angle binoculars, but he did not think so. The excavated limestone had turned up a generous supply of fossils, up to and including something like a small crocodile. That such evolutionary development should end with a single species of herbivore as the planet-wide dominant life form, bothered Ben. "We'll send teams out to gather the moss-grass," he said now, "but I want them to stay close and I want armed guards with them."

"All right," said Lee, agreeably. "I'll start dismantling the recycler again and moving the sections outside that I'll want."

So, as Polaris climbed in the sky, Ben stood on the wall with the mask attached to his oxygen backpack pressing hard against the skin of his face and the curve of the binoculars above them bumping his eyebrow ridge, as he watched the teams from the ship gathering the local herbage. But there were no incidents. The herbivores shied and galloped off when they were aproached, and the teams, investigating the vine clumps from a distance, reported that the big vine stems, a foot or more in diameter farther back toward their roots, became so tangled just beyond the edge that no animal much larger than a squirrel could crawl through them.

By noon of the next day, Lee had in operation what everyone was already beginning to call the glucose factory. The moss-grass yielded not only this, but a surplus of sorted water, which, distilled out, went to replenish the water stores of the phase ship. This relieved Ben, who had foreseen the problem of sending out a team to the nearest small lake just beyond the western hummocks, out of sight of the ship, for water.

On the morning of the third day, as he was standing on the wall, he heard footsteps behind him and turned to see the masked figure of Lee, recognizable by the way he walked, and carrying a glass-covered container.

"Look at that," said Lee, hollowly, but triumphantly, through the voice-box diaphragm of his mask.

Ben took the box and looked. Under the glass cover, he saw what looked like a mass of fine reddish-black grains.

"You remember those two herbivores we killed for specimens yesterday?" asked Lee. "Guess what you're holding?" Behind Lee, the massive figure of Walt climbed onto the wall, followed by the tall, thin figure of Coop.

"What?" asked Ben.

"An artificial protein," Lee said, excitedly. "I reduced some of the herbivore flesh to its constituent amino acids and recombined those into this—we can eat it, Ben. It's as nourishing as freeze-dried steak, dry weight, ounce for ounce. And the amount of flesh we have to process to get it is less than two to one by weight as opposed to over twelve to one of the moss-grass we're processing to get glucose!"

Walt spoke over Lee's shoulder, his deep voice vibrating in the diaphragm of his mask.

"We can send out a couple of teams," said Walt, "and drive enough herbivores into this area in two days to supply us with all the native flesh we can process."

"They drive easily—" put in Coop, eagerly.

"Yes," said Ben. It all seemed too good to be true— but that, he told himself, was bending over backward to find fault. Among all the kinds of worlds there must be in the galaxy, some worlds had to be park-like and completely harmless and bountiful. He gazed out over the peaceful landscape and the innocently grazing forms of the herbivores. It would be unthinkable to pass up the chance of storing up on as desirable a foodstuff as this artificial protein. He put the niggling doubts in the back of his mind firmly aside.

"Yes," he said decisively. "Two teams. I'll make up a list of who's to go."

□ CHAPTER 6 □

EARLY THE FOLLOWING morning, two teams of four men each, one led by Hans Clogh and the other one led by Coop, left the fort, hiking east and west. As Coop had said, the herbivores were not hard to drive, provided you did not hurry them. They would let anyone approach to within a critical distance of about thirty feet. Closer than that and they would move off about another thirty feet at a trot, provided the one approaching stood still. If he tried to follow the herbivore, all others close to it would go into a panic-stricken, stampeding flight. They would gallop in all directions, not stopping until they were tired.

It would therefore be necessary, Ben reminded himself, standing on the wall beside Polly Neigh, that the drive be made slowly and patiently. The two teams were to circle to the south and make a half day's march in that direction. Then they were to start back, driving herbivores before them. Night would fall before they were more than halfway back, but it had been observed that the herbivores did not stray far during the dark hours. In fact, they had a tendency to cluster together. The next day should see the two teams joining the herds they were driving and bringing them in together to the fort.

Ben was aware that Polly had lowered the binoculars with which she had been watching Coop's team disappear over the hummock horizon. He lowered his own binoculars and turned to meet her gaze.

"You're responsible for them," she said. Turning, she went, a little awkwardly with her artificial leg, back down the inner slope leading to the wall top. Ben stared

after her for a second, startled. It was quite true that he
was responsible, but Polly had not meant that, clearly.
She had meant that she was holding Ben personally responsible for the safety of Coop. Ben did not know
whether to be pleased that there was at least one person
who shared his misgivings about Old Twenty-nine, or
disturbed by this evidence of the intensity of Polly's
feelings. This was still the shake-down cruise. If, when
they came to their real task, thousands of light-years
from home, he should be faced with Polly putting
Coop's safety before the welfare of the ship and the rest
of those aboard—he filed the thought for future reference.

Both teams were out of sight now. He turned and left
the wall himself and went down the slope into the enclosed area surrounding the ship.

Already it looked like a slaughterhouse. The previous
day, they had killed and brought into the fort some
twelve of the beasts. Each animal yielded about fifty
pounds of usable flesh that could be turned into half its
weight in edible protein grains. Three hundred pounds
of grains—it was a good beginning.

The phase ship, the shutters drawn back over its observation window on top, gleamed in the bright-yellow
light of distant Polaris, looking hardly larger than the
Sun from Earth's surface. Below the ship, a dismounted
section of the recycler chugged away, extracting and
freezing oxygen from the small amount in the native
atmosphere to replenish ship and back-pack supplies.
Up beyond this section was the so-called digestive section of the recycler at work on the soup-like liquid Lee
was producing in a large plastic vat of diluted acids
from herbivore flesh.

The stench was undoubtedly abominable—to judge
by the small amount of it that had clung to equipment
and clothing and so gotten into the ship's air, which was
also recycled with oxygen in the backpacks to let the
crew members breathe outside the ship. Given time, the
whole inner atmosphere of the phase ship could be
flushed and the odor removed from it—but there was
no time now. On the verge of working up a resentment

against the odors he was breathing, Ben remembered that the two teams out driving herbivores would be facing the fact of living with the same odors, carried in their backpacks for the next two days.

Thought of the driving teams recalled him to the reason that had brought him down to the slaughterhouse area. He had wanted another look at one of the herbivore carcasses. Working on a table set up outside the ship the day before, he had made a general dissection of one of the bodies, but it had just now occurred to him that he might have overlooked the forest on examining its trees, so to speak. He found a whole carcass in the pile of unprepared flesh and pulled it out on top of the heap to examine it.

It came out stiff with rigor mortis. Ben laid it out on its side and ran his eye over it.

It was a slightly-furred animal, four-legged, barrel-bodied, somewhat resembling the small camel-like llama of South America, back home. The differences were a neck mounting almost vertically from the shoulders, a huge chest, and a literally tiny head with black eyes facing forward to give binocular vision, instead of the wide angle of single-eye vision typical of Earth's wild herbivores who must keep steadily on the watch for predators.

All told, the herbivore would have weighed about a hundred and fifty pounds on Earth and would have been easy prey for just about anything large enough to pull it down.

It was, for one thing, practically brainless. The tiny skull contained a sort of primitive end-brain, possibly housing the flight, feeding, and breeding reflex patterns of the creature. At the far end of the nerve cable leading down the long neck, however, there was buried between the shoulders a large, complex nerve center that probably took over some of the instinctual reflexes and duties ordinarily housed in the brain case of Earthly mammals. Any shock to this buried nerve center seemed to kill the herbivores immediately.

Ben stooped to examine the hooves. They were split, two-toed, like the hooves of the Artiodactyla of Earth;

and like the hooves of deer in particular, their edges
were razor sharp. Ben ran his finger along the sharp
edge of one of the forehooves before him, and made up
his mind. He had seen an incautious biology lab atten-
dant back on Earth badly slashed by a buck deer who
had just had its horns removed, a deer that the atten-
dant had mistakenly thought was therefore harmless.

Lee was busy with his protein cookery. Walt was
occupied with his duties as Duty Officer, a job he was
now holding down around the clock to free Lee for the
other work. Accordingly, Ben hunted up Kirk Walish
and told him to get together a working party of at least
three other off-duty people—preferably men only. Then
he went in search of Nora, finding her also off-duty and
engaged in the feminine occupation of washing her hair,
and therefore unavailable beyond the door of showers
and washroom on the women's side of the ship. Informed of what Ben needed, however, she sent out Tessie Sorenson with directions and the storeroom keys.
Ben led his crew down and broke out some twenty
small explosive packages and two hundred yards of cable explosive—of the type developed by underwater
demolition teams twenty years before.

"All right," said Ben to Kirk and Kirk's three drafted
assistants, when they were out beyond the wall. "We're
going to lay out two lines of explosive cable, with
charges at ten-yard intervals along them."

"Can I ask why?" inquired Kirk, dryly.

His black eyes met Ben's—but without the smolder-
ing anger Ben used to find there before Achernar One.
It was hard to decide whether Kirk had decided not to
be a rebel, or just to stop advertising the fact he was
one. Ben decided to give him the benefit of the doubt—
particularly since the other three crew members were
listening intently.

"I'm going to set up a slaughter pen," he answered.
"Shooting those twelve beasts yesterday was one thing.
But when the two teams under Coop and Hans get here,
they ought to be driving at least a hundred animals in
front of them. Killing them one by one while the others

mill around isn't going to be either safe or efficient. So, we'll do it this way."

Kirk nodded. And, under Ben's directions, the five of them laid out the two lines of explosive cable thirty feet apart and running from the wall around the phase ship almost to the vine clump at the base of one of the surrounding hummocks. The explosives packages, each with a killing circle twenty feet in diameter, were attached at their proper intervals. So spaced, the killing circles of the two lines overlapped to make a long rectangle.

"Well," said Kirk, with apparent satisfaction when they were done, "that'll take care of a hundred herbivores—or more. The only trick will be herding them inside the area."

"Yes," said Ben. He did not mention that in his opinion herding the animals into the area would be the least of their troubles—to say that would betray his hidden reason for setting out the explosive cables and charges. "We'll bury the cable and charges and run the cable underground and through the wall, so that it can't get cut by accident."

They did so, bringing the cable inside the wall and up to its top to the firing box. Standing by the box and looking out over the space before him, Ben noticed that the shallow basin had once more filled with grazing herbivores. There were more there now than there had been yesterday when Lee with his team had caught and slaughtered the dozen. More, in fact, than there had been in the area since the phase ship's landing.

Ben turned and called to the masked figure of Lee, beckoning him up on the wall. Lee waved back, finished whatever he was doing at the processing end of the digestive section of the recycler, and turned to climb the slope. He came up to stand beside Ben, who pointed out over the area.

"Maybe we better round those up," said Ben, "before they stray off again and leave us with just a handful around the ship."

"Yes," said Lee. He nodded, his dark hair joggling

forward on his forehead above his eyes and face mask. "There's no reason we can't run the processing through the night as well, and to do that, I'll need twice again as much as I've got in the way of raw material."

"There ought to be that much out there," said Ben. In fact there was. He had made a rough count of over forty herbivores. "I'll take a crew and round them up. Oh, who'd you use before? I might as well take experienced people while I'm at it."

"Mostly women. They make better drivers than the men—more patient." Lee's eyes above his mask met Ben's and Ben understood. Lee was putting in a pitch for the women to be allowed out beyond the wall—something at which Ben had hesitated largely so far. "Ask Tessie Sorenson—she'll get them together for you."

"All right," growled Ben.

"I'll get back to work, then," said Lee. He turned about and went down the slope to the recycler section. Ben, after a second, followed him and cut off toward the ship.

The drive worked out excellently. By midafternoon, thirty-four more carcasses—eight hundred and fifty potential pounds of protein powder—had been added to the pile awaiting processing. Curiously enough, new herbivores were already beginning to drift into the area. Ben frowned to himself. If they had been prepared to take time, as much as a week, and had known that the herbivores would not be driven off by this kind of harvesting, they could have sat tight and not sent out the two teams to make a drive of the animals to the ship.

But, Ben reminded himself, sitting down finally in his office to examine privately the newest star charts made by Observation, he had not known. And in any case, on principle, he wanted to spend no more time on the surface of any ineligible planet than the ship had to spend there.

He became involved in the charts and the problem of the best stellar neighborhood to investigate first, fifteen thousand light-years in toward the center. He did not notice the passage of time within the windowless walls of his office until the chart he was studying suddenly swam out of focus before his eyes. He blinked and straightened up, suddenly conscious that his neck was stiff and his back was aching from bending over the charts. He looked at his watch.

It was five hours since they had finished the herbivore drive in the area around the ship. Midafternoon had become midevening. He had worked through the normal sunset dinner hour. For a moment he thought of going down to the lounge for food now—then decided it was sleep he needed more than nourishment. A short nap. . . .

He locked up the star charts and the notes he had made on them in his walk-in safe and went into his bedroom. He dropped on the bed there and closed his eyes.

For a few minutes as he lay there with his eyes closed, he thought that he would not be able to sleep after all. There were too many different problems chasing each other like wildcat kittens at play in his brain. Then, somehow, without even realizing he had fallen asleep, he was being roused by someone shaking his shoulder.

He sat bolt upright on the bed, reflexively. Walt was towering over him at the bedside.

"What is it?" Ben asked.

"Reports from both the driving teams," said Walt, deeply. "They've been attacked."

"Attacked—I'll come!" said Ben, lifting his still sleep-numb body from the bed in the same second and heading for the door. With Walt following him, he crossed his office, walked through a deserted Control Section and a deserted Computation Section into an Observation Section with half a dozen people in it, clustered around the side-by-side TV screen that connected with the portable transceivers, one of which had been carried by each team.

Ben licked his lips, coming to a halt behind them. His mouth was cinderous and his head was like a block of wood. The collar of his white coveralls was damp where it touched his throat, sweated through in the heaviness of his slumber.

"Do we need all these people here?" he said harshly. "Let's have everybody not on duty out of this Section."

Three of the people present reluctantly abandoned their position and went out the further door to the corridor and the Lounge beyond. A fourth person defiantly stayed put. It was Polly.

"All right, Polly," said Ben, knowing that by making an exception he was tearing down the image of implacable authority he had tried so hard to build up for himself. He turned his attention back to the screens. Both showed the four men of a team, masked and backpacked, sitting on laid out and inflated sleeping bags on the ground, their half-guns uneasily in their hands, gleaming in the glare of the portable searchlights set up to illuminate the fifty feet of area surrounding. Before the party in the right hand screen, a dark thick shape the length of a man lay like a chunk of blackness along the moss-grass.

"What's that?" Ben asked Walt.

"What attacked them," said Walt. "With Hans' team's case, something came out of the darkness into the light and got away again before they could get a good look at it, when they fired. But with Coop's team—" he gestured to the right hand screen, "three of the things came right into the light, sat down, and looked them over before one of them decided to charge. They killed that one and Coop thinks they wounded the two others."

"Yes," said Ben. He leaned forward, pressed the transmit key below the right hand screen, and spoke to the group pictured on it.

"Coop? Let me have a closeup picture of this thing you've killed."

One of the masked figures came toward the screen until it blocked out everything else. The scene swayed up into the air, approached the shape of darkness on the grass, and swung aside to let the light fall on the dead creature as the transceiver itself was set down on the grass. Ben looked at furred legs and a furred belly of pale tan color.

"No," said Ben, "Hold it up—so I can look down on the animal."

The transceiver was lifted. Ben looked from an apparent distance of two feet down at the dead body of the attacker.

Its resemblance to the herbivores was apparent in the huge barrel-chest, and in the upright, if shorter, neck, and the eyes set side by side at the front of the head for binocular vision. But it was the *differences* that one noticed most.

The body was long-bodied, shorter, and heavier-legged than that of the herbivores. It was much weightier and more powerful in appearance. The legs did not end in hooves but in three toes with soft pads and hardened or horny front edges undoubtedly serving the same purpose as claws. All in all, the body was somewhat weasel-like on a large scale, allowing for the upright neck and the skull-case, which was large and intelligent-looking—almost domed in human and anthropoid fashion. The most remarkable parts of the body, however, were two hairless appendages sprouting from the front base of the neck.

"Let me have a closer look at one of those things on its neck," ordered Ben. A hand reached out from beyond the screen and stretched out one of the appendages. It was something like a thin, hairless whip, almost as thick as a man's wrist at the base where it joined the neck, but tapering to what seemed to be a horny or hardened point nearly three feet from the base.

"They seem to be able to use them the way South American monkeys use their tails—prehensile," said someone behind Ben, having found the word he was searching for at the beginning of the comment.

"Let me see the teeth," ordered Ben. The hand holding the furless whip dropped it and reached down to lift the lips from the right side of the dead muzzle. Ben counted two spade-like incisors and a heavy, dagger-shaped canine in front of only three other essentially flat-topped grinding teeth. It was plainly the jaw-armament of a carnivore.

"That's all right. I've seen enough," said Ben to whoever was holding back the lips. The fingers let go. Ben turned to Walt.

"Well," he said, "that's what ordinarily feeds on our herbivores." His voice was bitter with the inner self-reproach he was feeling. "Anyone who'd ever heard the word ecology should have known that with herbivores like this there would be plain evidence of a cursorial carnivore just around the corner."

The moment the words were out of his mouth, he regretted them. They had all the ring of an invitation to the others to excuse him for his negligence and carelessness. It had been up to him to trust to his suspicions about the danger beneath the bucolic landscape of Old Twenty-nine. He had not done so, and beating his breast over the fault in front of the rest of the crew was not going to remedy the matter.

"Coop!" he said harshly. "Hans!" He had reached out and was holding down the transmitter keys below both screens. A masked face filled each screen, inquiringly. "Keep someone on watch at all times until sunrise. And, as soon as there's light at all to move by, I want you to start back. Forget the drive."

"But we've got a herd of at least fifty moving—" it was Coop's voice.

"Forget the drive!" Ben heard himself snapping at the screen. "Get back here to the ship as fast as you can. You understand me?"

There was ready assent from Hans, grudging assent from Coop's voice.

"All right," said Ben. "That's all for now, then." He let go of the transmitter keys and straightened up. He looked at Walt. "Who've we got standing guard out on the walls," he asked.

"Ralph Egan," said Walt.

"Just one man? I want four," said Ben. "One to each wall. Find them. I'm going out now, myself."

He took a pair of night glasses and went back through the sections, into his office, and opened his walk-in safe. Just inside the door was a rack holding three of the hunting rifles. He took one and a loaded clip of ammunition and locked the safe again. He went out toward the airlock, fitting the clip into the rifle.

When he emerged from the airlock with oxygen backpack and mask on, he found the recycler sections still at work, Julian Tyree standing in Lee's place near the acid vat recognizable by the dark expanse of skin above his mask. Ben went to him.

"Anything happening outside the walls?" he asked.

"Not so far as I know," said Julian. His eyes were inquiring. "Lee's getting some sleep," he added, unnecessarily.

"Maybe you should, too," said Ben, recalled for a moment to other things. He had only Lee and Julian aboard who knew anything about chemistry—and in addition Julian had the same odd sort of technical genius that Lee had. He could not afford to lose either of them. "Can't this apparatus run itself for a while?"

"Yes . . . but," said Julian. "I'd rather stay with it. I've had a good deal of sleep, you know."

"Well—all right," Ben swung about and went up the ramp toward the half-gun-armed figure on the wall, which turned to meet him as he came. "Ralph—everything quiet up here?"

"Yes." The young, blue eyes of Ralph above the mask he wore were inquiring. Ben turned to look out beyond the walls and stared at a fifty-foot searchlighted strip of ground—beyond which was darkness. "Cover your eyes," he told Ralph Egan.

"Cover—" Ralph began.

"Just do it!" snapped Ben. He watched as Ralph put a hand over his eyes above the mask and then turned to call to Julian. Seeing the big figure of Walt just emerging from the airlock, he changed his mind. "Walt!" he shouted.

Walt lifted his head.

"When I yell at you," Ben called, "cut all lights."

The figure of Walt nodded and waved an acknowledgment. Ben, shielding his eyes against the glare of lights below him, stared up at the sky. It was clear of clouds and all three of the planet's rather dim moons were in the sky at once. Their light should be equivalent to fairly bright moonlight, once the artificial light was out. He covered his own eyes as tightly as he could with his free hand and slowly counted to one hundred.

"Now!" he shouted over his shoulder. "Lights out!"

He counted to five more and uncovered his eyes. For a moment he thought that covering them had not worked, and then he realized that he was still facing inward and down into the lightless depths of the fort. He blinked and the scene resolved out of the triple moonlight. He turned and looked outward.

On a now-silver carpet of moss-grass there was a clump of dark shapes huddled off to his right, with the long, foolish necks and little heads of the herbivores. But, as he swept his gaze from right to left, he saw other shapes, individual dark shapes of longer, more squat outline, sitting or pacing at distances of a hundred yards from the fort on every side. Turning slowly, he counted fifteen of them.

Slowly, he slipped the leather sling of the heavy rifle over his head and left shoulder and locked his supporting left arm with it. He took careful aim at one of the sitting figures. The triple moonlight ran down the length of the barrel and gilded the front sight. The edge of the leather sling bit hard into his forearm under the coveralls. He pressed the trigger and the seated figure leaped into the air, scrabbled about on its side, and lay still.

The other figures raced like ghosts to the nearest vine clusters and vanished under the outer vines, bellying down to the earth as they disappeared.

"So that's it," said Walt's voice.

Ben turned to find Walt standing beside him on the wall.

"That's it," said Walt dispassionately, "they have dens dug out among the roots of the vines underground—and as long as they came out only at night, we'd never have known they were there."

"I want two men to help me," said Ben, unslinging his rifle. "The rest of you cover us from here, with the lights off."

They brought the body back in, not without some labor, for it weighed perhaps half again as much as one of the herbivores, and the guards patrolled the wall with all lights out. However, no other vine-tigers—the name had come to everybody's lips seemingly out of nowhere—showed themselves. And with the coming of daylight, Ben began his dissection of the one he had shot.

It was similar in internal structure to the herbivores. The complex nerve center at the base of the neck was no larger, but the skull-enclosed brain was surprisingly large, with a volume of over eight hundred and thirty cubic centimeters, less than a hundred cc. smaller than the brain of *pithecanthropus erectus,* the fossil preman of Java, and only a couple of hundred cc. short of the brain volume of the smallest-brained modern man known.

Ben washed up in a plastic container of water brought to him outside the ship and called a conference of Lee, Nora, and Walt in his office.

"They're bright," Ben told the other three, once they were seated around his desk. "I couldn't find any sure evidence of a speech center, but they must have some means of communication. It's interesting to note that they paid no attention to us until we started slaughtering the herbivores."

There was a moment in which none of the others seemed to understand. Then Walt spoke.

"You mean the herbivores are their cattle?" Walt asked.

"Either by conscious breeding or an accident of parallel evolution," said Ben. "Notice, there're no other large carnivores to dispute the herbivores with these vine-tigers? Notice how the herbivores bunch up at night when the vine-tigers are out and let them or us get within easy charging distance—thirty feet or so—before panicking?"

"Still," said Lee. "Even if it's true, what can they do to us?"

"I don't know," said Ben. He had engaged in some private speculations on that question, but caution stopped his tongue now. If he was right, they would all find out about it, anyway. If he was wrong, there was no point in mentioning it. "But we're not going to wait around to find out. As soon as the two teams are back here, we'll lift. Lee, how long will it take to put those recycler sections back in place on the ship?"

Lee's teeth flashed cheerfully in his brown face, which had almost miraculously regained a share of its original tan in these two days of Polaris sunlight.

"We can have them back on board in half an hour," he answered. "And reconnected and working in a couple of hours aboard ship after that—I've got assistants that're used to the work, now."

"Fine," said Ben. "I want you to work up to the last possible minute, but no later. Walt, I want the Observation, Computation, and Control Sections aboard ship here manned, and the ship ready to lift at a moment's notice—" He broke off. There had been a knock at the door to Control Section. "Come in!"

Kirk Walish opened the door and stuck his head in.

"Calls from both teams," he announced. "They're getting crowded by herds of herbivores moving in the same direction they're going. They may have to take shelter in vine clumps until things thin out."

"Get me a hand phone!" snapped Ben, getting to his feet. "Bring it to me on the wall outside. Come on!"

The last two words were addressed to Walt, Lee, and Nora. They also rose and followed him out of the ship and up onto the south wall outside.

"Look at all those herbivores!" said Kirk, whistling.

In fact, the shallow, basin-like area surrounding them was full of the native animals, dashing about constantly as a chain reaction of excitement kept a portion of them always in a panic. Kirk appeared on the wall beside Ben and handed Ben the black shape of the hand phone.

"Where did they all come from?" Nora was asking.

"The vine-tigers are driving them in," said Ben, briefly, and was vaguely surprised to see the others on the wall staring at him. There were no vine-tigers in sight, but the responsibility of the native carnivores for what was before them was so obvious to Ben that he had to make a momentary mental adjustment to understand that it might not be obvious to the others.

At any rate, there was no time to explain himself now. He lifted the hand phone to his lips.

"Give me Coop and Hans both on a combined hookup," he said to Observation. "—Coop? Hans?" The two voices answered. "Coop, you answer me first. Hans, second. Now, are you both sure you can't keep coming?" He listened. "All right, then—you're both with your teams inside the edge of a vine clump now? —And the herbivores don't come close to the clumps? All right, how far from the ship are you?"

"Less than a mile," answered the voice of Coop. "A mile and a bit," said Hans.

"Can you see each other?" asked Ben. "No? All right, I'm looking in your direction. Each of you send up one smoke signal. Let me know when you shoot."

He stood watching, above the milling herbivores, already pounding the moss-grass into nonexistence, so that the grayish-brown gravelly earth showed under their hooves and above the hummocks forming the horizon two hundred yards to the south of the wall. For a moment there was only the blue sky beyond with a single cloud shaped like a white puffball, and then two thin plumes of gray smoke rose in the distance, as two voices spoke over the hand phone in his ear.

"I see," Ben answered. "You can't be more than three hundred yards apart at the most. Now, here's what I want you to do. If you get a chance to move toward the ship, move—but keep us informed here. Otherwise, as soon as it gets dark, the herbivores will start quieting down. Then I want you to start moving, regardless. Head straight for us here, and you should meet just beyond the hummocks to the south of us. But together or apart, keep coming until you get to the vine clump on top of the hummock dead in line with the southwest angle of the wall and the ship inside. Got that?"

He waited while the voices of the two men acknowledged.

"When you get that far, wait," he said. "I'll tell you what to do after that. Now each of you—Coop first. Repeat what I've just told you."

They repeated.

"All right," said Ben. "Remember, keep in contact. I'm going to cut my connection with you now, but there'll be someone at the other end in Observation from now on." He hesitated. "Any questions?"

There were none. He gave the hand phone back to Kirk and turned to Lee, pointing down into the trench in front of the wall. Several bodies of hervibores lay there—beasts who had been crowded by their fellows into a fatal fall.

"There'll probably be more of that as the day goes on," he said to Lee. "See if you can't rig up some kind of grappling hooks, and fish the bodies up so that you can use them. I want you to keep the processing going as long as you can."

"If I can keep it going until night," said Lee, "we ought to end up with a ton and a half of protein grains. That'd be enough to take care of us for nine months."

"Good," said Ben. "All right, everybody get busy. Walt—keep anyone you need in the Sections to get the ship ready to lift, but send me at least four more armed men for the walls, here."

They went about their various duties. Ben stood on the wall a little longer to check his conclusion that the number of herbivores in the basin area surrounding them was increasing still, then went back down the slope and into the ship. For him there was nothing to do now but wait until sunset.

A sensible man who had been running short on both food and sleep would take this opportunity to get some of both. Ben went down to the lounge and ate, then back to his own quarters and lay on his bed. A sensible man, he reminded himself again, would get some sleep. But he did not.

He lay on his back on the bed, staring at the ceiling of white-painted metal over him while his imagination threw up possible accident after possible accident in the process of getting the eight men back safely inside the ship—and tried to come up with a solution for each contingency.

After a while, a curious vibration attracted his attention, felt through the very structure of the bed he was lying on, and the floor and walls around him. He got up, masked, and went outside and discovered what it was. The basin was now filled with herbivores, thousands of them, and the constant drumming of their charging, panic-stricken hooves was sending a vibration through the ground all about.

He stood on the wall looking out. Lee was beside him, watching the grappling up of some of the dead herbivores crowded into the trench—a trench already filled level with the ground about them by those same bodies. Now, weaker herbivores were being crushed to death by their fellows against the stone face of the wall.

"If they keep that up," said the voice of Lee in Ben's ear, "they'll be over the top of the wall before too many hours."

"Yes," said Ben shortly. There was no point in discussing the obvious. He glanced at the sun and at his watch. It was midafternoon. He decided to stay on top of the wall for a while in case things should get worse.

The ground cover had long ago been hammered into the hardpacked earth by the hooves of the herbivores. Now a steady fog of dust was rising. Rising, too, was the tide of dead and trampled herbivores at the outer face of the wall. Below Ben a ramp of dead and dying animals was building ever closer to the point at which they would spill over the wall. By sunset the backs of the stampeding animals were just below Ben's feet. He could have stepped out on them.

The animals were voiceless, but the sound of their running and snorting for breath was now a deafening roar. As the sun touched the horizon, Ben went down to speak to Lee. He had to shout with his lips close to Lee's ear to make himself understood.

"Get your equipment aboard!" he ordered. Lee nodded.

With the setting of the sun the herbivores farther off began to slow down with their evening quietude. The three moons were already high in the sky. But those in the flat area close around the walls, long since lost to anything but the reflex to run, run, and keep running until danger was left behind or exhaustion dropped them, continued their milling. Their backs crowded against and above the wall now like the backs of steers in a pen.

"Ben!" It was Lee on the wall at his side, shouting in his ear. "They've reached the vine clump you told them to come to—both Hans' and Coop's teams! They say the herbivores are quieting down somewhat out beyond this basin—but the vine-tigers are out." He pushed something into Ben's hand. Ben looked down and saw it was a hand phone.

"What're you doing up here?" he demanded.

"No one else to spare!" shouted Lee. "I've got everything aboard and I—"

Something came out of the smoke-like dust and the tricky moonlight, running with incredible speed across the backs of the racing herbivores and launched itself through the air and onto Lee. They went down together on top of the wall, the shape of the vine-tiger on top. Moving without thinking, Ben took one long stride toward them, lifted his right hand, and brought the metal weight of the hand phone down with all his strength between the shoulder blades of the carnivore, above where the large nerve-complex would be.

For a moment the alien shape sprawled limply. In that moment, Ben dropped the hand phone, grasped the upper part of the furry body, and, using all his strength, hauled the heavy creature free of Lee. Just as it began to struggle once more, he sent it toppling inside the wall. It twisted in the air, falling, trying to right itself like a cat before it hit, but as it landed on its side, half a dozen half-guns from the surrounding walls hammered it into death and stillness. Ben snatched up the hand phone.

"Help, up here on the wall!" he souted into it. "Lee's been savaged by one of the carnivores! Get Nora. Get some men out here to carry him back in." He remembered suddenly the purpose for which Lee had brought him the hand phone. "—And connect me with Hans and Coop in the vine clump!"

"You're connected—" It was the voice of Kirk Walish. "They'll be right up to get Lee." There was a moment's rushing silence in the earphone, and then Ben heard Coop's voice.

"Ben?"

"Coop? Listen to me!" said Ben harshly, holding the mouthpiece close to his lips. "The herbivores'll be over the wall here in fifteen or twenty minutes, and they'll swarm over the ship and crush her—and we'll have to lift. That means you and Hans have to come in—now!"

"We can't—"

"I know!" snapped Ben. "But I'm going to clear a path for you." He turned and ran down to the corner of the wall, where the firing box stood, the ends of the two explosive cables plugged into the first two of the seven detonator sockets in front of the vertical plunger. He spoke again into the phone. "Now listen. Get ready to run, single file. I'm going to blow a path for you right through the middle of these herbivores. When you see the explosion, start running, and don't stop until you're up on the wall here. Understand me?"

"Yes," said the voice of Coop. There was a little pause. When Coop spoke again, Ben heard an odd note in his voice. "I'll let Hans and his men go first."

"All right," said Ben. There was no time to discuss the matter. He reached down and jerked one cable end out of its detonator socket. "Ready?"

"Ready," said Coop's voice.

"Then go!" Ben pushed down on the plunger. A great, hundred-yard long knifeblade of fire and upflung black bodies sprang suddenly and momentarily into being in a line between him and the vine clump where the two teams were sheltering.

The explosion rocked the ground. For a moment everything was still, and then the herbivores were in scrambling stampede away from the line of the explosion. Ben stared at the vine clump, dimly visible through the settling dust in the triple moonlight, but no figures had emerged from it. There were still some scattered herbivores in the fifty yards between the far end of the explosive line and the vine clump, and the first few of the herbivores were beginning to be pushed by their struggling mates back across the path of the explosion.

"Run!" shouted Ben into the phone. "What's wrong there? Run!"

"—No . . ." A babbling, yammering voice, a man's voice distorted by terror, which Ben could hardly recognize as the voice of Hans Clogh, came from the receiver of the hand phone. "We can't make it! They're closing in already. Tell them to bring the ship and get us! Bring the ship—"

Hans' voice was cut off.

"Hans!" shouted Ben. "We can't bring the ship—you know that! We'd have to shift out to orbit and in again. It'd take us hours! Run—" But, with despair rising in him, he saw that the open lane through the herbivores was already closing. He took a deep breath. "Coop!"

"Yes, sir?"

"Can you stay put in that vine clump for as much as ten hours?"

"No," answered Coop. "Not for one hour. There's vine-tigers all around us and more coming in all the time. Sooner or later they'll come in after us."

"All right, then!" said Ben. "Listen. I can do it once more—open things up like I did just then. Get ready. I'm going to do it, and when I do I want you to start in with everyone you can bring—in Hans' team as well as your own. Those who won't come you'll have to leave behind. You understand me?"

"Yes."

"Right, then." Ben reached down and put the remaining cable end into a detonator socket. "Ready?"

"Ready."

"Go!" shouted Ben.

Once more as Ben pushed the plunger, the line of fire spouted. For a second Ben saw nothing—then, through the thinning dust he saw black figures straggling along the blasted line toward the fort. There were three . . . four . . . six of them—and that was all. Running last, he saw the gangling figure of Coop.

"Guns! Rifles!" shouted Ben turning around—because big, weasel-like figures were humping their way at full gallop across the backs of the stunned and milling herbivores to cut off the runners. Ben's own fingers twitched—foolishly, he had forgotten a rifle for himself. But weapons were sounding on the wall on either side of him.

The runners came on, slipping and staggering on the bodies under their feet. The open lane began to narrow and close . . . Herbivores were breaking across it. Now, the first man was staggering up the slope of herbivore bodies to the walls, making the last dozen feet on hands and knees. It was John Edlung.

Behind John was a masked face that in this wild moment Ben did not recognize. Then another . . . and another. Then, last of all came Coop, reeling, beating his way through the increasing waves of scrambling herbivores, like a fullback. Then Coop was on the wall.

"Everybody into the ship!" roared Ben.

He threw an arm around the staggering exhausted Coop and brought up the rear of the rush for the airlock below. In seconds, they were all aboard, and the airlock closed behind them. Ben let go of Coop, and the younger man, gasping, fell to his knees.

But Ben had no time to spare for Coop now. Others could take care of those who had just run the gauntlet of the herbivores. Ben, himself, ran down the hallway into his office and from his office into Control Section.

Control Section was manned and ready. Walt was standing above Tessie Sorenson, seated at the Control panel. Ben glanced into the screen above Tessie's head and saw a view of the south wall they had just left. Already, herbivores were being shouldered over it, and the figures of vine-tigers were appearing upon it.

"Ready to lift?" he asked Walt.

"Ready to lift," answered Walt, expressionlessly. Tessie looked up sharply.

"But Hans and somebody else are still out there!" she said.

The herbivores, like a river in flood topping a levee, were pouring over the wall now and down upon the ship itself. The outer hull rang now to what sounded like muffled blows against it. Ben leaned forward over Tessie's shoulder and pressed the intercom key for Observation.

"Observation," he said. "Can you still connect me with Hans? Can you get an answer from either of the transceivers out in that vine clump?"

There was a moment's silence, then the voice of Kirk Walish.

"No answer—sir."

"Thank you." Ben let go of the intercom key. He straightened up. He was aware of Walt watching, of Tessie staring at him. He felt the crew around him, holding their breath in expectation of one more miracle.

He looked at the screen. The herbivores were already piling up around the ship, and as he looked, the hull creaked to the mounting pressure of their bodies. There were no more miracles.

"Prepare to shift," he said to Walt.

"Prepare to shift," said Walt emotionlessly to Tessie. She hesitated. Ben stared at her with burning eyes.

"Report," she whispered into the phone before her. "Match," said the dry voice of Kirk Walish.

There was a moment's hesitation and then Computation Section spoke.

"Match."

"Match!" whispered Tessie, looking up at Ben.

"Sir," said Walt. "Ready to make the shift."

"Shift then," said Ben. The universe moved imperceptibly under their feet. The screen above Tessie's head showed only the stars. "Begin Observation and Computation to one light-year's distance from Polaris."

He turned on his heel, not waiting for Walt's acknowledgment of the new shift order. The door to his office was open, and standing by his desk was Nora. She had heard it all. He went into his office, closing the door behind him. He felt half-blind with the emotion of the order he had just given.

"What is it?" he asked her numbly.

"The six who came in. I just wanted to report they're all right," she said. "I've given them sedatives."

"Good," he said, thickly. He looked into her face, expecting to see there the horror of him that he felt must be in the minds of all those aboard after his order to shift out and abandon the two men below. But in Nora's face he could see only sympathy for him and something else that might be an incalculable tenderness—a tenderness he did not dare to believe. He stood, helpless, staring at her.

"Oh, Ben . . ." she said, taking half a step toward him. He woke suddenly to the act of weakness he had almost let himself slip into committing. He stiffened and stepped back.

"That's all, then," he said gratingly. "I think it's high time I had some sleep myself. Try not to disturb me for the next few hours—if that's possible!"

He turned and stumped into his bedroom. And only when he had slammed the door behind him did he admit to himself that he had not dared, after saying these harshest words he could dredge up to throw at her, to stay and look her in the face.

□ CHAPTER 7 □

THE PHASE SHIP was on "hold." All three Sections had locked their instruments to maintain the ship automatically in its present position in the universe relative to the Galactic Centerpoint. All aboard—with the exception of Lee, sleeping under electric sedation in the dispensary—were present in the Lounge. Ben, Walt, and Nora came in, Walt and Nora finding seats near the entrance of the room, Ben continuing on until he could mount the little platform against the wall and turn to face everyone present.

"This is to be a brief announcement of a decision I and Captains Bone and Taller have just reached in conference—" Ben broke off as John Edlung, next to Coop the youngest man aboard, started abruptly and jerked his head around to stare behind him at the Lounge entrance. He looked back immediately and guiltily. His oval face under its almost-white blond hair, was paler than Ben had ever before noticed its being. The past experience on Old Twenty-nine, thought Ben, must have hit John hard.

Ben looked on into the entrance and saw the cause of John's start. Sprockets, the cat, had just appeared there, and the small jaws were still gaped in what must have been a querulous meow.

"Well," said Ben, dryly—by now the whole room had discovered the cat's presence, "come on in and join us."

Sprockets hesitated, tail-tip twitching. Then he walked forward to the side of Polly's chair and waited for Polly to pick him up. Polly did so, and the attention of the room came back to Ben.

"—Our decision," went on Ben, speaking to them all, "is one we'd have come to eventually, I think. But it's been hastened by the latest reduction in crew numbers." He was making an effort to speak as dispassionately, in as machine-like a way as possible. "We've landed on two worlds now, and each time we've lost people. We can't go on like this."

He paused for a bright, stark moment of silence to emphasize that fact.

"Accordingly," he went on, "I've given orders to Captains Bone and Taller that from now on no landings will be made on any world that doesn't seem, from orbit, to meet all the qualifications of the planet we've been sent out to find. In other words, we will land from now on only to confirm or reject what appears to be a completely safe and humanly habitable world."

He paused and looked around them. They were all listening.

"In order to improve our chances of finding such a world," he went on, "I've decided to make the large jump immediately from here halfway in toward the center of the galaxy, where the chances will be increased greatly by the increased number of stars in a given area of space. This means our next destination is approximately fifteen thousand light-years away. This will undoubtedly take us twenty-five or thirty shifts to correct estimated error before we arrive in the area I have picked out. So, we'll get back to our Sections, now, and get to work immediately."

He stopped speaking.

"That's all," he added as they continued to sit still and silently.

He got down from the platform and made his way back through the room where everybody was beginning to stand up and talk. No one stopped him to ask him questions, and he was able to get out of the Lounge, down the corridor on the men's side, and back into his office and back to his study of the star charts. Those charts would improve with each new shift toward their destination, but what he could discover now might make him quicker-eyed to see things in the more detailed charts that would come after.

They had hesitated here, one light-year from Old Twenty-nine, just long enough to hold the conference that preceded his announcement to the crew and to allow those aboard to recover somewhat from the shock of the experience on the world they had just left. The long-range effects of that shock, Ben told himself now, were yet to be discovered—like the full effect of the wounds Lee had taken from the carnivore; though at first examination these appeared, if painful, superficial enough. What was certain in the case of the crew, though, was that everyone aboard had suffered a heavy emotional blow, and the effects of that blow had to show up somewhere.

It could, thought Ben, spreading the charts out on his desk, turn into resentment of him, as the man who ordered the takeoff that left two men behind. In fact, that was the most likely and—he thought a little bitterly—probably the safest course it could take. He would have to watch the crew closely for signs of reaction as they shifted inward toward midpoint to the Galactic Center. "Ready to shift," announced Coop, rousing him from his work some four hours later. Coop had been assigned Duty Officer status along with Walt, now that Lee was out of action. "First gross shift."

"I'll come," said Ben.

For the first time they were really up against the mathematics of phase shifting. Theoretically, they had only to calculate the point of arrival they wished, and a single shift would bring them to it, across the whole fifteen thousand light-years of distance. Practically, it was a matter of making that calculation with correct values of distance and position. Observation, after all, could only give them approximate figures for both the distance of their present position and the distance of their point of destination from the Galactic Centerpoint that was the reference point of their calculations. In fact, that Centerpoint itself was only theoretical and its position approximate.

So, until Observation could make a direct, line-of-sight measurement on some star near that destination point, all phase shifts were "gross"—movements to an approximated and unseen destination point. Once such a star could be sighted on and measured they would become "fine" phase shifts—still with a varying quantity of built-in observational error and computational limitations, but with a lesser scale of problem.

The first "gross" jump would be practically a blind jump halfway to Galactic Centerpoint. They would emerge in their new position, if they were lucky, not more than a few thousand light-years in error. Then, as the hours of calculation and observation grew on each successive shift, they would try to decrease that error, and decrease it again, and so on until a stellar reference point could be established and the whole business would begin over again on a finer scale.

"Prepare to shift," said Ben now, emerging into the Control Room. Ralph Egan was in the chair before the control instruments while Coop stood behind him.

The sensation of shifting struck hard this time. Ben felt his stomach lurch as if it had been turned inside out—which, topologically and theoretically speaking, it more or less had been, along with the rest of him. It was no help to him to realize that this feeling was entirely subjective and after the fact—that the shift itself was instantaneous and it was merely the memory of it that nauseated him. But the fact that, looking around him now, he could see that Coop and Ralph had been similarly affected did help. He straightened up and looked into the screen above Ralph's head.

The difference was there to see. Just where they were now, it would take some hours, perhaps even days, to calculate, but there was no doubt about the difference in this their present position and the fact that it was far closer to the Centerpoint than they had ever been before. The screen showed a scarcely-broken carpet of stars in all colors.

"Call me once our position's established," said Ben harshly, breaking the spell that tempted him to stand marveling at the star-scene, like a hoard of jewels, thrice-ransom for an emperor, spread out before him.

He turned sharply seeing Coop and Ralph stirring dazedly out of their own reaction at the sight of the alien stars, and went back into his office, shutting the door behind him.

But once the door was closed he sat down at his desk and turned on his desk screen to show a view of the thick-clustered stars here, halfway to the center of the galaxy.

He sat looking at them. They were beautiful—almost too beautiful to believe. But as he sat staring, he felt rising in him the same stiff coldness of fear he had felt in orbit around Alpha Centauri as he had sat looking out at the stars his screen showed there. Now, at last, they had stuck their heads into what might be a den of lions.

It was inevitable and necessary that they finally come here. But that did not lessen the dangers inherent in their coming. They were like the members of some primitive tribe, descending from their bare and starving mountaintop into the richer valley lands below. On the mountaintop they had gone hungry, but also they had gone unchallenged. Here, they should not go hungry, but no sensible man could believe they could go forever unchallenged—where there was so much richness to dispute. With an abrupt effort of will, Ben pushed it from his mind. He switched off the screen.

There followed, after all this, days stretching into weeks—stretching at last into a month—of strange peacefulness. For the first time aboard the phase ship they went week after week, day after day, without sighting a single star close enough to think of as a sun. Always the thickly carpeted space of stars surrounded them on all sides—so numerous that it was only by laying one star chart made by Observation next to another that the untutored eyes could see that a shift had moved them at all. Under these conditions, the crew of the ship seemed to retreat into themselves and the artificial universe of phase-shifting mathematics, as they had in the first few weeks after leaving Earth.

Lee was not healing as he should from the wounds

the vine-tiger had given him. He had been scratched on the upper thighs and upper chest and had tooth puncture wounds in his upper left shoulder. In addition, one of the neck-base tentacles of the vine-tiger had evidently whipped him around the neck, leaving a shallow scoring in the flesh, though not deep enough to cause dangerous bleeding from any of the blood vessels there. There was no evident infection or undue inflammation. But the wounds were healing with extreme slowness. They were as painful now, six weeks later, as they had been the day after the attack. And under the scourge of the constant pain, Lee was becoming aged and gaunt.

"What's wrong with me, Ben?" he asked, almost fretfully.

"I don't know, Lee." Ben had come by Lee's stateroom, now converted into a hospital room of sorts, not because there was anything he could do for Lee physically, but to tell the other man that the next shift should bring them within sight of their first point of destination—a system with a Go star like Earth's Sun and a very good chance of an Earth-like planet orbiting around it.

"You must have some idea!" Lee moved his head restlessly on its pillow.

Ben, about to say no, changed his mind. Suddenly he had remembered his own resentment in the past of physicians whom he had suspected of not telling him as much as they could about his ailments. He understood those physicians now—a guess could turn out to do more harm than good if it were wrong. But he had no professional authority to maintain, in any case.

"It's just speculation," he told Lee now. "But I don't think you're the victim of an alien virus or anything like that. The original idea that alien life forms couldn't infect us or vice versa seems to hold up as far as that goes."

"Then why don't I heal up?" demanded Lee

"Well, I think it may be something simply chemical in its action," said Ben. "Something I don't know enough or don't have the equipment aboard here to identify as being in your wounds—but something that chemically inhibits the natural process of cellular re-growth."

"Then I'll never get well!" Lee's head rolled on the pillow again, revealing the whiplike laceration, like a black line with the clotted blood in it.

"Yes, you will," said Ben. "You're healing up in spite of this. And I think you're healing a little faster all the time, which would mean the chemical action is weaken-ing as the chemical itself is being destroyed or somehow expelled from your body." He saw Lee was not com-forted by the explanation. Perhaps he had been wrong to tell him of it, after all. "Why don't you clip your electrodes on again and get some rest?"

"Rest!" said Lee. "It's like spending part of my time being dead." He did not object, however, as Ben picked up the clips and replaced them on the shaved areas of his scalp, so that the electric anesthesia provided by the slight current through clips and scalp and skull could put him into an easy sleep.

Like being dead it might be, thought Ben, looking down now at the immediately sleeping man. But if he had been forced to combat Lee's constant pain with something like barbiturates, Lee would be in a sad state by now. Electrical anesthesia was a godsend to this kind of situation.

He turned about and left the stateroom. Coop was waiting for him just outside the door.

"Ready to shift to orbit around Destination Star One," said Coop.

"All right. I'll come."

Destination Star One was a Go star, the first of a cluster of six such Sun-like stars scattered in an area of about two hundred light-years in diameter. The odds were strong that it would possess planets; and when they had shifted to it, they found that it did. But none of them were habitable.

"Very well," said Ben, after four days' search of the area about Star One. "We'll go on. Star Two."

Star Two, only sixty light-years away, also possessed planets but these were also uninhabitable. And so the search continued. When this area was exhausted, Ben, in conference with Walt and Nora and Coop, chose another and they began all over again. Every so often they were tempted with a world that seemed to have only one flaw—an atmosphere just too low in oxygen to be breathable or a planet barely too scant of water—but Ben held firmly to his decision not to land unless the world seemed completely habitable from orbit.

In this atmosphere of search and search again, Christmas came and then the New Year aboard the phase ship. By Earth calendar they moved on into January and then February. On February 16th, they had barely shifted into orbit around a Go star, when Walt stepped into Ben's office.

"Possible planet," said Walt. "It looks good."

Walt's face was as expressionless as usual, but there was an intensity about him like the glow of invisible heat from a metal ingot not yet fired to the point of changing color, but already dangerous to approach closely.

"Ready to shift to it?"

Walt nodded and stood aside as Ben rose from behind the desk and walked past him into the Control Section.

"Prepare to shift," Ben said, turning formally to Walt as he entered, closing the door to the office behind him.

"Yes sir." Walt turned to Tessie Sorenson. "Prepare to shift."

"Report," said Tessie into her phone to the other Sections.

There was a pause as the other Sections waited for Observation to report first. The pause extended itself with no answer—and suddenly there was a hoarse yell from Observation and the sound of some thing or things falling, heard not over the phone but through the connecting entrances between Sections.

"Hold!" snapped Walt, turning toward the entrance to Computation Section. But Ben was already ahead of him, striding through Computation, past the two people on duty there, and into Observation.

The shutters were back over the Observation window overhead, and the stars outside were so bright with their

total light that they made themselves seen through the
window even in the face of the interior illumination of
the Section. Of those on duty there, one was still seated
in his chair, while Kirk Walish the Section leader, was
squatted before John Edlung who was crouched in a
corner, shivering, his hands over his face.

"What's the matter here?" said Ben. Kirk looked up.
For once the sharp-voiced, balding man looked bewil-
dered and at a loss.

"I don't know, sir," he said—and the fact that the
"sir" was said ungrudgingly was an index of Kirk's loss
of aplomb. Ben had given up trying to maintain that
element of military order except among the on-duty
people, but Kirk had continued to resist it even when
leading his Section. "—I just said he was being a little
slow," went on Kirk, "and he dived at me, as if he was
trying to choke me." Kirk's hand went wonderingly to
his own throat.

John Edlung continued to crouch, shivering with his
hands over his face. For a moment Ben thought the
man was weeping, but it was simply hoarse and tortured
breathing he heard.

"All right," said Ben, "help me get him down to the
dispensary. Captain Bone, find somebody to replace
him, and run through the shift on your own authority—
but write it up in the ship's log when you're done."

"Yes sir," said Walt. Ben and Kirk between them
were lifting John by hands under his armpits and guiding him up through the Sections, through Ben's office,
and out the door on the women's side to the dispensary.
They sat him down in the chair in that white room with
its glass cases of equipment and medicines and its
white-clothed narrow table on which Polly had lost her
leg. He still had his hands over his face.

"All right, Kirk," said Ben. Kirk went out, closing
the door behind him. Ben sat down on an edge of the
narrow table, waiting. After a few minutes John's hands
came slowly down from his face revealing eyes that
were bloodshot and with the skin under them puffed
and darkened.

"What is it?" Ben asked.

"Nothing," said John almost whispering. He did not look up to meet Ben's gaze.

"You haven't been sleeping—is that it?" asked Ben, evenly.

John shuddered with his whole body. The shudder sent little waves of movement through his pale, lax cheeks.

"Nightmares," he said. "—I've been having nightmares." His voice was just barely above a whisper.

"Why didn't you come to me about this?"

John shuddered again. His hands twitched as if he would have liked to put them up to his face again, but he held them down on his knees.

"I'm going to die," he said. "I know I'm going to die. I'm never going to get home. I wasn't going to let anyone know. I thought I could make myself not think about it, but I keep dreaming it, night after night . . ."

The dammed up horrors inside John came tumbling out. It seemed that as a boy he had lived with his parents in a small seaside town in the state of Washington, where there were a couple of fish canneries. The town was plagued with large, gray wharf rats, and in an abandoned warehouse next to one of the canneries the rats swarmed thickly. The children had a story about a King of All the Rats, as big as a man, who lived in the warehouse; and one day a group of them including John had crawled in a broken window to explore the ruined structure. The rest had slipped away, leaving John, the youngest, behind. And when he went to get out, he found that the rats had blocked the entrance.

Fearful, hardly daring to breathe, he had crouched there on some ancient burlap sacks by the window, expecting the King of All the Rats at any moment. And time went by . . . And then he heard at last the voices of the other children coming to release him—but in that moment, he saw something move, in the farther shadows of the rafters and forgotten crates and boxes. Something as big as a man.

When the other children unblocked the window, they found him hysterical. This had frightened them, so that they had said nothing of what had happened, and nei-

ther had he. Over the years he had forgotten it until the
episode on Old Twenty-nine. Now, every night he
dreamed of it, dreamed of the King of All the Rats, who
was somewhere on one of the worlds among the stars,
waiting for him.

He broke down, telling Ben about it.

"I know it's my imagination," he said to Ben, chokingly. "It must have been imagination that made me see
something in the warehouse—or maybe it was just some
waterfront bum who'd crawled in there to sleep off a
drunk. I don't know. But it doesn't help! It doesn't help
to know it was imagination. Every time I fall asleep I go
right on dreaming about the Rat King!"

"Yes," said Ben, evenly. "Everybody's got something
like that. It's always something we've never told anyone—or something no one would believe when we tried
to tell it. Mine's a grizzly bear."

"Yours—?" For the first time John looked up.

"Up in the Canadian Rockies," said Ben. "When I
was seven years old. It was just about twilight and I was
cutting through a little patch of woods from one cabin
to another. I—thought I saw a grizzly."

He had not thought it. He had seen the bear, but for
John's sake he left the matter in doubt. Ben proceeded
to tell the story, and even here telling it brought everything back to him with a rush.

His father had been a geologist. It was a summer
camp to survey some mineral properties for a mining
firm. The camp followed the angle of a small river,
making an artificial L-shaped clearing among the trees.
Ben had been to the stables—why, he could not remember now—and running back to the family cabin at the
other end of the clearing, he had decided to cut through
the point of the woods in the angle instead of following
the clearing around.

He had been running as fast as he could go. Then,
running was something like breathing—done without
effort. His feet flew and his body rode them like gallop-
ing horses. He flew through the corridors of white birch
and pine. The scent of the pine needles was in his nose.
The twilight made everything different. He pounded the

earth with his feet and the world flew by around him.

Running so, drunk with his own speed, he was half-way across the small natural clearing before he saw. And he stopped. The world stopped. Just before him, on the edge of the clearing where he would have run into it in a few steps more, was the bear.

It was not black. It was gray, and it was bigger than any black bear. It was standing upright and facing him.

He did not move. He stood still, caught still in the open center of the clearing. Don't run—the thought hammered in him. He had been told that by everybody. Don't run from a wild animal. A strange coldness began at the back of his neck and flowed through him. He reached down without quite knowing what he was doing and picked up a stick at his feet. There was no reason for it. The stick was only a twig about two feet long and branched at the end. —When they come and find me, he thought, they will find I had a stick in my hand.

He looked up at the bear. Massive, towering, vast, it stood with one forepaw hooked over the horizontal limb of a small tree. The fur of the underarm was lighter and there was a streak of light fur on the loose skin of the throat. —And then he saw that the eyes of the bear were not on him. The underside of the bluntly v-shaped, dog-like jaw was raised to him. The black nose was search-ing the light upper movement of the air among the trees. All that had happened, from the moment he had stopped until now, had happened in next to no time at all.

He began to step quietly away, sideways, toward the trees. He did not think of the trees as a place to hide, he simply went to them, as he had stopped stock-still on seeing the bear, without thinking. He moved quietly sideways, and the bear stood, and after a little the trees were around him, and a little after that the bear was out of sight, and he ran on home.

Ben stopped talking. John Edlung was watching him, quiet now.

"So you see," said Ben. He turned and unlocked one of the glass cupboards. "Here," he said, taking out a small box and opening it to get a single green-and-white capsule out. "These are tranquilizers. Take a couple now, and take a couple more before you try to sleep. You shouldn't dream—of rats, anyway."

That was the end of the business, for the moment at least. Ben told John to stay off duty for a while and take the tranquilizers, then come and tell Ben if the nightmares had ceased. But the whole affair had set Ben to wondering. How many others of those aboard, he wondered, were being visited in their dreams by their own personal shapes of fear?

Meanwhile, the planet had been orbited, and Observation was beginning to check it out from an altitude of a hundred miles.

It was an amazingly Earth-like world, even to the two longitudinal ocean areas, and the continental masses in northern and southern hemispheres between oceans. The ecology was rich in varied animal life, shore, plain and upland varieties of game. The continental areas, aside from the desert sections were thickly forested. There was no sign of intelligent life on land or sea. Still, Ben kept the phase ship in orbit a week and a half, checking and rechecking before giving permission to land.

"All right," he said at last to Coop, standing in the Control Section, "prepare to shift to surface below."

"Prepare to shift," echoed Coop. The ritual was repeated, the ship shifted.

One moment it was out in space and the next it was on the ground. Local gravity took over from the phase oscillation of the ship itself. It was a slightly less gravity than that of Earth and the lightness of body Ben suddenly felt, with the rest, was an inescapable invitation to a lightness of spirit.

He looked into the screen.

The spot that had been picked was a small, natural phase ship's parking area. It was a tiny valley on a plateau, held between steep rock walls eighty to a hundred and fifty feet in height. The floor of the valley was relatively smooth and carpeted with a sparse growth of something very like grass, between large, whitish boulders evidently split off and tumbled from the surrounding cliffs.

In the floor of the valley, there were no trees. It was like some ancient dry riverbed scoured down to the rock. Only on the rock walls and on top of them were a few gnarly, small tree-like specimens of vegetation to be seen. The valley down which Ben looked on the screen was silent and still.

—Then, suddenly there was movement.

A flicker of movement at the far end of the valley floor, becoming suddenly a small object hurtling along the ground toward the ship. It came at an incredible speed, and as it flashed into near view Ben saw it was a small device of metal about as large as a child's wagon and floating barely inches above the ground. It shot forward, swerved to its right, and described a circle around the ship, abruptly laying behind it a wide track of yellow coloring.

It completed its circle, swung back, and approached one of the large boulders just inside the line. It nosed against the boulder and for a moment nothing happened—and then the six foot high chunk of rock moved. It teetered and rolled ponderously across the yellow line, out of the circle.

Immediately there was a wink of incredible light on top of the rock wall to Ben's right. In the same split-second there was a crack of noise loud enough to be heard inside the phase ship, and where the boulder had been was only a cloud of rising dust.

The metal device took suddenly to the air and flew back and forth, looping from the yellow line of the ground on one side of the phase ship to the yellow line on the other side.

When it was done, a hoop-shaped pattern of golden lines in the air above enclosed the phase ship like a cage placed over it.

"Take her up?" said Coop, urgently in Ben's ear. Ben, turning to look at him, saw the younger man's face pale and staring.

"No," said Ben, steadily, looking back at the screen. "I don't think we'd be allowed to make it."

□ CHAPTER 8 □

HE WAS BY no means certain of that—that whoever or whatever had reacted to the phase ship's landing could stop them from shifting off-planet and escaping—thought Ben several hours later in the privacy of his office, where he had retreated to think the situation through. He could not imagine how their unseen captors could know that they were going to phase shift, or inhibit the shift once it was triggered. But the fact that the ship's landing at this remote and apparently deserted spot should find defenses immediately ready and waiting for them was enough to make him cautious about testing the further powers to be found on this world.

The important thing was that Coop had accepted without argument Ben's apparent certainty that it would not be safe to try and lift the ship. By so much had all these past weeks of Ben's efforts to make himself independent and unquestionable in authority paid off. If the worst came to the worst, they could still try a shift off-planet. But meanwhile, Ben had the satisfaction of knowing the crew would obey him and follow his lead.

Already in the past four hours, they had cautiously explored the situation. Chemical tests run on the local atmosphere had proved it eminently safe and breathable. Heat radar pictures taken by Observation had established the existence of metal devices about as large as a small military tank just out of sight on the cliff above them at four points surrounding them. And by each metal device had been heat images that moved about and had about the same characteristics as the body heat human beings would show. Finally, a volunteer—Kirk Walish—had left the ship and walked around inside the yellow line on the ground, breathing the native atmosphere, and come back aboard unharmed.

The next move was undoubtedly up to their captors. That there would be a next move, Ben did not doubt. The fact that the cliff-top weapons had not simply blasted the phase ship without warning meant that their captors could not be completely sure of their superiority over whoever might be inside the ship. The natives—whoever they were—had taken the initiative. Aboard the space ship the humans had stood pat, refusing to be drawn into any retaliatory action. It was like a game of chess in the opening moves between two players who had never played each other before—both sides wanted to gain as much information about the opponent as possible, and give up as little as possible about themselves. The next move now was up to the phase ship's captors.

The very fact, thought Ben, feeling his mental machinery warming to the problem facing it, that their captors had hesitated was in itself a betrayal of information about them. Their characters must be such. . . .

The intercom on his desk came alive to interrupt his thoughts.

"Sir? Coop speaking. Observation has two upright, two-legged individuals coming in fast."

Ben reached out and pushed down the key on the intercom.

"How?" he demanded. "Coming in, how?"

"On one of the same sort of things that marked out the yellow lines."

The thought of the yellow lines struck a sudden spark in Ben's mind.

"Have Captain Bone meet me at the airlock," he said into the intercom. "I'll go out to meet whoever it is that's coming as soon as they get here."

"Yes sir—" There was perhaps a small note of surprise in Coop's voice over the intercom. He would not have thought ahead and foreseen, as Ben had done, that the next move in the present situation had to be some sort of interview between captors and captured.

Walt was already at the lock when Ben got there, and

he had the TV screen in the lockroom switched on. In it, Ben could see two slim, gray-furred creatures standing patiently just beyond the yellow line on the ground with the long narrow stretch of the dry valley behind them.

"I expected this," Ben said to Walt. A stray observation intruded to distract him momentarily. For the first time, in all the years Ben had known him, Walt was unshaven. It was not a startling unshavenness, but the close stubble darkened Walt's chin and jaw, giving him a grim look. "I want you to go out with me," Ben went on, "to meet them. But there's something else. I want you to get Observation busy, and anyone else who might be able to help, at figuring out what those yellow lines, on the ground and in the air, are made of, and if it's the same thing in both cases."

"Yes," said Walt, as evenly as ever. "I'll see to it."

"Come on, then," said Ben. He reached out to press the control activating the airlock. It opened and they went outside.

Outside, he walked forward to the line, with Walt beside him, and stopped. Only a couple of feet beyond stood the two gray-furred beings. They were scarcely more than five feet tall, Ben observed, slightly boned, with four-fingered hands having each a single, powerful, opposable thumb almost as long as the fingers. The inner surface of the hands and some small circles of dark flesh around the eyes were the only unfurred areas of their bodies. They were almost neckless, and their round, dish-shaped faces had a straight, nearly lipless mouth and a rudimentary, barely projecting nose with small, triple, horizontal nostrils that squeezed themselves shut as he and Walt approached. Above the nose, two round, dark-corneaed eyes, with yellow "whites," and both upper and lower eyelids, looked at the humans with no expression that Ben could discover.

Ben and Walt stood on their side of the yellow line.

"Hello," said Ben dryly, to the alien faces.

As if the word had been a signal, the one on the left turned, bent down and took what looked like a black rod from the sled-like device beside him. He pushed the rod into the earth and he and the other backed off. Immediately, above the rod, the air fogged and appeared to resolve itself into a three-dimensional image. As Ben watched, he saw the phase ship imaged, saw the airlock door open, the figures of himself and Walt step out, walk up to the yellow line, and stop. He saw the rod driven into the ground. Then the imaged figures stopped moving.

Ben looked at the Gray-furs and saw them looking back at him. The two dish-shaped faces turned to face once more toward the pictured scene, and Ben turned with them.

The figures shown there began to move again. One of the imaged Gray-furs stepped forward and passed a small object held in his hand above the yellow line. The line vanished for a space of about three feet. The image of Ben stepped through and the Gray-fur waved the line back into existence behind him. The image of Ben and both Gray-furs stepped onto the sled, which carried them rapidly down the valley through a blur of motion and distance, and finally under huge trees and between white-sided structures. They were carried finally into a structure, where they got off. The image of Ben was met by four other Gray-furs. Another image maker was set up but the images it showed were out of focus to the real Ben watching from inside the yellow line. Then the imaged Ben and the two Gray-fur images remounted the sled and returned to the ship, letting Ben pass once more within the yellow line.

"All right," said Ben.

He turned to Walt.

"They want you to go with them, that's plain enough," said Walt. There was a strange look to the unshaven face. "Maybe we better talk it over in conference back on the ship."

"No," said Ben. "It's our move. We aren't going to learn any more unless I go with them." He looked intently at Walt. "You'll be in charge while I'm gone."

"If you don't come back—" Walt's tone was expressionless.

"Whether I come back or not," said Ben, "if, in your

opinion, the safety of the ship is threatened, you can try to lift out of here. If you do that, it'll be up to you to see that the ship goes on and does what it was sent out to do. You'll find the combination to my office walk-in safe in the office filing cabinet, under 'S'. In the filing cabinet inside the safe, under 'P,' you'll find a file folder of secret papers, including the full original order that sent us out here, and two orders I've written out, one appointing you commanding officer aboard the ship in my place, one appointing Lee. Destroy Lee's appointment and enter your appointment in the official ship's log. —Is that all clear?"

"Clear," said Walt, inclining his head slightly.

"All right, then." Ben turned back to the Gray-furs and saw a gap had already been made in the yellow line. He stepped through. One Gray-fur turned and stepped over to take the image-producing rod out of the ground.

Ben turned abruptly back to the yellow line, which had been closed up again.

"What is it?" asked Walt, on the other side.

"I want them to leave that there," said Ben. "If I'm right, it can give you a picture of everything that'll happen to me while I'm with them." The thought of this had come like an inspiration. Another inspiration followed hard behind it. "Walt," he added "have Observation film everything that's shown by this gadget. I want it filmed for detail, so we can study it closely, later."

"What do you want me to do now?" asked Walt.

"I'm going to turn and walk away a few steps down the valley," said Ben. "Don't watch me. Watch where that rod was, as if you expected to see what I'm doing shown there. If they're as bright as all this indicates, they'll get the idea."

He turned. Both Gray-furs were watching him. The one who had picked up the rod, still held it loosely. Ben walked off a few steps and stopped, hesitated a second, then turned around and came back. The Gray-furs were no longer looking at him, but at each other. The one with the rod drove it into the ground. An image of Ben appeared in the air above it.

Ben moved experimentally. The image of himself matched the movement.

"All right," said Ben. He turned and stepped up onto the small surface of the sled-like device. A Gray-fur stepped up in front of him, and another stepped up behind him.

"Good luck—" he heard Walt start to say . . . and then they were moving at steadily increasing, blurring speed down the valley just above the surface of the ground.

The wind seemed to part around them as they went. There was nothing to disturb their precarious-seeming upright stand on the tiny surface of the sled. Almost immediately they were emerging from the far end of the valley. They swooped down an almost perpendicular slope at a horizontal angle to the steeply inclined earth, and plunged beneath the shadow of green-topped, tree-like plants that towered above them. And suddenly they were among tool-made constructions—buildings with curving walls and domed roofs and arched entrances, all in a soft, smoothly gleaming white.

The vehicle under them kept going downwards. Now, either the ground had dropped away, or they were descending into some great, artificial, pit-like depression. They now moved and descended by levels, interspersed with the tree-like plants in all sizes, all filled with the curving white shapes of buildings. Then without warning they had flashed through an entrance and were inside a wide, white room, whose circular wall swept up to make a dome above it.

The aliens got off the sled, and Ben followed them. There were others of the Gray-furs in the room—four of them, working with four black boxes set on high tripods around Ben. The two who had brought Ben back from the phase ship turned and walked off, the sled following them like an obedient dog. Ben turned to follow them, but abruptly he was caught and held by a pressure as heavy as if he had been immersed in liquid mercury. He could not stir.

After the first surging attempt to break loose, he stood still, and the pressure relaxed. The four boxes were being moved in around him now, about fifteen feet distant in each case from him. And for the first time he was aware of a humming noise in the room, a humming set up by each of the Gray-furs, as if that was their way of communicating with each other.

The box on Ben's right put out a pale beam toward him, taking him by surprise, and Ben felt a warm touch on the right side of his head. His shoulder twitched once, undirected by his mind.

There was a warm touch on the left side of his head, another pale beam had reached out to him from the box on that side, and unexpectedly he found himself weeping. He was torn by a raging sorrow—he did not know why. And then, as suddenly, the sorrow was gone and his left leg had jerked upward as two other warm touches made themselves felt against his scalp. In a moment he was laughing uncontrollably.

He stood there, being worked like a puppet on strings by the four Gray-furs with boxes, and through the muscle spasms and the reasonless bursts of emotion that played through him, his mind fastened on an understanding. These Gray-furs were charting his brain, locating emotional and motor centers by noting what reaction they got by stimulating this or that area beneath his skull. It was an advanced method of what had been done back on Earth in the way of stimulating pleasure, pain, or motor centers in the brains of animals, by means of electrodes touching the animals' brains at certain points. What he was going through was impersonal and not cruel, but it was humiliating, emotionally shattering, and degrading. Ben burned with sudden anger.

Almost at once he was aware that the stimuli were no longer being applied to him. Of the two beams on the side and the one in front, he could see that the front and right side beams were pale, while the left side beam pulsed redly. Astonishment and sudden caution replaced the anger, and the red light faded from the beam on his left while the beam to the box straight before him brightened with a steady blue glow.

They were no longer transmitting stimuli to his brain. They were receiving—reading off the electrical dis-

charge of his own emotions. Ben made an effort to find
a point of emotional neutrality. For a moment his mind
scrambled for something to hang on to, and found nothing. The harsh scent of his own sweat was in his nostrils
and he felt like an animal in a trap—and then abruptly
his mind came clear and sharp and analytical. The
emergency had triggered the calculative element in him,
developed over twenty years of trying to fit himself into
the situations thrown up by his fellow human beings.
All at once his thoughts stood off to one side considering the situation with himself as only one of the factors
in it—and the three beams he could see shone pale and
colorless.

There was an outburst of humming from the Gray-
furs—and he was being manipulated physically and
emotionally again. But this time his intellectual detachment held good. When they stopped, he was still detached and thinking, and the beams flowed pale.

There was a change in movement, the box directly
before him shifted off to one side, and slowly three-
dimensional images formed in the vacated space. Ben
found himself looking at a world swimming in black,
star-swarmed space. No, not just a world—*this* world of
the Gray-furs, as he had seen it from the phase ship in
orbit.

The world dwindled, the view lengthened and became a model of the solar system to which the world
belonged. Twelve worlds circled about a Go type star.
Their circling ceased. They began to rotate backwards
and the flow of further stars beyond them began to flow
backwards. He was watching, Ben suddenly realized, a
reversal of time, a movement back into the past, into
history.

The speed of the backing up continued and increased
to blurring speed. The motion of the Gray-furs' world
was a constant ring of movement to the eye, about its
sun. Thousands of years back, perhaps a hundred
thousand years in ordinary space time was unreeled
before Ben's eyes. It slowed, it stopped, and the point
of view moved in close on the Gray-furs' single planet
again.

The motion of time moved forward. Tiny shapes that were long, flat, spacegoing vessels came out of the stars toward the galactic center, and landed on a world lacking much of the vegetative cover that shrouded it now. The motion stopped and reversed itself. Like a movie run in reverse, the Gray-furs who had come out of the landed vessels backed into them once more, the ships backed off into space and receded from this world and its solar system. As they receded the view lengthened until the fleet of vessels became a moving point of light.

The point of light became a bar stretching back toward the region of the Galactic Center. It stretched centerwards for perhaps a thousand or more light-years, and there it divided into a number of fingers, reaching out to end on a number of different planets on nearby solar systems. The ships landed and time moved back again for perhaps fifty or a hundred years.

Then time began to move forward again.

Cylindrical ships came out of space. They landed; and from them emerged tall, slim, golden-skinned and graceful-looking bipeds with strange, thin, lance-like weapons that glowed at the tip and wrought incredible destruction. The defeated Gray-fur survivors escaped to another world of their own kind, circling another star.

The golden-skinned aliens razed the eggshell-white cities of the Gray-furs and built slim, towering metropolises of their own. They attacked, conquered, and settled another of the Gray-fur worlds. Planet by planet, they drove the Gray-furs outward until only one, overcrowded planet remained in Gray-fur possession.

The Gray-furs assembled a fleet of the long, flat spaceships Ben had seen earlier. That fleet took aboard all the Gray-furs that remained and swam outward for a thousand light-years until it reached at last this world on which the descendants of its passengers and Ben now stood. The point of view moved back to give a view of the complete solar system and time blurred forward, slowed, stopped, and the point of view moved back in, down to this city, this room, and the present moment with a view of Ben standing watching the boxes, the Gray-furs, and the domed room surrounding him.

The images vanished. Ben tried to move, but the mercury-like pressure still held him captive.

There was renewed humming among the Gray-furs. The boxes were drawn farther off from him. Their beams lengthened. Still, he saw with a touch of self-congratulation, the beams were pale. Whatever reaction the history of the Gray-furs had caused in him, no betraying hint of it had been available for his captors to read. But now what?

They did not keep him in suspense long. Abruptly, he felt the restraining pressure vanish from around him. But at the same time, six feet away all around him, a ring of floor ten feet wide sank noiselessly and swiftly out of sight. He found himself marooned on a little island of floor space. He took one step to the edge of his island and looked down.

For a moment, dizziness swam in him and he felt an unexpected fear of falling that made one of the beams still touching his head flare yellow. The floor had sunk away an inconceivable distance. He could barely make out a circle of level, far below down there just before the shining walls seemed to come together with the illusion fostered by the distance. He was perched on a tiny platform twelve feet in diameter and at least a hundred feet above its base. He lifted his eyes quickly from that smooth depth and stepped hastily back to the center of his platform. Then he saw that something was happening at its further end.

The air there was thickening, changing. The room about him, beyond the circle of depth, was darkening and disappearing. In the thickening air above the platform, shapes like the three-dimensional images of the Gray-fur's pictures were struggling to be born.

The four beams still reached out to touch Ben's skull. Now, the touch of one of them warmed against the side of his head and without warning fear welled up inside him. Fear, then terror—then panic was being stimulated in him by the beam. Ben found himself crouching slightly at the knees, turning to look for a place to hide. But there was no place to hide on the small platform, and his turnings only brought him back to face the image that was struggling to be resolved.

But now it was resolving itself. And as he began already to realize what it would be, a purely instinctive, uncontrollable fear of his own producing leaped up in Ben. The pit of his stomach, the short hairs on the nape of his neck, the smooth muscles of his contracting throat knew what was taking shape even before it was recognizable. The fingers of his right hand flexed uncontrollably. He looked down. There was no flimsy twig in his grasp there—but his palm and fingers felt that it was there. Jerkily, his gaze moved upward again to the resolving figure and saw it taking plain shape at last.

Towering, as large, relative to his grown size, as its original shape had been to his seven-year-old height, the furred and mighty, gray-silver-haired body took form, standing manlike on its hind legs. One huge forearm was hooked over a shadowy tree limb, and the great dog-like muzzle was uplifted to sniff the air.

Ben took two instinctive, automatic steps backward—and felt the heel of his right foot come down on no surface. For a moment, under the momentum of his backward movement he teetered on the edge of the depth behind him. Then he caught his balance and took one hurried step forward again. He wet his dry lips and looked once more at the grizzly.

His mind told him it was only an image, but the fear impulses being pumped into him along the beams from the black boxes and his very nerves and cells leading to the old, primitive portions of his brain called his mind a liar. And then, slowly, the muzzle began to come down. It dropped, dropped, and tilted toward him. Gleaming in the dusk of twilight that surrounded him, two small and burning eyes lowered and focused on him.

The huge, upright shape swayed toward him. Fragments of forgotten fear-bright knowledge flickered wildly in Ben's brain—*Ursus Horribilis*—Rudyard Kipling's poem—*The Bear That Walks Like a Man* . . . *". . . Nearer he tottered and nearer, with paws like hands that pray—From brow to jaw that steel-shod paw, it ripped my face away!"* . . . Closer came the shape, shuffling, looming, burning-eyed. Fear packed Ben's body all within like wet clay. It was almost upon him and there was no place to run.

Then it was on him, one last step from him, and there was no hope left. Fear broke into desperation, an abandonment to fury, and Ben leaped forward and upward at the grizzled throat, hands outstretched—

He went sprawling on a hard surface, his hands as far as the elbows stretching out over emptiness. He lifted his head, dazedly. The shape was gone and the floor was rising swiftly toward him to fill in the space between him and the Gray-furs with their boxes beyond.

He got to his feet, becoming aware that the beams were no longer reaching out from the boxes to touch his skull. Now, two Gray-furs were coming forward with a sled like that on which he had ridden here. The sled sidled around to hang in the air just above the floor beside him.

Ben stepped shakily upon it. The two Gray-furs mounted also, one before and one behind him. The sled started to move.

They went out through the entrance, picking up speed swiftly as they did so, and the trip back to the phase ship was made in silence. When they got close to the ship Ben could see a number of the humans standing just inside the line, waiting for him. The sled reached the line, one of the Gray-furs opened it, and Ben stepped through. The Gray-furs remounted their sled and picked up the rod that was still imaging the scene around Ben back here by the ship. They went swiftly away.

"Ben . . . " began Nora, who was in the forefront of those waiting.

"Don't say anything now," said Ben, harshly. He had been thinking furiously on the way here. "Let's get back aboard the ship—all of us."

He led the way back in through the airlock. It had been late morning when the phase ship had touched surface here in this valley. Now, it was late afternoon and the sun would be down in another hour. Ben went directly to his office.

"Coop, Nora, Julian—somebody get me Walt." he reeled off the names, as he turned around. standing behind his desk. "The rest of you clear out of here." He stared at the crowd that had pushed into the office behind him. "Well?" he snarled, "What's the matter with all of you? Didn't you hear what I said?"

They stared back at him with what he suddenly realized were expressions of deep concern—and out of the blue it burst upon him that they had been worried about him and that that was why they were clustering around him now. It was a naked moment of sheer embarrassment.

"Will you get out?" he roared. "There's nothing out of the ordinary to stare at around here!"

At that they went, but as the door closed behind the last back, Nora spoke behind him.

"Ben?"

He turned around almost savagely.

"What?"

"Hadn't you better lie down? After all they—" the word seemed to stick in her throat.

"They what?" he demanded.

"Well, they tortured you! We saw them do it!"

Understanding broke upon him like a strong light. Of course, the whole ship would have watched everything that happened to him, imaged in the air above the rod outside the yellow line. He had not thought it possible to be more embarrassed than he had been at the realization that the rest aboard had been worried about him. Worried about Ben Shore—the man who had kidnaped them and already cost them four lives out of their number. But then he discovered an even greater embarrassment was possible.

It came home to him suddenly—they had all seen him. They had seen him weeping like a child and laughing like a fool. They had seen him jerking like a puppet and convulsed with fear before what they could only know of as an outsize image of a grizzly bear. So much for the arbitrary and awesome figure of authority he had tried to make of himself over the last long months. —But there was no time to mourn over that loss now.

"It wasn't torture," he said roughly. "It just looked that way." Just then Walt entered the office from the Control Section and Ben turned gratefully to him. "Walt. Good. Now listen to me, all of you. We're getting out of here tonight."

"Shift off?" asked Coop.

"Not until those weapons up on the cliff covering us are out of action," said Ben. "Now, first—" he turned to Julian, "give me an answer to a question. If we cut a section out of part of the ship's hull that's resting on the ground, in order to get at the rock we're lying on, can we weld that section back afterwards and have a safe hull again? Can you answer that—or do you want to check with Lee?"

"Why . . ." said Julian. "I think I can answer it all right. It's a double hull, you know, with insulation between. But provided the section is welded back tight without leaks and the insulation replaced, we shouldn't have any difficulty."

"Fine," said Ben. He turned to Walt. "What about those yellow lines? Did Observation find out what they're made of?"

"Yes," said Walt, "they're wire."

"Wire?" said Ben, frowning.

"Almost microscopic wires—the tensile strength of each individual strand must be fantastic, to make those bands of them stand up over the ship in the air the way they do. But we've examined them under high magnification and that's what they are. The wires put out a slight magnetic field, so that essentially we've got a bowl-shaped, weak magnetic field covering the ship." He looked curiously at Ben. "That's how they guarded against our making a sudden shift off-planet. The yellow lines are just a warning system—like a burglar alarm. The minute we activated the magnetic fields of the ship's receptors preparatory to making the shift, their field would be pulled out of shape."

"Then how—" began Nora, and stopped herself.

"We're going to tunnel out," said Ben, flatly, glancing at her for a second. He looked away again as her eyes met his, uncomfortable all over again with his embarrassment. "Julian, get some men busy cutting out a section of the hull where it lies flat against the rock. Then start your men with ultra-high temperature torches cutting through the rock underneath. Go down at least six feet and then tunnel horizontally toward the cliff on our right. That cliff face isn't any more than thirty feet away. You ought to reach it in four hours at the most."

"Yes sir," said Julian, turning toward the door.

"I'll need some commandos," said Ben. "I'm going to take four men out that tunnel and put those weapons and their operators out of action. They'd better be people who can climb, as well as fight. We're going to have to climb the cliff face to get up there. Coop?"

"Yes," said Coop. "I'll be one."

"Who else? Who do you suggest? Kirk?"

"Kirk would be good," said Coop. "And Ralph Egan."

"You'd better take me," said Walt.

"No," said Ben. "I want you here to take over if anything happens to me."

"Why don't you stay here and I'll lead them?" asked Walt.

"Because that's the way it's going to be!" snapped Ben. He could not tell them that he did not trust anyone but himself to handle the silencing of the Gray-fur weapons. Walt was easily the most powerful individual aboard the ship—but he was a theoretician by nature, not a man of action. He should, Ben accused himself in the following second after his outburst, have been able to come up with an excuse, a reason of some sort. But he was too tense at the moment to be politic.

"Take me," said Julian at Ben's elbow. "I've had commando training." Ben turned to stare at the slight, dark man.

"All right," said Ben, swallowing his surprise. "Walt, I want you to signal the minutes from the time we leave the ship in flashes, on the minute, through the Observation window. After we've been gone one minute, show a single flash, after two minutes, two flashes, and so forth . . . With our watches, it will serve as an extra time check. It's a good thing the watch cases are plastic."

"I'll do that," said Walt.

"Let's get busy then," said Ben. "I want to be out in the open at the base of that cliff in four hours." He checked himself. "Plastic watches and flashlights are okay even if the Gray-furs have metal detectors up on that cliff, but we can't use guns or knives." He turned to Julian who had paused on his way out the door. "What's your suggestion, Julian? I was thinking of something like sandbags for blackjacks?"

"Very good," said Julian politely. "And short lengths of plastic cord with handles for strangling ropes. You can break a neck with a length of tough plastic cord quite easily if it's properly handled."

"Yes," said Ben, striving to hide the internal shudder that went through him. He did not enjoy the prospect of breaking any neck, even one belonging to a Gray-fur. "Get busy then," he said, trying to match Julian's calmness of voice.

The meeting split up and the work began swiftly. Outside the phase ship, the sun was already down and the dry valley was a river of darkness with the streak of star-studded, moonless sky overhead. It was a little less than four hours later that Ben and the four others emerged from the mouth of the tunnel up into the darkness at the base of the right-hand cliff.

A tap of Ben's forefinger on Julian's shoulder and a light shove started Julian off along the cliff away from the encircled ship, until it should be judged safe for him and the two with him to cross over to the cliff on the other side. Ben turned to Coop, the only one to attack the right-hand cliff with him. In the darkness he could not see Coop—both of them were darkness themselves, wearing coveralls hastily dyed black and taped tight at wrist and ankle—the tape and all exposed skin darkened with carbon black. He tapped Coop silently on the shoulder and urged him to the cliff beside them. Together, they began their climb.

It was not a difficult face to climb, even for amateurs. But the darkness made it tricky, and Ben—in spite of the regular physical exercises he demanded of himself as well as of the rest of the crew—found his muscles out of condition for it, his wind short. The eight-inch length of sandbag-style blackjack, pendulum-ing at his belt, was a nuisance. So was the cord, which managed to catch itself on bosses and projections of rock as they climbed.

They crawled out at last, panting, onto the level top of the cliff, and Ben looked down at the Observation window of the ship. He saw darkness—and then twelve spaced flashes. Twelve minutes since they had emerged into the darkness at the base of the cliff. They could lie here a second and catch their breath. Their efforts must be timed with Julian's, on the opposite cliff top; and Julian had considerably more distance to cover— although, where he would be climbing the opposite cliff with his two partners, the rise was only about two thirds what Ben and Coop had just come up.

The night was dry and cold—bathed in sweat inside his black coveralls, the coolness bothered Ben not at all. He lay watching the glowing numerals of his watch face. When twenty minutes had elapsed since they had left the tunnel mouth, he tapped Coop on the shoulder. They roused and crept up along the cliff top toward the nearest Gray-fur weapon.

There were only two upright, man-like shapes black against the sky there, as the two humans approached the weapon. Ben and Coop, like Julian, Kirk, and Ralph, would be coming up safely from downwind— Ben remembered how the triple nostrils of the Gray-furs had closed protectively when he and Walt walked up to the yellow line earlier in the day. Provided they were quiet, the Gray-furs on the weapons should have no warning.

Ben, with Coop lost in darkness at his right, was al-most upon the weaponeers now. Ben reached out and touched Coop's invisible shoulder, giving it a light push. He felt the shoulder go away from him and began to count seconds slowly under his breath. Thirty seconds, it had been agreed, would give Coop time to circle behind the other Gray-fur.

The one in front of Ben was only a few feet away, standing behind the eight-foot high black mass of the weapon. The weaponeer moved a little, restlessly, looking out across the valley with his back to Ben. The second hand Ben glanced at was rapidly approaching the thirty second deadline. He took the heavy shape of the "sandbag" from his belt and weighed it in his hand. A suddenly horrible pity for the intelligent creature he was about to strike down gushed suddenly up in him. The second hand touched deadline. He rose behind the five foot black shape and struck out and down with all the fury of revulsion against what he was doing, and desperation.

The figure dropped before him. He found himself leaning over it, panting in the starlight. He jerked his head about and saw what was obviously the human figure of Coop like a black cutout against the pinpoint-blazing sky. They stood alone.

But there was no time to be wasted if they were to stay on schedule with Julian and the others on the opposite cliff top. They went on, and some forty yards back past the point where they had climbed the cliff they approached the second weapon on this side.

As with the earlier weapons, the two weaponeers here fell without a protest or a struggle under the blows of the sandbags. Thank God, thought Ben, he had not been called upon to use the strangling cord. Now that the need was past, he found himself wondering if he would have had the courage to use it—he forced that question from his mind. He looked again at the dark Observation window and waited—then counted twenty-nine flashes. A minute yet before Julian should have completed his work on the opposite cliff.

A low whistle came from across the canyon of darkness that was the valley, seen from the cliff tops. Ben whistled back. —A moment later a light gleamed on the other cliff top and blinked twice before being extinguished. Julian had been successful.

Ben reached into a pocket of his coveralls for the plastic flashlight there. He took it out and shone its light cautiously on the weapon. This was the moment he had not been able to prepare for in his plans aboard ship. It was one thing to put the Gray-fur weaponeers out of action—quite another thing to put the weapons themselves out of action. For all he knew they had been set to fire automatically at any attempt of the phase ship to take off. Now, his small flashlight revealed an incomprehensible piece of metal equipment consisting of a large box-shape about eight feet on a side, connected to a smaller, rectangular shape with a sloping face from which protruded inch-thick studs, or rods, of lengths varying from a fraction of an inch to several inches. The only thing resembling at all the business end of a gun as humans knew it was a stubby, yard-high antenna-like projection with a loop at the top, facing in the direction of the phase ship below.

Ben flashed his light toward the underside of the weapon. Yes, it was mounted on the same sort of barely-floating sled on which he had traveled to the Gray-furs' city. This sled of course was much larger, but—experimentally he leaned his weight against the weapon and pushed. It moved, yielding position reluctantly, but definitely, for several inches.

"Help me, here!" said Ben in a low, but urgent tone to Coop.

Together, they put their shoulders to the weapon and urged it toward the cliff edge. It did not resist their efforts so much as it gave to them, slowly. Slowly, like pushing a truck through hub-deep water, they approached the cliff edge—and suddenly the mass vanished before them, and they fell on their faces.

Fantastically, there was no crash from below. Ben crept to the very edge of the cliff face and peered down, vainly trying to see the weapon on the valley floor. Evidently the sled on which it was mounted had somehow preserved it on the way down. —But the important thing was that the weapon could no longer be aimed to do the phase ship any damage.

"Push them off the cliff—the weapons!" shouted

Ben across to Julian, between cupped hands, throwing discretion to the winds. He turned to Coop. "Come on!"

He led the way at a run back down to the other weapon on their side. The dark masses of the fallen Gray-furs still lay beside its mass. Had they killed the weaponeers with those sandbag blows? In any case, there was no time now to find out. He and Coop together leaned and pushed against the other weapon. It slid slowly, tipped—and fell.

Then they were scrambling down the cliff and running for the airlock of the ship, which now stood open for them. Julian's team met them at it.

"Both weapons down on our side, sir," gasped Julian.

Ben nodded, too winded to answer, and led the way into the airlock. Walt was waiting for them there.

"Ready to lift as soon as the airlock's closed," Walt said.

"Let's go!" said Ben. He charged down the corridor toward the Control Section with Walt at his heels. In a moment they had passed through the office and were standing above Tessie Sorenson at the Control instruments.

"Prepare to shift."

"Report."

"Match!"

"Match!"

"Match!"

"Sir, ready to shift."

"Shift, then!" said Ben, too out of breath to worry about any of a thousand possible chances, including the fact that the Gray-furs might have had more than one means of destroying them at any attempt to lift ship.

They shifted. And suddenly they were among the stars.

"Captain Bone," croaked Ben, breathlessly, "shift again as soon as possible on your own authority to a distance of at least a light-year. I think I'll take this chance to catch a little rest."

"Yes sir," said Walt.

Ben turned and went through the connecting door to

his office, and from his office into his bedroom. Wearily, he stripped off his coveralls, socks, and shoes and crawled under the covers too tired even to wash the lampblack from his face and hands.

Sleep descended on him like a stooping hawk. —But there was yet time before it claimed him, for him to remember how he had jerked and reacted under the beams of the Gray-furs, and that the whole ship had witnessed these actions. Convulsed with humiliation, he buried his face in the darkness of the pillow.

☐ CHAPTER 9 ☐

"MAKE STAR CHARTS from our film of the Gray-fur images?" echoed Coop. "Why, yes sir, I guess so. You mean the part where they showed you how the Golden People drove them off their home worlds?"

"Yes," said Ben. The phase ship was safely lost in space again, a full light-year from the Gray-furs' planet, and he had called a conference of the senior officers—Coop, Walt and Nora, as well as a pale and scarecrow-thin Lee Ruiz, for the first time in months. Suddenly, as if the blocked-off natural healing processes and of his body had broken through whatever had been holding them back, Lee had mended. Now, all that was visible of the open slash around his throat was a red line like a welt.

Whether Lee's presence at this conference would help or hurt, Ben could not tell at the moment. But Lee could not very well be excluded. And, Ben reminded himself, he had even considered calling a full meeting of the ship's company instead of this conference to announce his present decision and the reasons for it. But such a meeting would have been an open invitation to debate about the decision, silent or otherwise, a debate in which he would be on one side and the rest of those aboard on the other.

No, he thought again, now. This way was better. A decision coming out of conference, even though it was his decision, implied the agreement of the senior officers with it. But it would call for careful handling to present not only the decision but his reasons for it as if they arose spontaneously out of the conversation of everyone there. In Ben's mind he juggled, like different

weights against each other, the agreeableness of Lee,
the stolidity of Walt, the protectiveness of Nora, and the
impulsiveness of Coop. Coop would have to be his pi-
geon, this time.

Ben roused from his thoughts to see all four of them
looking at him curiously.

"Have the charts made as soon as possible, then,"
Ben said. "We'll be going to take a look at those
worlds."

It took a moment for his words to sink into them.
Ben saw a variety of expressions, from Nora's of shock
to Lee's of dismay.

"Going there?" said Lee. "But I thought we'd be
heading home, now?"

It was a dangerous question, expressed aboard a ship
where there could hardly be anyone who did not long to
head homeward. Ben, even with a court-martial and retribution waiting for him, felt that longing himself. There
could be no temporizing with such a question.

"We haven't yet found a habitable world, Captain,"
said Ben formally.

"But the world we were just on—the Gray-furs—"

"Happens to be populated," said Ben, dryly. "We're
not out to find worlds to conquer. We're out to find
worlds to settle."

"But—" it was Coop finally, unable to resist the impulse to get into the discussion. Ben turned to him almost in relief. "If we had to run away from the Gray-
furs and the Gray-furs had to run away from the
Golden People, what good will it do us to go look at
planets the Golden People've taken over?"

"Our job," said Ben, "is to investigate all potentially
habitable planets. If the Gray-furs lived on them, those
planets are potentially habitable."

"But isn't it our duty not to risk—" Nora began and
broke off. "I mean, if a race of conquerors like the
Golden People find out about Earth, they might want
our world, too." She hesitated, plainly on the verge of
saying something more then changed her mind. It was
not necessary for her to say anything more. They all,
including Ben, knew what she was talking about. It was

the same ancient fear Marsh Otam had expressed back on Earth the day they had first lifted ship, the fear that was in all of them including Ben himself, deep and unkillable. The fear of the night beyond the firelight, of the dark depths of the unknown forest, of the western edge of the flat world where the seas went pouring off into space.

"They won't find out," said Ben. "We can make sure they don't. There's no one aboard this ship that knows the way home." He looked around at them, at their startled faces. "Have you forgotten?" he said. "The only way we can find our way back to Earth is by using the data stored in the tape decks of the memory tank in Computation."

They had none of them thought of it, Ben saw. Or rather, they had known it so well that they had ceased to think about it. It was the stored data of past computations, and the distance and direction of their shifts, that alone would permit the ship now to figure its way to one small Go star lost among billions of other stellar bodies. Destroy those tape decks and the phase ship would never get home. Even one long shift from the Sun—even at a thousand light-years distance—they would be condemned to wander forever without the tape decks and their store of data.

"We're going to pull those tape decks," said Ben. "I've got fresh ones in my safe here to replace them with." He glanced over at Lee. "That's why I asked Captain Ruiz to sit in on this conference, although he's just barely up and around again. The original decks will be kept in the safe here with a device that'll destroy them instantly on a signal from me, or if any attempt is made to force the safe. If this ship should be surprised or taken by aliens and in my judgment there was no hope for us, I'll destroy the tapes immediately."

There was a fresh silence at that. Like a man who has just been informed by his doctor of a dangerous weakness in one of his vital organs, the other four were feeling newly aware of their dependence upon the tape decks.

"I want that film studied," Ben went on, "and star

charts made from it showing the way to each of the worlds pictured. We'll come as close as we think safe, shift quickly into camera range of each world, take sixty seconds worth of film, and shift out again automatically. Then, safely off in space, we can examine the pictures before going in closer."

"But still, what's the use of it all?" persisted Coop, daring to argue more than he had ever done before. "The Gray-furs are stronger than we are—"

"No," said Ben. He had encouraged Coop the last few weeks to come up with this very type of protest in conference. So that he would have somebody to bring out the questions he wished to answer for all those present. It was the role Lee had originally filled, of interlocutor. "The Gray-furs are at a disadvantage with us. Why do you think we were able to dispose of those weapon crews and get away as easily as we did?"

"Why, you took them by surprise—" began Nora.

"But why were we able to take them by surprise?" interrupted Ben, turning to her. "It had to be because there was no sense of originality in what they were doing to guard us. Observation can probably slow the film down and get an idea of the time span involved, but the Gray-furs have been on that world, according to the images they showed me, for at least a hundred thousand years. It's a hundred thousand years since they ran away from attack. A hundred thousand years since they've been in a combat situation. Our landing triggered off an automatic ancient pattern of defense, but that was all. Do you all understand that?"

He looked around at them.

"N-no," said Coop, hesitantly, but honestly.

"The pattern," explained Ben, "was to immobilize any unknown space ship making a landing, to take a sample individual from those abroad it, and find out if he had the same conqueror-type characteristics as the Golden People had displayed. The Gray-furs wouldn't want to destroy such an unknown ship until, first, they knew it was safe to do so, and, second, they were sure they'd found out all there was to be known about the race it came from."

There was a murmur from the others. Ben saw he had brought them that far in understanding, at least.

"The quickness of their reaction to our landing, the fact everything was ready," he went on, "shows that this pattern had to be prepared. But over the centuries and the generations, it must have become hardened into something like a ritual dance they went through without question and almost without thought. I think it's pretty clear that I reacted in a way they didn't expect with that bear image they confronted me with."

"In a way they didn't expect?" asked Walt, his deep voice striking like the sound of a gong into the conversation.

"Yes," said Ben. It was emotionally painful to speak of his experience in the hands of the Gray-furs even now, but he put his head down metaphorically and plowed on. "They got the image of the grizzly bear from my mind by stimulating the part of my brain concerned with the reflexes of flight and fighting. Everyone has his own basic emotional image of what fear looks like. The bear was mine. I was supposed either to retreat from it, or attack it, in spite of the fact that intellectually I knew that doing either thing meant falling off the platform. When I stayed where I was until the bear came to me, I violated the pattern."

"What was the pattern?" Walt asked.

"If the subject retreated, ran away at any cost, he was of an emotional type like the Gray-furs," said Ben. "If he attacked the image of his fear, clearly, he was of a Golden People type. They had to face the fact that I, their representative human, was neither." Walt nodded, thoughtfully, as if some inner thoughts of his own had just been confirmed.

"But what's this got to do with why we were able to get away from the Gray-furs?" Coop asked.

"Think about it!" said Ben, sharply to him. "Use your head! They were faced with a breakdown in their pattern of handling alien visitors. A certain step in the pattern had failed to produce the information it was supposed to produce. Any thinking minds not crystallized into a rote-pattern of behavior would have stopped immediately at that point and begun to question and examine the pattern itself. They'd have begun immediately to stimulate other reflex areas of my brain, looking for other differences in reaction."

"Instead, they sent you back here to the ship," said Nora, suddenly. "I see! They ignored what they couldn't understand, pretended it wasn't there and that it'd go away." She looked at him with a curious light in her brown eyes. "And you figured out all that—while they were putting you through what they did."

Ben cleared his throat harshly.

"The point is," he said, looking back at the others and away from Nora, "that the same thing held true for the Gray-furs with the weapons covering us. The pattern told them to stand guard against any attempt by the ship to lift off or any try by its crew to step over the yellow line on the ground. We were supposed to recognize the fact we were prisoners, and accept it. The thought we might not accept it, that we might try to do something about it was simply not considered by the Gray-furs. Maybe those on the weapons even heard or smelled us coming at them along the cliff tops—but because they didn't have any idea of what to do in an unpatterned situation, they simply stood and let themselves be knocked on the head."

It took a few seconds for that to sink in on Ben's listeners. But when it did, the next objection came from the thin face of Lee.

"Even if that's true, though," said Lee, "the Golden People are still the race that drove the Gray-furs out of their home worlds when the Gray-furs weren't yet acting by pattern and rote."

"Exactly," said Ben, turning briskly to him, "—they were the race that drove the Gray-furs off their home worlds. But that was a hundred thousand years ago, for them too. The Gray-furs have had time to reduce themselves to the lowest common denominator of their racial character. So, maybe the Golden People have too, by this time. They may even have killed themselves off. In any case, there's more than a dozen habitable worlds whose location we can determine by studying the film we made—and we're going to have a look at them."

The last words came out flatly—flatly enough to close the mouths of Coop and Lee, who looked to be on the verge of continuing their protests.

"I think that's all then," said Ben, recognizing the psychological moment for putting a definite end to the conference. "Coop, you take charge of the business of making the star charts from the film. Nora, I wish you'd take inventory of our stores and give me an estimate of how many more days of food and supplemental water supplies we have—as well as listing any unusual shortages in other stores. Walt, you take over as full-time duty officer until Coop has the star charts made. Lee, I wonder if you'd stay a few more minutes, I'd like to talk to you about the business of taking the tape decks out."

The members of the conference awoke to the fact that Ben's words were a polite dismissal of everyone but Lee. The others got up from their seats and left the office. As the last door shut behind those leaving, Ben looked across his desk at Lee.

"Coop can just as well go on holding down his turn as one of the duty officers," said Ben. "But meanwhile—are you sure you feel up to getting back to work on something like this tape-deck change?"

For a moment the ghost of the former buccaneer's smile returned to the bony face before him.

"Never felt better in my life," said Lee. But the smile slipped away and the voice did not have the old vibrancy and enthusiasm. Several months of constant pain had filed away at the full strong body of that voice and made it thin and a little ragged. "Anyway, there's no real job to changing those tape decks. No problem, I mean. It's just a matter of some rather complicated disassembly work."

"I see," said Ben. If Lee was willing to get back to work it would be no kindness to stop him. "All right then, what do you suggest about a gadget to destroy the tape decks if that turns out to be necessary . . ." In a moment they were deep in a discussion of explosive packages and radio fuses.

What was finally decided on—and put into practice in the last days of the following week, after the main computer had carefully been half disassembled to get the tapes out of the memory bank—was an explosive package containing the tape reels and two fuses. One was a radio fuse keyed to a small transmitter that Ben could carry in his pocket, and the other was a fuse wired directly to the locking mechanism of the safe itself.

Meanwhile, the laborious and tricky job of reassembling the main computer was being completed. The tapes had not been designed to be replaced anywhere but at home on the surface of Earth, with the phase ship itself partly dismantled for general overhaul. Theoretically the tapes were good for five years of ship operation, and in fact Ben had had to smuggle the replacements aboard originally. He found some small cause for self-congratulation about this, now, but it did not have the effect of cheering him up so much as of increasing his worries. The thought of it reminded him of all that he had forseen that was, presumably, yet to come; and he was left to wonder if his provisions for those situations still in the future would be as good as this had been.

But meanwhile, the star charts made from the images the Gray-furs had shown to Ben of their defeat and exodus from their home worlds, were also finished. Magnification of the film of those images for detail had turned out to be limited only by the grain of the film itself.

"I've never seen anything like it!" said Kirk Walish, genial for once with enthusiasm, spreading the star charts out on Ben's desk for Ben's inspection. "We couldn't have done any better if we'd taken the ship there ourselves."

"Then we're ready to go?" Ben said.

"As far as Observation's concerned, we are. Sir," said Kirk, almost happily.

"Computation will take about three days for the first gross shift," put in Coop, who had come in with Kirk.

The first gross shift, in fact, came five days later, rather than three. But as if in compensation it took them, both by luck and by virtue of the new star maps, within less than a dozen light-years of the first of the star systems they wanted to investigate. This particular star system had only one habitable planet, according to the star maps made from the Gray-fur images.

"We can put the ship in orbit around that planet in three shifts," said Walt.

"All right," said Ben. "But I'd rather approach in a larger number of shifts and make sure when we come in that the last shift to orbit the planet is from a safe distance out. How far out can we be and still make the shift to orbit the planet in one jump?"

"I'll check with Observation," said Coop.

Observation, consulted, gave its opinion that the maximum distance from which it could pinpoint a jump into orbit, close enough for detail picture-taking of the world in question, would be about eight hundred million miles. Or slightly less than the mean distance between the solar system orbits of Earth and Saturn.

"Then make it four shifts to orbit," said Ben. "Three to the eight hundred million mile approach position and one from there to orbit. Then one full second of camera work and jump immediately to a distance of three light-years."

They moved in. The first three shifts took place without a hitch.

"There it is," said Kirk Walish, coming back from Observation to point to the screen above Tessie Sorenson. Ben looked. Among the starlights thick on the screen, Kirk's long, tapering forefinger indicated a small, bluish pinprick of light.

"Thanks," said Ben. "How soon can we shift into orbit."

"Right now," said Walt behind him.

"All right, prepare to shift, then."

The chant of orders before shifting rang in Ben's ear. As always, the moment before shifting brought a slightly cool feeling to the back of his neck.

"Cameras ready?" he asked over the intercom to Kirk in Observation.

"All ready."

"Shift!" ordered Ben, watching the screen.

Suddenly, before them was the day side of a world with one sprawling rectangular continent in its northern hemisphere connected to two southern continents by narrow land bridges. Here, from four hundred and fifty miles up Ben could see no signs of civilization, but the cameras of Observation would find out. Ben forced himself to stand impassive. But the blood pounded in his ears with each beat of his heart and he found himself counting the seconds by it, all the time his imagination was evoking lances of fire, or dark shapes of strange missiles leaping up at them from the tranquil surface below.

Then, the automatic shift away. His stomach reacted to the jump and without warning the screen was filled with nothing but the peaceful stars.

He heard the sound of breath being exhaled in relief from Tessie below him and Coop behind him. The tiny sounds woke him to the fact that he, too, had been holding his breath during the minute of their close orbit. He caught himself just in time from making the same audible exhalation.

"Call me as soon as the pictures are ready," he said stiffly to Coop, and went off through the door from the Control Section into his office—where at last he could sigh in privacy. It was a little thing, but he was determined to regain as much ascendancy over the rest of those aboard as he must have lost by their seeing him jerking and weeping in the control of the Gray-furs. Here in the territory of the Golden People the phase ship's real challenge was probably still before it, and his power to command could be more vital than ever for the sake of everyone's lives.

He went across the room to the log cabinet to make an entry noting the recent close orbit and picture-taking in the official ship's log. He was just finishing the entry, when there was a knock behind him and the door from the Control Section opened.

"Pictures ready," said the voice of Coop.

"Thank you," said Ben. He closed the log and locked it away, then turned and followed Coop back into the

Control Section and through Computation into Observation.

In the oval-shaped Observation Section, the shutters were closed over the observation window overhead, but the large, curving screen in one side of the room was alight. Before this sat Polly Neigh, with Ralph Egan across the room in the other chair. Beside these two seated were Walt and Kirk standing, which made with Ben, himself, and Coop, in all six people in the small section. Moreover, there was an air of expectancy in the room like a bubble about to burst; and with his uncomfortably sensitive emotional perceptions, Ben understood instantly that it was directed at him.

They had discovered something they thought would please him. It was as if they were all only waiting for the moment to leap up about him and yell "Surprise!" He writhed inwardly at the thought of being that easy to manipulate—it was his embarrassing exhibition of helplessness in the power of the Gray-furs that had given them the idea—and looked desperately about for some excuse to show himself arbitrary and unpredictable. As luck would have it, he was able to spot some whiskers poking out of the darkness under the desk board of the control panel above Polly's feet.

"What's that cat doing in here?" he snapped—and Polly's face fell instantly into an expression of guilt.

"He just likes to lie by my feet," she said, stooping to pick up an unwilling Sprockets, who glared and hissed around the room with fine impartiality as he was passed from hand to hand until he could be thrust out through the door facing the lounge.

"Polly's trying to teach him to purr in time to save his reputation when we spot a habitable world," said Kirk, waspishly. Ben was surprised to see not only Polly but Coop look furiously at the balding Observation Section Leader. Evidently the old prediction that Sprockets would purr for the first time when they sighted the world that would fulfill their mission had come to be a matter of gibe and countergibe aboard.

"He'll purr!" said Polly, angrily. "You'll see. Maybe not for the world, but he'll purr!"

"Have Coop build him a mechanical purrer—" Kirk was beginning.

"All right!" snarled Ben at him, interrupting. "Are the fun and games over with?" They were, he noted with a sort of mean satisfaction. For a moment he felt guilty—then he reminded himself that anything was better than to let them all think that they had a commander who could be manipulated. "Let's see those pictures."

"Here," said Polly, indicating the screen.

Ben turned and saw what they had all been waiting for him to discover and react to, on discovering. On the screen was a view from an apparent height of two hundred feet, courtesy of the telescopic equipment of the Observation Section's cameras. It showed a city such as Ben had seen the Golden People building in the images shown him by the Gray-furs.

Tall, slender buildings. Narrow arches. Walkways looking as thin as spider thread, without protective railings, and stretching at throat-tightening heights from one high tower to another. A city of concentric streets, streets with curving, spiral-making connections between them. A city of reds and yellows and grays.

Then Ben's attention suddenly sharpened. He had been about to look for signs of life among the circling streets and the narrow buildings. He had not seen any yet, and he saw now why there might well be none there. At first sight the buildings and streets had seemed as clean and colorful as if they had been built yesterday. But now that he looked closer, he saw marks upon them—not only the marks of time, but the marks of destruction.

Vegetation stained their lower walls. Here and there a spider-web walkway had parted and the air gapped between broken ends. Also, here and there, a wall had fallen inward on towers or lesser buildings, and—now that he looked very closely—Ben could trace lines of destruction, like monstrous whip-marks up to a quarter mile in length, scarring the face of the city below.

"You were right!" said Coop at Ben's shoulder. The words seemed to explode out of him, as if they had finally refused to be bottled up any longer. "They've killed themselves off! The Golden People've killed themselves off. There's no one down there."

Ben felt a sort of thrill race through him that was hot and cold as the same time. He got a firm grip on himself and kept his voice flat as he straightened up and turned to Coop.

"There's not?" he demanded. "And why do you think you can be sure about that?"

"No heat images!" said Coop, in triumph. "Heat radar shows no moving images, and no images the size of a man."

"They could be in the buildings," said Kirk, across the room. "They could all be under cover."

"All?" said Coop, turning on him. "In a city that size? Even if they'd known we were there when we popped into orbit position, they wouldn't have all gotten out of sight in sixty seconds."

There was a silence in the Observation Section. Ben turned fully and looked at Walt. Walt's face was as impassive as ever. He could call a conference, thought Ben—but no, his instincts told him this was not the same for a conference.

"All right," he said, turning to Coop. "Ready a shift to the next closest Golden People world, and call me when you're ready to shift."

Coop stared at him for a moment, then blinked. He wet his lips. Clearly, he was working up the courage to ask a question. Ben waited for it. He wanted the whole ship to be informed of his reasons.

"You aren't—" Coop fumbled. "Isn't the ship going to land?"

"Not until we look at the other worlds first," said Ben. "I want to know if this is an isolated phenomenon, or if they're all like this. —I might remind you all," he said, looking around the room, "that we've run into the unexpected on every planet we've set down on. From now on, expecting the unexpected is going to be a rule on this ship. Just because heat radar can't find anything down there, doesn't mean there's nothing down there. It may only mean that whatever's down there is something that we're not clever enough to find."

With that he turned on his heel and went up through the silent Sections toward his own office, congratulating himself on regaining some of his Gray-fur-impaired authority. Once the door from the Control Section to his office was shut behind him, however, he found himself gulping with excitement.

It must be true that somewhere in this arbitrary and unfeeling universe, chance had to fall their way on occasion, rather than always turning against them. Why shouldn't it turn out that for once there were no unpleasant surprises below and that the Golden People had conveniently all been killed, or had killed themselves off? After all his planning, all his risks and efforts, why shouldn't luck favor him, just once?

The truth of the matter was he wanted to go down onto the surface of the world they had just seen as badly as Coop or anyone.

□ CHAPTER 10 □

BUT THE OTHER fourteen worlds taken by the Golden
People from the Gray-furs, as they were visited one by
one, showed the same ancient scars of destruction and
air of desertion. The worlds themselves were spread out,
never more than two among the planets of any solar
system, through some eighty-odd years of space. Observation, taking surveys as the ship went, had already
established with over ninety percent of certainty that
they were the only planets with a possibility of being
habitable by humans (and therefore by Gray-furs and
Golden People) within a fairly large area of space. For
one thing, even in this relatively overcrowded area of
the galaxy where the stellar population was a number of
times that in the skies around Earth, there were no Go
stars the size of Earth's Sun for nearly a hundred light-
years in any direction.

Ben was beginning to think—and Observation tended
to agree with him—that humanly habitable planets were
rarer even than estimates back on Earth had figured
them to be. Although it could be that the phase ship
had simply found itself in areas where Sol-like Suns
were scarcer than normal.

All the same, thought Ben at his desk in the office, as
the phase ship was completing the last jump of the shift
he had ordered back to approach position on the first
Golden Peoples' world they had investigated, there was
something almost eerie about the situation. If another
conquering race had passed by here, defeating the
Golden People as the Golden People had defeated the
Gray-furs, the conquerors had not stopped to reap any

profit from their victories. They had simply killed and passed on.

That was against reason for any technologically civilized, intelligent mind of which Ben's human mind could conceive. Of course, among the trillions of stars making up the galaxy it was possible to imagine that there could be civilized and intelligent space-going races that would operate in ways making no sense at all to a human mind. But still . . . reasonless extermination was what had happened to the Golden People.

A knock on the door of his office brought Ben out of his speculations.

"Ready to shift," said Walt, opening the door from the Control Section.

"Coming," said Ben, briefly. He got up from his desk and followed Walt into the Control Section.

"This time," Ben said, "we'll shift into orbit position, take pictures, and shift out again after sixty seconds, as before." He closed the office door behind him. "After we compare this set of pictures with the last, we'll think about going down to surface. Not before."

"Yes, sir," said Walt, calmly.

"Prepare to shift."

"Prepare to shift—" Walt was beginning when there was an interruption. A sound of shouting, jeering voices from the front part of the ship, echoing through the metal walls and doors of the Observation Section and making itself heard up through the Sections even to the Control Section at the end.

"Report!" Tessie Sorenson was beginning, speaking into the phone before her, but Ben put a hand on her shoulder.

"Hold that!" he ordered. He walked forward through the Sections and pushed open the door from Observation to step into the corridor facing the Lounge entrance.

Ridiculously and without reason, a small riot seemed to be in process there. The corridor and the Lounge before it were filled with arguing off-duty crew members, at the center of which was Polly, pale and upset, holding the cat, Sprockets, in her arms. Beside Polly was

Coop, his face white and furious, standing almost nose to nose with Kirk Walish. Seeing them bristling at each other like this, Ben was suddenly reminded of how small Kirk actually was—no more than average height, if that much, and thin to boot. It was his challenging attitude and sharp tongue that gave him always the impression of being so much bigger than he really was. Young Coop, facing him now, overtopped him by a full head and must have outweighed him by thirty or forty pounds, but of the two it was Kirk who looked more in command of the dispute.

"But I tell you, he did!" Polly was insisting. She looked on the verge of tears. "He purred!"

"Just happened to," sneered Kirk. "Of course! Just before we shift in above the planet everyone knows is okay. And just when there happened to be no one else around to hear. Too bad!"

"Listen—" said Coop thickly to him, "you're calling her a liar, are you?"

"Why, I'm not calling her a liar." Kirk grinned up at him. "I'm just pointing out a few facts. Facts—"

"Shut up!" roared Ben, reaching the three of them at last. He found himself seething with rage. "Shut your mouth, Kirk! You too, Coop. All of you—*shut up!*"

The voices around him fell still abruptly. The silence, during which he glared around at all of them, even at Polly who stood awkwardly on her one artificial lower leg, holding the irritated and hissing cat protectively to her.

"What is this—some sort of Sunday picnic?" Ben's genuine fury put a ring in his voice that he saw having its effect upon the faces within his field of vision. "We've got a world to land on in two hours time—and we don't 'know it's okay!' All we know is that we can't find anything to guard against down there. Two hours from now we may all be dead! And you've got nothing better to do right now but get into a fight over whether a cat purred or not!"

He glared around at all of them again, but apparently there was no one hardy enough to argue with him.

"That's all I want to hear of this kind of noise!"

Turning on his heel, he went back into the Sections. He did not hear the sound of the argument starting up again.

They shifted in close to the world, took their pictures, and retreated sixty seconds later. A careful study of the pictures this time with the techniques evolved for the analysis of aerial photos showed no meaningful difference from the pictures they had taken on their earlier visit.

Standing over the matched photos on Observation's large screen, Ben hesitated. There seemed to be no good reason why the phase ship should not shift back into the orbit position they had just left, and from there down to the surface of the Golden People's world.

"All right, we'll go down," he said, turning to Walt. "But I want to shift no closer than a hundred feet from the ground and hold while we look over our landing area before touching down."

"Yes sir," said Walt, as calmly as ever. But it seemed to Ben that Walt's eyes paused a moment, considering Ben, before the big man turned away to give the necessary orders. For the first time, wildly and irrationally, the suspicion awoke in Ben that his momentary hesitation over going down had caused Walt to doubt him— even to think him a coward. It was the first time it had ever occurred to Ben to think that Walt might doubt his will to succeed and his right to command aboard the phase ship.

That could be a more serious matter than settling an argument over whether a cat had purred or not. Walt was over-sized, both physically and mentally, and a man of unswerving independence. He could not be fooled and he could not be bullied. —Ben put the matter out of his mind and followed Walt back to the Control Section.

They shifted down within a hundred feet of the ground over a small open area of raw earth and scrubby vegetation—it might have been a park once—among the buildings of the city. It was early morning, and the tall slender buildings around them looked like fanciful stage settings for an imaginative play. Nothing stirred in the hot, bright sunlight below and around them. Again, the heat radar showed nothing. Air samples and all other tests showed favorable.

"Shift to surface!" said Ben.

There was a tiny touch of shift-nausea, and the screen over Tessie Sorenson's head, before Ben, now showed a view from ground level, a view of the bases of the slender buildings only forty or fifty feet away beyond the bulge of the outer airlock door, hiding the lower left corner of the screen. Ben felt the phase ship settling almost imperceptibly under him as local gravity replaced the internal and artificial force of shift oscillation.

"All right," he said, speaking stiffly with the tension of the moment. "Captain Bone, come with me to the airlock."

They went through the office to pick up two of the Weyerlander half-guns, then down the short corridor to the airlock. It was all but filled. Most of the off-duty people were there, eagerly waiting to pour out through the airlock's double doors as soon as they were opened.

"Stand back," said Ben, grimly. "We'll take a look outside first."

He pressed the button that swung open the inner door of the airlock and stepped through it. He pressed the second button and heard the heavy interior door swing closed behind him. The outer door began slowly to swing wide. He looked out at sunlit-brown earth and weeds, with the curved sides of buildings a short distance off—empty and peaceful. He turned back and pressed the button that would open the inner lock without closing the outer one.

As he watched the inner door swung open. He saw the faces of the crew looking past him—then suddenly they contorted, changing. Somebody shouted. Ben swung around to look out upon the open space beyond the outer door of the airlock—and coming toward the ship with giant strides, he saw half a dozen tall, thin, golden figures with slim, short rods like javelins in their hands.

Ben's hands shot out and jabbed the "close" button

on the outer airlock door. The door stirred and began to
swing toward him, to close again.

The leading golden figure lifted his javelin. It glinted
in the sunlight—and then from its tip raved forth a bolt
like a lash of silver lightning against the closing door.
There was a crash and the whole phase ship rocked.
Ben staggered, trying to keep his feet and desperately
blinking the lightning dazzle out of his eyes. As he began to be able to see again, he perceived the outer airlock door, sagging half-torn off its massive hinges and
distorted by a smoking cleft in its upper edge.

Then, the circle of sunlight where the door had been
was being blotted out by thin giant shapes, scrambling
into the airlock. Ben and those around him were being
herded outside into the sunlight beyond the airlock,
while others of the tall golden figures plunged on into
the further depths of the phase ship.

Ben and the others in the airlock went numbly and
allowed themselves to be rounded up outside and kept
standing under the impersonal, oval, olive gaze of two
of the attackers. Ben held the half-gun still in his hand
as did Walt, but their guards made no attempt to take
the weapons from them. It was very possible that the
guards did not recognize the half-guns as weapons. In
any case, he felt no impulse to try and use the one in his
hands. Compared to the casual bolt from the slender
four-foot rod that had torn the heavy outer airlock door
half off the ship, a half-gun could be no more than a
toy—a toy pitiful in its limitations.

The hot sun warmed the top of Ben's head. Through
the open airlock he could hear sounds of things broken
or torn loose inside the ship. He expected at any minute
to see those crew members who were still inside the ship
be herded out by the lightning-bearing javelins of the
Golden People who had entered. But they did not come.

After a little while, however, the Golden People who
had gone into the phase ship began to come out. They
were carrying all manner of things—chairs from the
Lounge and tools from the machine shop on the lower
deck—Ben even saw one carrying a copy of Nora's

Stores inventory report that had been on his desk. One of them, who was particularly overloaded, stopped to share his burdens with one of the two guarding the knot of humans outside the ship—and the two large golden figures went off together.

The humans outside the ship were themselves beginning to become restless and dart unhappy glances at the open airlock beyond which the fate of those still inside the ship was hidden and unknown.

"Stand still!" muttered Ben, without moving his lips, as another one of the Golden People came out of the airlock, carrying Ben's desk armchair with one long, javelin-bearing arm wrapped around it. "Don't talk."

Those about him fell silent. But his voice, pitched low, did not carry its warning to those farthest from the airlock. Just at that moment, the voice of Burt Sullivan, out there at Ben's left, came clearly to Ben's ear.

"Why doesn't somebody try to slip in through the airlock when these watchdogs aren't looking at him?" Burt was saying. "Then he could—"

The Golden alien carrying the armchair halted almost in front of Burt, turned slightly still holding the armchair so as to face the humans, and without loosening his grip pointed his javelin at the group. From its tip lashed out a wire-thin, smaller, paler version of the bolt of silver lightning that had halted and torn loose the airlock door. Ben could see Burt go down out of sight behind the intervening bodies as the bolt struck. And then the silver lash leaped again, and whoever was standing next to Burt went down as well.

The Golden alien turned and went on without pausing. In eight or nine long strides, while the humans stood stunned, his great legs carried him to and around one of the surrounding buildings, out of sight. As he disappeared, the human group came out of its moment of frozen shock, and with a little moan, sagged back from the two fallen figures.

Ben could see them now. One was faceless, almost headless, and unrecognizable. But that one must be Burt because the body slashed and burnt across the chest lying next to it bore the face of John Edlung, who had been so sure that he would die before he could get back to Earth.

Their single remaining guard had taken a step toward them, now, his javelin half-lifted at the sound of their moan, and their movement.

"Stand still!" snapped Ben, low-voiced between his teeth. But Kirk, fists clenched and shoulders quivering, was already stepping forward out of the group toward the guard.

"You want to kill somebody?" Kirk's voice went up on a rising note. "You want to kill somebody—" He was advancing toward the guard hands now open and up as he talked, with every evident intention of leaping for the narrow golden throat, nearly four feet above his own head. The guard lifted his javelin as if to shoot, apparently changed his mind, and struck out and down with it as if it had been a slender club.

The sheer size of the guard made the movement awkward. Kirk dodged under the blow and for a moment it looked as if he would reach the guard's throat after all. But then the javelin swept down at an angle again; and Kirk, trying to dodge, backed up against the hull of the phase ship with no room to slip aside.

The rod caught him across the side and the back, about waist high, as he was trying to duck away, and slammed him up against the hull. He fell to the ground, made an effort to scramble to his feet, and was defeated by the fact that his legs were no longer responding. He shouted something furiously up at the guard, as the tall, golden body moved between him and the other humans, blocking off their view as it struck down again.

The hidden blow cut off abruptly the sound of Kirk's voice. But the guard, half squatting from his nine feet or so of height above where Kirk lay, continued to strike, the way someone with a horror of vermin continues to beat an already motionless rat or snake to make sure it is dead. The body of watching humans swayed forward all together with an instinctive movement.

"Still! Stand still!" cried Ben, raggedly. He threw up an arm in time to get his forearm across the throat of

Coop, beside him, who was going forward yet, unhearingly. Coop checked, choking, and a moment later Ben saw him encircled and held by the massive arms of Walt. The movement stopped.

The back of the guard was still to them.

"Stay here, all of you!" muttered Ben harshly. "And don't twitch a finger!" He turned and slipped off to the right, up the foot high step into the airlock. Within, all was quiet. He ran as silently as possible on the tips of his toes down the short corridor and into the corridor on the women's side of the ship. The back of a tall, golden figure was to him, evidently dragging something heavy out of one of the staterooms.

Ben backed up a step, opened the door to the Special Stores Room, slipped inside, and closed the door. He stood with the silent and apparently untouched cartons around him and the automatic light on overhead, his ear pressed to the cold metal panel, listening. After a little he heard something heavy and apparently metallic being dragged, squeaking and screeching down the corridor to the entrance to the short airlock corridor, then off down the airlock corridor and into silence. He opened the door a crack and peered out to find no one in sight. He slipped out into the corridor himself, again.

Opposite him was the door to his office. He laid his ear against the upper panel, heard nothing, and opened the door a crack. The room within was empty. He slipped inside, closing the door behind him.

Now, for the first time, pausing in the familiar surroundings of his office, he felt the helpless fear, which had been pushed into one corner of his mind by the emergency up until now, threaten to rise and overtake him. He felt it coming up like a sour acid in his throat and dissolving all the drive and purpose wakened in him by the sight of the guard clubbing Kirk. —He must not continue to stand here, he told himself, with a silent gasp of panic. If he did, all the courage in him would leak away and he would think of nothing but finding some cupboard or shielded hole of the ship to crawl into and wait, either for the going of the Golden People or the moment when they would find him there.

He broke the paralysis holding him with a wild effort
and stepped to the door leading to the Control Section.
He jerked it open without even putting his ear to it first,
and stepped through.

In her seat before the Control instruments, Tessie Sorenson looked up at him with a face as pale as the paper
of the Presidential message that he had altered to bring
them all here. He looked down through the openings
between the various Sections to the closed door at the
far end of the Observation Section. He saw the on-duty
members of the crew seated at their instruments, but no
towering golden figures.

"Were they in here?" he demanded, in a hoarse, low
voice, of Tessie. She nodded. "You all sat tight?" She
nodded again. "What happened?"

"They took—" her voice was a whisper, "anything
that was loose, and went out." Talking seemed to give
her courage. A little color came back into her face and
her voice broke out of a whisper into low, speaking
tones. "The door at the end down there was open a little, so they came in. But they don't seem to understand
about locks. They didn't try to open the door to your
office. So when they went, we locked the end door
again and no more came in."

"Good. Stay put," said Ben. He went hastily on down
the line of the Sections, shaking his head at those who
wanted to ask him what had happened and was happening outside their three enclosed Sections. At the end
door, he put his ear to the panel, but heard nothing. He
cautiously cracked the door and looked. The corridor
and the Lounge were empty. He stepped through the
door, closing it behind him.

The thought of Lee Ruiz erupted so suddenly in his
mind that for a second he was ready to believe he had
heard Lee's name spoken aloud. He looked around
sharply but saw no one. It was possible—very possible—that all of the Golden People who had entered the
phase ship had now left it. Ben swore at himself silently
now for not having had the presence of mind to keep
his head and count those who entered. But there was no
help for that now—and the lack of sound from both the

lower and the upper decks, from the whole ship, agreed
with the evidence of his eyes that the aliens had left. He
must find Lee quickly.

Lee had not been among those in the airlock who
had been herded outside and put under guard. So far,
Ben had not seen him inside the ship. —What had Tessie said? That the aliens had not seemed to understand
fully the concept of doors and had not tried to open any
that were locked.

He turned to his right and went swiftly down the corridor on the men's side of the ship to the door of Lee's
stateroom. He put his hand on the handle, found it unlocked, and shoved the door open.

Lee was inside on the bed, huddled as far back into a
corner as he could go. His face was gaunt and savage
and he held a long, thin screwdriver in one hand blade-
end-upward like an experienced knife fighter. For a
second, Ben was reminded of the twig he himself had
held as a child, facing the grizzly. Lee's eyes stared at
him for a moment without recognition.

"Lee!" said Ben. "It's me—the aliens've gone!"

For a second longer, Lee's eyes continued to stare.
Then his face loosened all at once, as if the tension
holding it together had evaporated, and his hand that
held the screwdriver began to tremble so badly that he
put the tool down on the bed.

"Gone—" he said, chokingly.

"Yes." One stride across the tiny room brought Ben
to the side of the bed. "But they've got one of them still
holding more than half the crew outside the ship. I need
your help. Here's what you've got to do—"

He broke off, for Lee's head was wobbling on its lean
neck as Lee shook it.

"I can't, Ben," said Lee, "I can't help you. I can't
take any more—"

"You were ready to try to stick that screwdriver into
the first golden face that poked itself through the door,
just now," said Ben, brutally. "I'm not asking you to do
any more than that. —Listen! Are you listening?"

"I'm . . . " Lee made a great effort and managed to

straighten himself up so that he no longer huddled in the corner, "listening."

"All right," said Ben. "Walt, Coop, and nearly everyone off-duty are outside the ship under guard. I want you to take command of whoever's still aboard here. There's a full crew in the Sections. Have them compute a shift off-surface, anywhere, but not out of the atmosphere. Meanwhile, you see what can be done to get that inner airlock door to make an airtight seal—"

Lee's head wobbled on his neck again.

"Do you think the Golden People'll let us take off—" he was beginning. Ben cut him short.

"Never mind!" Ben snarled. "Never mind anything. Just do what I tell you. Do it! Have you got that?"

Lee nodded. His head was steady again.

"If you can get a seal with the inner airlock door, and I'm not back in—" Ben paused to glance at his wristwatch, "two hours at the outside, make one large shift off-planet—try it anyway. If you get away, head for Earth. Don't stop to worry about me or anyone outside the ship. If you can't get a seal, at the end of two hours try to make a shift to somewhere else in the atmosphere of this world, but off-surface and away from here. Understood?"

Lee nodded.

"All right." Ben turned once more toward the door of the stateroom. As he opened it, he looked back. Lee had not moved. "What're you waiting for?" snarled Ben. "You're in command, here now!"

Lee started up off the bed like someone coming out of a dream. Ben stood aside to let him out and saw him go down the corridor and in the door opposite the Lounge, into the Sections. The door closed behind Lee, and for a second Ben, himself, leaned wearily against the corridor wall. It was wonderful to let down for a second—just for a second.

Then he became suddenly conscious that he did not want to start up again. The temptation to give up was as crushingly powerful as the thought of sleep to a man three days without it. The fear he had pushed back earlier rose within him. He remembered that to do what he

had decided to do meant that he would have to go outside the ship again—out where the Golden People were.
For a few unchained seconds his imagination ran riot.
He saw a javelin lancing its silver fire at him, he saw
himself sprawling in the dust with a broken back, while
one of the aliens squatted above him to beat him to
death.

For a moment his spirit failed him. He could not do
it—not when without effort he could turn back from the
airlock, claim that there was no chance of his getting
out without being seen and killed, and help Lee get
away with those who still remained aboard ship. No one
would ever know. Even if they knew they could not
blame him—one man against a city of aliens with weapons gods might have made and put in their hands.

He sagged like a terrified child against the wall—and
then, through all the horrors of his imaginings, he became slowly conscious of a small, rhythmical sound that
he realized now he had been hearing for some time. He
lifted his head. It was coming from down the corridor
on the women's side of the ship.

He pushed himself away from the wall and went
slowly, wonderingly toward it. Halfway down the corridor, he found its cause. It was Polly Neigh, crouched in
the little wall indentation of the drinking fountain there,
her artificial leg tucked clumsily under her out of the
corridor, crying above the body of Sprockets in her lap.

Ben looked down at her dark head, bowed above the
body of the cat. Sprockets was as unlovely in death as
he had been in life. He had been half-crushed by a blow
across the chest area of his body—Ben could imagine
what had dealt the blow. Sprockets' mouth was caught
open in a snarl, showing his needle-sharp teeth. Perhaps
he had had the hardihood to scratch or bite one of the
Golden People, thought Ben, and at that thought he
found a new kindness toward the cat.

But Polly had become aware of Ben's presence. She
lifted her face, puffed and wet with crying. She did not
seem surprised to see it was Ben, rather than one of the
aliens, standing over her.

"He didn't purr—" she choked. "He never really did

purr. I made it up." She began to sob again and bent
head head once more over the dead animal, her tears falling on the grizzled fur as she stroked it blindly. "—It
wasn't his fault," she wept, rocking back and forth. "He
wanted to purr, but no one understood what happened
to him. He never knew how to purr—and nobody gave
him a chance—"

Suddenly Ben understood. Her agony and her loss
came clear and real to him. Her figure became indis-
tinct before his eyes and his throat seemed to contract
in the cruel grip of a dry and hurtful fist. The dark
shape of her artificial lower leg and the dark shape of
the cat blurred and seemed to flow together so that they
were one and the same thing.

An iciness of fury began to form at the back of his
neck, and as it spread his vision cleared once more. He
stood looking down at Polly and the cat who had never
learned how to purr and the coldness spread, across his
shoulders and down his back like an armor-coat of ice
forming around him. The dead cat swam in his mind
together with the mental pictures remembered of Burt
with his head unrecognizable, and John Edlung dead,
and Kirk struggling to get up from the ground.

The ice armor spread out all over him. He reached
out his hand to lift Polly to her feet, and then changed
his mind. He turned on his heel and strode down the
hall and back into his office. He crossed the office, unlocked the safe, and ripped down from its rack one of
the hunting rifles. He filled his pockets with clips of
shells, locked the safe, and went swiftly back out into
the corridor. He stepped into the sick bay, opened a
drawer, and took out a dissecting knife. He wrapped its
keen blade in a towel, put it in his pocket, and went out.

When he got to the airlock, he fed a clip into the rifle,
jacked the first shell into position, and looked cautiously out from the shadow within one side of the
opening.

The crew members under guard outside the ship had
been moved off a distance of about thirty feet. They
were all sitting on the ground now—whether of their
own volition or because the guard had made them do

so. They sat with their backs to the ship. The guard squatted over them, facing directly toward the airlock, but so screened by their bodies that Ben's half-raised rifle sagged in his hands again. A shot at the guard that did not kill immediately would be worse than none at all.

And now another of the Golden aliens, wearing a brown blanket from one of the ship's beds around his neck like a scarf, came out from between the buildings and squatted down next to the guard. For a moment they were looking at each other and the guard's attention was withdrawn from the prisoners and the ship. Ben ducked quickly and silently out of the airlock and started around the back curve of the ship to put its bulk between him and the eyes of the two aliens.

At that moment, the guard looked back. Ben froze in midstride, half-crouching against the body of the ship. The guard's eyes stared over the heads of the seated prisoners and directly at Ben. The other alien stared as well. Ben stayed crouched, motionless but in plain view. The two golden heads seemed to be pondering whether he was actually there before their eyes or not. Perhaps their vision was not good at over a few yards of distance—or maybe they were having some debate the human ear could not hear over which one should have the pleasure of using a javelin bolt on him.

Their two heads swung back to face each other. Their eyes were off the ship. Ben jerked into movement again and bolted around the end of the ship. With the dark steel alloy of its side curving up to hide him from the eyes on the other side of it, he paused to catch his breath. His eyes ranged the open space and the bases of the buildings beyond. There was no living thing in sight.

The murderous iciness that had come over him as he watched Polly weeping over the dead Sprockets still held him in a grip like iron. He felt a moment's vague wonder at where his fear had gone, but it had evaporated. Where it had been, there was now the cold determination to rescue the human prisoners and kill any of the Golden People who had stood in the way of his doing it. Also—there was a grim suspicion in the back of his mind that must be investigated if he could manage to kill one of the aliens and examine both it and its javelin weapon.

But first came the matter of releasing the human prisoners. To do that, he would have to dispose of their guards, and, for that, he must be able to get in a position giving him a sure-and-certain-killing first shot at the aliens.

He would have to go into the buildings and, using them for a screen, work his way around behind the two Golden People now squatted, facing Walt and the others.

He went at a run for the nearest buildings. It was not until he was safely behind the curving side of its rose-colored wall that he paused again to catch his breath. He crouched low, next to the ground, the rifle with safety off and ready to use, himself ready to freeze instantly into immobility if an alien should spot him.

But there were no aliens in sight—only a streetless area of weed-covered earth and the curving sides of the slender, tower-like buildings in various solid colors. In here, among them, even the breeze was cut off. The sun shone hot and he could feel his chest shaken by the steady pounding of his heart.

After a bit, he went on, sidling around the curves of buildings, dashing across open space, trying to get no deeper than the immediate ring of buildings around the cleared space where the phase ship lay, so as not to lose his way.

Finally, he came around the bulge of a light gray tower and caught a glimpse of golden skins before him. He drew back instantly, looked around behind him to see still only silence and emptiness, and began cautiously once more to peer around the building.

Inching forward, he caught sight of the prisoners and both aliens with their backs to him, squatting in silent conversation. Beyond these two were the faces of the seated humans; but, although they were looking in Ben's direction, so far they had not seen him. That was all to the good. Their staring at him might make the aliens turn around to look also.

With one more glance around him to make sure no other alien was approaching, Ben dropped on the ground and into a prone position with his rifle. The range to the two guards was almost ridiculously small—less than fifty feet. But to balance this was the fact he was not sure where in the golden bodies a single shell should be put to kill instantly. Any failure to do so could raise a hunt for him and leave the prisoners without hope of rescue. After a moment's debate, Ben decided on head shots. Those skulls should house the alien brains, large as they were—bigger even than human skulls, although the alien's height and long necks made their heads seem small for their bodies.

But before he could fire, the original guard rose suddenly to his feet. Carrying his javelin, he turned and stalked off—not in the direction of Ben, but between two buildings beyond the green tower at Ben's right. The rifle wavered in Ben's grasp. He wanted that guard. He wanted him very badly. Compared to the alien just leaving, the one left behind with the brown blanket around his neck was almost unimportant.

There was no time to lose. He cramped the sun-warmed butt of the rifle hastily to his cheek, looked down the blue steel barrel at the back of a golden head, and fired. The blanket-scarfed alien pitched forward on his face and lay still. Without waiting to see the reaction of the prisoners, now freed, Ben scrambled to his feet and ran after the other alien.

The other was not in sight among the buildings—and then Ben caught sight of him, moving away rapidly in the direction in which Ben had seen him disappear. Ben ran after him. The walking stride of the alien moved him at a good eight miles an hour and Ben was hard put to follow. There was no stretch among the buildings open enough for him to stop, take aim, and shoot before the other had disappeared behind some further curving wall.

Ben had assumed the alien was heading for some place only a short distance away. But the other kept traveling. Ben began to get winded. Months aboard the ship, even with a daily routine of exercise, had not put him in training to make a long-distance run. Eventually, the alien turned around a corner and came to a building with one of its walls half fallen away. He passed through the gap into the ruined building and approached a wall in which were a number of oval recesses. He stopped, reached into an apparently empty recess, and pulled out a large cube of grayish material, which he began to chew.

Ben, checking his pace, stole up behind the tall, golden back. For a moment it looked as if Ben would be able to come right up to him—but in the last few feet the Golden alien seemed to have heard something, for he turned about, still holding the stuff he had been eating. His oval, olive eyes looked down into Ben's.

For a second the eyes stared. Then the javelin came up like a club and the alien threw himself at Ben. The rifle in Ben's hands exploded, as if it had a mind of its own, and the grayish lump of edible material went bouncing and rolling aside as the alien sprawled at Ben's feet, the top of the golden skull blown off.

Ben reached out gingerly with the barrel of his rifle and attempted to lever the body over on its back. It turned more easily than Ben expected, as if it could not weigh much more than Ben, himself, for all its size. Possibly the long bones of its tall frame were hollow like a bird's bones—but that could be investigated later if there was a chance. Right now, Ben snatched up the javelin weapon the other had dropped.

He examined it feverishly. It had a color and sheen like dark metal. There was the javelin-like point at the front end, a raised ridge like a ring about halfway back from the point, where the big golden hand had held it. It was heavy and hard, in spite of its slimness, but somehow not with the hardness of metal. Ben fumbled in his pocket, got out the dissecting knife, and unwrapped it. He took the knife and made an attempt to cut into the ring-area of the rod. The surface resisted for a moment, then the blade bit in and a part of the ring as well as about six inches of the rod peeled up like a splinter from a piece of wood.

Ben looked at the cross-section of the ring, where the knife had cut into it. He could see plainly that it was simply a raised part of the material of which the rod was made and that the rod itself had been stained to give it the color it appeared to have on the surface. Little dark threads of the stain made ragged the lower edge of penetration of the coloring into the color of the rod's pale substance.

Ben glanced around him. Here in this half-ruined building he was shielded from view by the walls that still stood. He dropped on one knee by the dead body, looking even larger than in life, stretched out flat on the bluish surface that had been used for the building's flooring, and took the knife to the ruined skull. But before he could begin the rough dissection he had in mind, his hand was arrested by the distant sounds of gunshots.

He snatched up the cloth, rewrapped the knife, and picked up the rifle along with the javelin. He headed out of the ruined building at a run in the direction from which the sound of shooting came. It was the short, rapid bark of the half-guns he heard—there had been half a dozen more of those besides the ones he and Walt had taken from the open gun rack in his office.

He had tried to keep an idea of direction in his mind as he had been following the alien he had shot. Now, as well as he could judge, the sound of shooting seemed to be coming from back where the phase ship was. He went in that direction as fast as he was able.

It did not seem such a long way back, but he was forced to stop twice to rest. After that first burst of firing, there had been no sound; and as he broke at last into the little clearing where the ship lay, it was empty.

At that moment there was a new burst of firing and a distant sound of shouting not far off among the buildings to Ben's right. He spun about and headed in that direction. The firing was stilled, but the sounds of human voices, rising to shouts at times, were like a beacon guiding him. He came around the curve of a gray tower, finally, and came upon Ralph Egan, half-gun in hand, stooping over the body of one of the Golden aliens.

Ben pounded up to halt before him. Ralph had just picked up the dead alien's javelin. He stared at Ben. Ben opened his mouth to speak, found he was too out of breath for words, and instead snatched the javelin out of Ralph's grasp. Tucking the other javelin and the rifle under his arm, he examined the weapon he had just taken from Ralph. It looked identical with the one he himself had been carrying, but it was more a metal-weight and feel, and the ring on this one moved.

"Where are they?" he snapped at Ralph, as his wind returned.

Ralph pointed ahead between the buildings.

Ben ran on, hearing Ralph behind him. He burst out from between two of the buildings and found himself in a little, bowl-shaped open area, midway between a dozen men from the ship at his left and five aliens at his right. One of the aliens was down. The other four had apparently just emerged from the buildings on their side of the open area. They stopped now and looked at the downed alien and the humans, only seventy or eighty feet away. One of them whipped up his javelin and a thin silver line arced toward the humans, but fell short by a dozen feet.

"Don't shoot!" shouted Ben, beginning to run toward the men. But Walt, in the lead of them, was already firing, and a second later the rest followed his example. The tall golden bodies tumbled.

"Damn you!" gasped Ben, running up between them and the aliens. "Don't shoot, I said!"

They stared at him. Across a couple of yards of distance, Walt's eyes stared straight into his.

"Look out!" shouted somebody behind Walt. "One's still coming!"

Ben turned to see one of the fallen aliens, trailing a broken leg, crawling forward at them with his javelin still clutched in one hand. A shot rang out and the alien dropped flat, unmoving.

Ben spun back to face them.

"Put your guns down!" he snarled. "That's an order!"

He glared at them. Several of those standing back slowly and reluctantly lowered their half-guns to the earth. Walt and Coop as well as some others behind Walt did not.

"That one was still coming at us," muttered Coop, rebelliously.

"Of course he was still coming!" snapped Ben. "That's instinct in them, to attack anything that looks like an enemy. But that's all it is—instinct. They've regressed. They're like animals—can't you see that? Most of those weapons of theirs are just carved imitations of the real thing. Just sticks. Look!"

He threw at Coop both the javelin he had cut into and the one he had taken from Ralph Egan. They bounced off Coop's chest and fell to the ground. Coop bent down to pick them up and compare them curiously. He and the others let their guns drop. Walt had not moved.

"If they're animals," said Walt, calmly, "they're dangerous animals."

"We'll decide about that later," said Ben.

He became suddenly aware that Walt still held his half-gun in such a way that the muzzle was pointing forward, hip high, aimed in Ben's general direction. And the hunting rifle in his own hands hung half-ready and nearly aimed at Walt. Across the two yards of distance between them they stared at each other. There was no expression at all on Walt's face.

Ben waited. The group around Coop behind Walt were all occupied now in examining the two javelins Ben had thrown at Coop. They did not see what was going on between Walt and Ben, but in a second someone among them would notice, and then there would be no backing down quietly for either Walt or himself. Walt's gun could go off now, apparently by accident, and while some of those behind the big man might suspect, the damage would be done—

Walt lowered his gun while Ben was still in midthought; and Ben with an inward sigh of relief let his rifle sag also in his grasp, so that its muzzle pointed earthwards.

"Let's get everybody back to the ship," said Ben.

"There's an alien body back aways I want carried to the ship for dissection, and I think we better discuss the situation here in conference in my office. Things are a good deal different than we suspected."

"Yes sir," said Walt.

They returned to the ship. None of the Golden People attacked them on the way back, and the body of the alien they brought back with them for dissection was sealed in a canvas freeze-sack outside the ship until Ben could get to work at it. For there was something to be done first, a sad job that took precedence over everything else.

This was the burial of Burt Sullivan, Kirk Walish, and John Edlung, the first of the dead of the phase ship to be put down under alien soil with ordinary rites. Burt Sullivan had been listed in Ben's files as a Catholic, Kirk was down as Lutheran, and John Edlung had nothing at all in the blank where religion was supposed to be entered. When Ben came out to read the burial service over them with all the ship's company standing around, he saw another, smaller—in fact, cat-size—grave had been dug not far from the two human ones that were themselves only a dozen yards or so from the ship.

He made no comment. If the restless and lonely ghost of Sprockets was within range of his voice, it would do him neither harm nor good to hear words of a nondenomination burial service read over him. Ben read the words steadily. He felt drained by exhaustion, emotional as well as physical, and the phrases he spoke seemed to have little reality to him. He could not think that they had won any kind of victory. He could think only of John Edlung. John had been right, clairvoyantly right, in his belief that he would never live to see Earth again; and now he was dead, only because he had happened to be standing beside a man who spoke and invited the alien lightning. —But maybe that belief of John's had caused him to make some small gesture that invited it, too.

□ CHAPTER 11 □

"WE'LL GO HOME," said Ben.

It was a week since their landing on the Golden People's world, a week since he had known that he must say these words and still he had to nerve himself to say them. A little sigh went through the group of senior officers sitting in his office as he spoke. They—Nora, Lee and Coop, with Walt as the only possible exception—had been like all the rest aboard ship, longing for the day when they could turn the phase ship and their thoughts Earthward, once more. Their dreams of home were all bright dreams.

It was different with Ben. To turn back toward Earth, for him, was to turn back to face the judgment of law for what he had done in stealing the phase ship and kidnaping its crew. Trial—probably a general court-martial—certainly a long term of imprisonment, and quite possibly execution if a murder charge could be brought on the basis of the deaths among the crew, were what he must be ready to expect. It was a prospect from which anyone could be excused for shrinking; and inside himself Ben was quite ready to shrink—except that if they did not return, and the phase ship brought back no word of new worlds for men, there would have been no point to everything that had been done so far.

There could be no question about their going back, now that they had found what they had come to find.

"For the record in the official log," said Ben, speaking with the harshness he had found successful in hiding any leakage of his emotions into his voice, "I'd like to have your individual reactions to my own belief that we've done what we were sent out to do. Not only this

159

world, but all the worlds the Golden People took from the Gray-furs ought to be habitable by humans. And—going by what we've run into here, the few Golden People left on those worlds won't be any obstacle to colonization." He looked to his left. "Walt?"

"Yes," said Walt—after a slight hesitation. "I agree with you."

"Nora?"

"Yes."

"Lee?"

"Yes."

"Coop?"

"Yes," said Coop. "They won't even come near us now. You don't even have to stand still to keep them from attacking you. They turn away so they don't see you the minute you come into sight."

It was true, thought Ben, grimly. As he had thought, that first day after watching them, the Golden People had degenerated almost to the animal level. The one trait remaining to them was the reflex to attack in the face of any challenge. But that attack, except in the case of the rare, ancient, javelin weapons that still worked slightly, was suicidal, facing the human guns.

It was possible that there was only one fully working alien weapon in the city—the one in the hands of the leader of those attacking the phase ship the first day. The other javelins the humans had seen were little more effective than flashlights with dying batteries, or they were carved imitations of the real thing. And the aliens carrying them were equally reduced in effectiveness. They had attacked the phase ship and looted it, evidently, out of reflex and instinct alone. All the loot they had taken the humans had found dropped and discarded the next day within short distances of the ship.

Since then, following the slaughter of their numbers the first day by Walt and those with him, they had begun to avoid the humans. At first the crew members needed to stand still to keep from triggering the attack reflex in the tall golden bodies. But lately, as Coop said, it was the aliens who turned away at the first chance of meeting.

"They've fallen apart worse than the Gray-furs," said Nora.

That too was true, thought Ben. The Gray-furs had only ceased to develop as a race should. They had been caught and embalmed like an insect in amber, in a pose of fearful flight. They had been frozen in an image of the Conquerable.

The Golden People had been frozen in the far more destructive image of the Conquerors. It was not like amber, but acid, the character in which they had tried to embalm themselves. Friezes and murals on the inner walls of the buildings around the ship hinted at part of the story. The Golden People themselves had been driven from their own ancestral worlds, farther in toward the galaxy's center, by a rotund, furry race that seemed to carry no weapons but yet were superior to the javelin weapons. Hunting for new homes, the Golden People had adopted the character of Conquerors, and after taking over the Gray-fur worlds, could not, or had not been able to, release themselves from those characters again.

Conquerors with nothing more to conquer, they had apparently fragmented as a people, fought with themselves, dwindled in number, and degenerated over the equivalent of a hundred thousand Gray-fur years, until now they were in worse condition than the race they had conquered. Ben felt a coolness like horror inside him at the thought of it. Here were two plain paths to racial death, one taken by the Gray-furs, one by the Golden People—and the human race would need to learn how to chart a path between, like a ship between hidden reefs, to survive.

". . . Soon?" Coop was saying. Ben woke to the fact that the others had been talking while he thought, and now Coop had asked about the time of lifting ship for Earth.

"If Stores are sufficient—" Ben turned to Nora, who nodded.

"Plenty, if we're going to shift straight home," she said. "I can take inventory of the Survival Stores if you want—water, food, and so forth."

"Do that," said Ben. He turned to Lee. "How about the outer airlock door where the bolt from that javelin weapon hit it?"

"It's all right," said Lee. "We've built up the burned-away part with welding rod and we'll have it ground down to make a seal in another day. The hinges are fixed, the operating instruments the Golden People took that first day have all been found. We're set."

He had answered cheerfully, but he did not look directly at Ben as he spoke. In spite of being left in command of the ship, Lee had failed to keep Walt from arming the men and taking them out after the Golden People that first day. The failure had shown, for all to see, that Lee had no real authority. There was no way to give it to him, now. It was a cruel universe, thought Ben, in that sooner or later it put everyone to the test. Walt had been Lee's test—Perhaps, thought Ben, remembering the moment in which he and Walt had stood with guns half aimed, face to face, Walt would end up being his test as well. With an effort Ben shoved that thought from his mind.

"Then there's no reason not to leave in a day or two," he said.

"No," said Walt, now, unexpectedly. They all looked at him. "Provided," he went on evenly, "we want to cut our stay here that short."

Ben eyed this man he had known over half his life, but never fully understood, with a sudden new wariness.

"Our duty," said Ben, "is to get back as soon as possible."

"Yes," said Walt. "That's true. On the other hand, if anyone ever earned the right to this world, we have. But we've spent only one week on it—and if we go now, the chances are we'll never see it again."

He looked around from Ben at the others.

"Never see it again?" said Coop, after a moment, frowning.

Ben opened his mouth and closed it again. At once there had burst on him a suspicion of what Walt was trying to do.

"There won't have been any new phase ships under

construction," Walt was saying calmly to Coop, "seeing ours disappeared the way it did and hasn't been heard from since. When we do get back to Earth, construction and phase ship work'll have to start fresh. Even if they decide to use this ship again, it'll need to be completely overhauled, no doubt with all sorts of changes and new wrinkles added."

"But what's that got to do with us?" asked Coop.

"Just," said Walt, "that by the time the next ship's ready to go out, three—maybe five—years'll have gone by. And by that time there'll be a surplus of new, young, specially trained astronauts ready to man it. The way this ship was intended to be manned in the first place. Nobody on this ship can ever reasonably hope to go beyond the solar system again in his lifetime."

Walt stopped talking. All the time he had been speaking, he had never lifted his voice above its normal tones, and the quietness of his speech had made what he said doubly effective.

"But what can we do about it?" asked Lee, finally, a little hoarsely.

"I think we ought to stay awhile," said Walt. His eyes were not directly on Ben, but Ben felt that the words had a special direction toward him. "I think we owe ourselves that much—to learn about this world we've found. In fact—" Walt seemed to think for a moment, "it's not an impossible thought that we might want to do something more. Set up permanent quarters here, residences, and some of us stay behind while the others go back . . . when they do. Possession may not be ninetenths of the law, but it certainly gives us a claim. And it seems to me we've earned a claim, at the cost of seven lives out of twenty-four, to find these worlds."

It was well argued. Over the months those aboard the phase ship had come to identify themselves with it, and with the worlds they were then searching for and now had found. The idea that what they had discovered might be forever barred to them, while men and probably women, who had not even been with them would follow the path they had blazed among the stars, had its effect. At the same time that effect hid the fact that the argument was not actually aimed at them. Its true target was Ben, himself, the one person aboard who could actually do something about the phase ship staying on the Golden People's world—if he should be so tempted.

And, for a moment, Ben could not deny to himself that he was tempted. The possibilities Walt's words suggested leaped into being in Ben's active mind like a series of bright pictures. If a permanent settlement was made upon this world where the phase ship now sat, he could remain behind with those who stayed while others went back. Not only that, but those who returned, in bargaining for recognition of their claims to these worlds, could also bargain for forgiveness for Ben himself. Of course, the rest aboard the phase ship did not yet know what Ben had done to them—but, weighing his crimes, once they knew them, in balance with the fact that he had made them part-owners of fourteen valuable worlds should surely win him some measure of their forgiveness.

Even if they would not fight for a pardon back on Earth for him, he could at least stay here and be safe, one of the founders of the new human society that would be springing up on here and on the other Golden Worlds— The bright series of pictures disintegrated like the dreams they were. Of course he could not do any such thing.

He had not struggled with this race of men and women with whom he so deeply longed to fit in, even while he despaired of ever fitting in with them, without learning that they shared his own faults—in a lesser degree, perhaps, but still they shared them. Like him, if there was a chance of doing things wrong, they would do them. He had learned long ago that only the selfless individual could be trusted to see a situation clearheadedly and carry it through to the end. Anyone who let selfish desires intrude developed a blind spot in the area of his selfishness, and on such blind spots plans were wrecked.

And Walt had selfish reasons for wanting the ship to stay. That much was plain. Ben, himself, on the other hand was selfless—not out of any particular virtue in

him, but because nothing he could ever do would make
him one of those around him. The one way he could
reach through the barrier of his outsiderness and touch
other men and women of the world on which he had
been born was to give them this new living space the
way he had planned to do. If he failed in this, what
good would it do him to extend the number of years in
his own life, here, on a world far from home? Better
facing a death sentence back on Earth than living on
here, knowing his one worthwhile effort had foundered
and failed because he was afraid to face the conse-
quences of his own actions.

"Those seven lives you talk about, Walt," he said, as
acidly as he could, "weren't lost in an attempt to make
the rest of us rich, but to find living room for a world
full of nations bursting at the seams and ready to explode into nuclear war.—And we aren't exactly free-
lance prospectors, either, but members of one of the
armed services of a country who paid for the ship that
brought us here and the very clothes we wore while
coming."

Out of the corners of his eyes he examined the faces
of the other three in the office and thought he saw his
words strike with good effect.

"We're under orders—more specifically," he went
on, "everyone on this ship is under my orders. And my
orders are that we keep faith with the world that sent us
out by getting back to it as quickly as possible with the
news of what we've found here."

Even as Ben said it, the last sentence struck him as
pompous, and to keep it from lingering in the ears of
those he was talking to, he hastily scraped back his
chair and got to his feet. Forced into it, the others rose
also.

"That's all, then," he said. "Everybody get to work."

They filed out. As the door closed behind Coop, who
was last to leave, Ben sat down in his chair behind the
desk again. But barely a couple of minutes thought
brought him to his feet once more.

He crossed his office and stepped out through the
door into the corridor on the men's side of the ship.

There was no one in the corridor and all the staterooms were either empty or had closed doors. With the ship on surface, most of the off-duty people spent as much of their free time outside as possible. That was good. Any change from routine aboard ship was a cause for comment—and it was a change of routine for Ben to go calling on any crew member who was not sick or incapacitated.

He went down the corridor and knocked on Walt's stateroom door.

"Come in," said Walt's voice. Ben stepped through the door, closing it behind him. Walt was lying, fully clothed, on his back on his bunk. Like the golden alien Ben had shot, stretched out Walt looked enormous, too big for the bunk he occupied.

"Ben," said Walt, looking at him briefly and then looking back up at the curving underside of the ship's hull, close above his face.

"I thought I ought to explain something," said Ben, standing over him. "I didn't mean to imply your suggestion of setting up residence here was completely reprehensible." Even as he said the words, he hated himself for the lie implied in them, but too much was at stake here to quibble over implied lies.

"Of course," said Walt, without removing his gaze from the ceiling. "I understood."

"It's our duty to go back," said Ben. "That commits us."

"Yes," said Walt.

"If it wasn't for that—but everyone aboard wants to get home."

"Do you?" said Walt.

"Why—yes," said Ben. "Don't you?"

"No," answered Walt. He was still watching the ceiling overhead. "I've had a number of years of the animals back there." His voice was perfectly calm. "At least the animals we've had aboard the ship here are clean animals. Maybe if we started a new colony here with them, it'd stay a clean colony."

Ben stood looking at him.

"I didn't know you thought that way," said Ben, at last.

"Didn't you?" said Walt, without altering his voice or the direction of his gaze.

"No," said Ben.

"That's because you still think you can make something out of them," said Walt. "Sooner or later you have to give that up. You make something beautiful for them and they take it out and use it to hit other animals over the head with. It's no use—self-protection's what you come to in the end. You'll come to it, too."

"No," said Ben.

There was a moment of silence that grew longer and longer. Then Walt sighed.

"It's too bad, Ben," he said. "You were the one human being I knew."

"Thank you," said Ben. He reached back and put his hand on the knob of the stateroom door. "I'll be going, then."

"All right," said Walt, closing his eyes. "Will you make sure that door latches when you close it? I'm going to take a little nap."

"I will," said Ben. He went out. Outside in the corridor, he stood for a moment, mentally running over a blueprint of the operating equipment of the ship. He turned and went back to his office. He unlocked the arms rack there, took down all the Weyerlander half-guns and locked them in the office safe. Then he went out through the door into the corridor on the women's side of the ship.

He stepped off sixteen feet and stopped to examine the blank metal wall on his right, beyond which was the equipment of Calculation Section, and specifically the tape deck of the memory tank. All the other equipment in the Sections could be sabotaged only at the cost of making the phase ship permanently unable to shift. Deprived of the reels of tape in the memory tank, it could still shift—it just would not be able to find its way back to where it had been previously.

When they had changed the tape decks before shifting into the area of these worlds the Golden People had taken over, Lee had required several hours to dismantle the memory tank and get at the reels. But he had gone at it from inside the Computation Section. Someone bent only on destruction could cut or blow his way through this outer wall, and the tape decks would be the first part of the memory tank he would reach.

Of course the important tapes—the original ones with the records of their shifts out from Earth that would be needed to show them the way home—were still in his office safe. Ben turned, walked on down the corridor and turned in through the door opposite the lounge leading into Observation Section.

"Yes sir?" said Ralph Egan, looking up surprised. He was on duty alone here with the ship grounded, and he had one of the cameras half-apart, working on it.

"You're senior officer in Observation now, aren't you?" said Ben, staring a little at him. The personality of Kirk Walish had so dominated this Section that Ben had forgotten who would replace him in authority here.

"Why, yes," said Ralph, a little shadow crossing his thin, youngish face. It was remarkable how everyone missed Kirk, thought Ben. Sprockets, too, had left a hole in the atmosphere.

"Then I've got a question for you," Ben said. "You'll need the original tapes to find our way back to Earth—we all know that. But even without them you could get closer to home than we are now—you could work us into the stellar neighborhood of the Sun, couldn't you?"

"Well . . ." Ralph frowned. "It'd be a pretty big neighborhood."

"But for example—?"

"Well," said Ralph, wiping his hands on a waste cloth absent-mindedly. "We know we're some sixteen thousand light-years in toward Galactic Center from the area where the Sun is. We could begin by moving out in a straight line, more or less, for sixteen thousand light-years and then trying to correct for what we estimate we made in movement off direct line to Galactic Center, during our trip in from Polaris. Oh, we could make a stab at it. But we couldn't hope to come closer than a thousand light-years—unless some fantastic, lucky error happened to land us within viewing distance of the Sun. And the odds against that—" he hesitated, then gave up. "They're impossible."

"Never mind," said Ben. "I want us to try it. This will be a chance to find out just how far we can go solely on observation and calculation. When you admit yourself stuck, I'll break out the original tapes and we'll calculate our way home from wherever we happen to be then. But let's see how close we can come without them."

Ralph's face lit up with sudden enthusiasm for the idea.

"Say," he said, "that would be something to try, wouldn't it?"

"Yes," said Ben. "I'll see that everyone else is notified." He turned and went up through the two other empty Sections and back into his office. He closed the door to it behind him with a small measure of satisfaction. The tapes with the information that would alone bring them home to Earth were secure, for the present at least, in his safe under lock and explosive booby trap. And the excitement of heading for home should make everyone on board unresponsive to any suggestion by Walt that they do anything else, for the present.

At the same time he did not underestimate Walt. The man's mind was such that it was literally impossible to estimate in advance what he might do. Nor would a lack of courage make him hesitate in carrying out whatever decision he might make. Now that it was too late, Ben thought of a hundred different indications, small things said or done by Walt, that should have been warnings that Walt was slipping over the mental line. It was plain that Walt's loneliness and differences from ordinary people had become, by tiny degrees, a mania. Ben had recognized the possibility of such a slipping in himself, on occasion, when long hours of work and insufficient sleep had filled the world with a gray fog of fatigue.

He should never have allowed Walt to be one of those aboard the phase ship when he tricked it and its

crew off the surface of Earth. Subjecting Walt to this
final strain had probably been the straw to break the
camel's back of his sanity. Unsparingly, Ben reproached
himself. In the final analysis he, himself, was responsible.

But, as the ship finally lifted two days later and began shifting homeward, it was without any sign of trouble from Walt. The enthusiasm of everyone on being
headed back to Earth, the excitement of seeing how
close to it they could come without having to fall back
on the tapes of the voyage out—these things together
made a climate in which trouble was not likely to flour-
ish.

Experimentally, they began by shifting directly outward from Galactic Center for sixteen thousand light-
years to a theoretical point referred to as Estimate
Earth. When they had finally corrected down their
shifts to arrive at that particular destination, they found
as they had expected nothing but empty space, surrounded by an unfamiliar wilderness of stars. From
then on they began a three-dimensional—actually four-
dimensional if you included the temporal involvement
of star movements—version of a standard spiral search
pattern. The three-dimensional version could be likened
to the winding up of a length of string into a ball; where
the thickness of the string was the sphere of "observable" space, close to a hundred light-years in diameter
with the phase ship at its center, within which the Sun
or some other familiar star could be positively identified
by the instruments in Observation.

They proceeded in shifts equal to the radius of their
observable space, or for fifty light-years at a time. This
was equal to half the diameter of the string, and progress was slow for all that—. Expressed in miles—the
figures they dealt with were huge. But the fact that their
chances of finding a familiar star by this method were
almost no chance at all gave some indication of the size
of space itself. Nevertheless, it was interesting and in-
structive to try.

Sooner or later if phase ships began to move between

the stars in any numbers, thought Ben, methods of location and navigation would have to be developed that did
not require the memory tanks—though these would
probably always be useful.

But meanwhile, those aboard the ship were becoming
restive. The human, like his draft animal the horse,
tends to become more eager to be home the closer he
approaches his dwelling place. The day came when Ben
sat alone in his office, frowning at the latest estimate of
the search pattern's progress during the next five-day
period before him. Ralph Egan's opinion was that the
Sun of Earth was within less than a thousand light-years
of them—but it could be within less than five hundred
light-years and they could search this way for the rest of
their lifetimes without finding it. On the other hand,
they could feed the route they had taken since replacing
tapes to Computation, replace the new tapes with the
original ones with their data, and the phase ship would
be home in less than three days, and possibly as little
time as ten hours.

But putting the original tapes in the memory tank
would make them vulnerable to destruction by Walt. It
was the tapes, Ben was sure, that Walt's overstrained
mind had fastened on as a means of stopping the phase
ship from returning to Earth. Once in the tank, a
quarter-inch corridor panel of aluminum alloy would
not protect them; and with the original tapes destroyed,
they would be left with the replacement tapes and no
place to go but back to the worlds of the Golden People.

Ben drummed with his fingertips on the desk top. He
could arbitrarily arrest Walt and order him confined
until they landed on Earth. But then he would either
have to give the crew his reason that he believed Walt
was mentally unbalanced or refuse to give any reason at
all. Either course would look strange to the rest of the
crew, and Walt had probably already made plans to
turn any such unusual behavior on Ben's part to his advantage. Ben remembered how Walt had always been
obeyed by the others aboard in spite of the fact he made
no great effort at command. There was something about

Walt's sheer contempt and indifference to whether he was believed or not that made his lightest statement sound like gospel.

What if he tried to confine Walt and Walt claimed that it was Ben who was going insane and this desire to lock up Walt proved it? Faced with a choice, the crew would of course obey their true commander—or would they? Nora was not the only one who had at times spoken to Ben about getting more sleep. Harmless warnings, but—the point was, thought Ben drumming restlessly on his desk top again, in dealing with Walt, he had to assume that Walt could out-think him—had already out-thought him.

The conversation that day in Walt's cabin had been, innocent as it sounded, a declaration of war. Ben knew enough about Walt to understand that. Walt had made plans to keep them from ever going back to Earth; and as long as Ben did not know what they were, he could not take the chance of exposing the tape decks that alone could get them home.

He had put things off this long with the attempt to navigate home without the taped information, hoping that some stroke of luck, some miracle would intervene. But now time had run out.

He got up, went over to the safe, and opened it. Inside were the racked rifles, the pile of half-guns from the office rack, and in a corner, the filing cabinet that held the booby-trapped tape decks. He turned to the bottom of the rifle rack, opened a drawer there, took out a short-barreled .38 caliber revolver, and loaded its six chambers.

He put the revolver into his pocket, left and locked the safe, and went across from his office to the dispensary to take a hypodermic syringe from one of the glass-fronted cabinets in the drug room. He filled the syringe from a small, clear-glass container of sodium pentothal and carried them both back into his office. He laid syringe and container on top of his desk. He took the gun from his pocket and laid it beside them. After a second, he changed his mind, took the revolver, and put it down in the lowest right-hand drawer of his desk—but left the drawer open.

He sat down at his desk, punched the intercom to connect him with the Sections where Walt was on duty, and spoke.

"Captain Bone?"

There was a slight pause and then the steady tones of Walt's voice answered.

"Yes sir?"

Ben paused. The sound of his voice from the intercom in front of Walt would be reaching the ears of all those on duty in the three Sections. There would be no hushing up what Ben intended to do so far as the phase ship was concerned.

"I'm going to have the tapes now in the memory bank replaced with the original deck," said Ben, "so that the ship can proceed home from here as quickly as possible. Will you put a stop to the search pattern, call Captain Ruiz to take over in Sections and begin work on the memory bank, and come here to my office, yourself, to help me get the tape decks from the safe?"

There was the slightest of hesitations.

"Right away, sir," said Walt. Ben let go of the key under his forefinger and the intercom connection was broken.

Ben waited. More than a minute or two went by—and then there was a knock, not at the door from Control Section, but from the corridor door on the men's side of the ship.

"Come in," said Ben.

Walt opened the door and stepped inside, closing the door behind him. Standing with his back to the door, he loomed in the small office in his white coveralls, his long arms hanging relaxed on either side of him in their loose sleeves, the powerful fingers of the left hand slightly flexed, those of the right half-curled, with the broad back of that hand toward Ben. Ben stood up behind the desk.

"Walt," he said. "before I take the tapes out of the safe I'm going to give you an injection, and I want you to go back into my bedroom here and lie down on the bed. The injection will make you sleep and I'll give you others in the next ten hours to three days it takes us to get back and down on the surface of Earth."

He stopped speaking. Walt looked back at him calmly, but without stirring from his position by the door.

"That's an order, Walt," said Ben. He found himself staring at the still face before him. It seemed completely sane, completely unchanged. It was incredible that this man that Ben had known over the years could have altered so much without showing the smallest sign of it. It seemed unthinkable that it should not be possible, even now, to reason with Walt—to talk him back from that far, high, bitter land into which he had wandered, from which all other men and women looked like animals. For a moment, Ben felt doubt sweeping him. Perhaps he had been wrong about Walt from the moment they stood facing each other, holding guns, on the Golden People's world.

Walt's lips twisted suddenly in a small, wry smile.

"All right, Ben," he said. "If you want me to."

Ben felt the breath leak out of him in relief—and for the first time became conscious of the fact that he had been holding it.

"Good—" he began, glancing down at the desk top as he reached out to pick up the hypodermic syringe. A flicker of movement, seen out of the corner of his eye, made him look up.

Walt's feet had not moved, but he was flinging his right arm outward and upward toward Ben. Sliding out of the sleeve of that arm like a hidden knife into the hand of a knife-thrower was the slim length of one of the javelin weapons of the Golden People.

Ben took an automatic step backward and tripped on the desk chair behind him. He dropped into the chair to keep from falling and ducked down behind the desk, reaching into the open drawer for the revolver there.

The lashing discharge roared above him, hammering on the surface of the desk as he ducked below it. Ben had his hand on the revolver in the drawer now. He tilted its barrel up, shooting through the wooden desk at Walt. The revolver bucked in his hand. He kept pulling the trigger, aiming by guess and instinct through the desk.

He checked his finger with one round still left in the gun. The room seemed full of smoke. The alien weapon was silent. Walt must be waiting for a clear shot at him. Ben thought—I'll stand up for one clear shot anyway. If he kills me, I've got to take him with me. Lee can figure out how to get the tapes out of the safe without blowing them up. He thumbed back the hammer and stood up.

The office was not full of smoke. It had been only dust from the bullet-hammered wood of the desk, though there was a black burn from the alien weapon directly across the desk top. Walt had fallen beside the door, which was now open—all the doors were open, with people pushing into the room.

Ben laid the revolver numbly on the desk top. The surface there was warm against the side of his hand as he laid the gun down. Nora was among those coming into the room.

"Nora," he said, hoarsely, "help me get him to the dispensary."

He came around the desk, and with more hands than was necessary helping, they carried the still figure of Walt into the dispensary and laid him down on the white table on which Polly Neigh's leg had been amputated. Ben closed the door upon all but Nora and bent to examine Walt.

But Walt was dead.

Ben was surprised at himself. He felt remote, untouched. He had expected some strong reaction, but the body on the table could have been a wax showman's figure for all the emotion it evoked in him.

"Take care of things here," he said to Nora.

He went back to the office and got the tape deck out of the safe. He handed them over to Lee. He was aware of Lee's strained, white face staring at him, but the sight did not affect him. It was as if he saw Lee through glass. He felt strangely outside himself, watching himself move and act. He got out the official ship's log, and sat down to the blackened desk top to write up a full account of what had happened.

He was just about finished with this—there would be statements to be taken from the crew members who had come in to find him standing, gun in hand, over Walt's body, but impartial authorities could take care of it once they were down on Earth—when Coop came in to tell him that the original tape deck was in. It turned out they were less than eight hundred light-years from home. They would be shifting down to surface in six hours. Ben hardly heard him.

Shortly after that Nora came into the office—for what reason was not exactly clear to Ben. He had finished the log by that time and he found himself, surprisingly, talking volubly to Nora about Walt, almost babbling.

"Even in college, as an undergraduate," he found himself saying, "they knew Walt had great talent . . ." He noticed a pile of things on top of a filing cabinet. "What's that?"

"Walt's personal things," said Nora. "You told Coop to get them."

"Did I?" said Ben. He could not remember. He went to look through the pile, and found something unusual. "Walt's personal log," he said. "It shouldn't have been in his room. It ought to have been in its locker with the others in the Special Stores room."

He took the personal logbook and carried it back to sit down with it at his desk. Nora followed him. He could feel her standing at his left elbow, looking down over his shoulder at the book as he opened it. He riffled through the pages. They were all blank. That would be like Walt—contemptuous of any need to put a record of his days down on paper in order to remember them. Nothing written anywhere in all that barren expanse of white paper—no, wait.

On one of the pages near the front, there were three inked lines in Walt's neat, up-and-down handwriting. Ben read the lines but his mind seemed to slide over them without understanding. He frowned and tried again—they were poetry, he even recognized them.

They were from Tennyson's *Idylls of the King*. The last part, titled *The Passing of Arthur*—there, now the words made sense to Ben's blurring eyes. He could almost hear Walt's voice, deep in the empty silence of his stateroom, murmuring them over as Walt's fingers wrote them down . . .

> *"I found Him in the shining of the stars,*
> *I marked Him in the flowering of His fields,*
> *But in His ways with men I find Him not—"*

The book began to shake in Ben's hand, uncontrollably. To stop the shaking, he closed the book and laid it away on the desk. He rose to his feet, trying to make his voice light.

"Did I tell you," he said, turning to Nora, "we were in high school together—" His voice suddenly stuck in his throat. He moved his lips, but not a sound came out of his straining throat. The world was breaking up around him—the universe was breaking up around him. Nora was in front of him. He reached out, panic-stricken, and felt his arms close around her.

"Nora—" he croaked. Her arms were holding him, and somehow her lips were against his. Her hands were touching him, stroking him, patting him gently.

"Dear Ben," she was saying now in his ear. "Dear Ben . . ." He clung to her, drowning in darkness, as if she was the one plank of safety in an ocean of fear and loss. Walt was dead—dead—and he, Ben, had killed him. That unquenchable torch of a mind, that one brother-light burning far off but clear above the smoky, guttering lamps of lesser minds. He had killed it, because he was too limited, too stupid, to figure out a way to save it from itself. Guilt clutched at him with giant hands, striving to drag him down, and he clung for his life to Nora.

But then he was not simply clinging to her. With the breaking of his self-control, rampaged forth all the damned-up emotion and instinct held back through months of loneliness and celibacy. His lips were searching hers hungrily—and then, like the invention of a bad playwright, came the sound of a knock and the opening of a door.

"Sir," said the sound of Coop's voice, "ready on the first shift to Earth—oh!"

It was ridiculous. It was unbearable. It was melodrama and buffoonery in the face of life and death. Coop was already starting to duck back out of the room, but the damage had been done. Ben and Nora had already, automatically, let go of each other.

"Wait. I'll come," said Ben, harshly. He turned and walked around the other end of the desk, unable to look Nora in the eye, and followed Coop into the Control Section.

When he came back after the shift, Nora of course was gone. The room seemed unnatural and empty. He sat down behind his desk and abruptly realized that he had nothing to do any more, but wait for the next shift. After all these months he sat with nothing to do but wait for the descent onto Earth and the arrest waiting for him there. Arrest—judgment—retribution. And he had killed his oldest, if not his only friend, and had not even been able to retain a little human dignity afterwards.

Ben began to laugh bitterly. It was too much—he had had everything stripped away from him. But as he laughed the bitterness drained away as he began to imagine how it must have looked to Coop, and all at once he was simply laughing at himself with no bitterness left. He continued to laugh, but silently, until he was laughed out. Finally, he sobered.

Astonishingly, he felt empty and greatly relieved. Somehow the laughter had drained him of everything— embarrassment, guilt, even the apprehension that had been growing inside him ever since he had decided on the Golden People's world that they must return now to Earth and—in his case—to the justice that could be expected there.

He felt strangely indifferent now to the fate waiting for him, and almost content.

☐ CHAPTER 12 ☐

THEY MOVED THE phase ship into matching orbit above the installation they had left, nearly nine months before, and a hundred and fifty miles up. Ben, listening over the ship's phone on his office desk, heard Coop put in a coded call, using the recognition signal they had used between ship and installation back when they all had been on the ground, making preliminary tests of communications.

There was no answer. Coop signaled again. The receiver hummed and broke into a scrambled voice signal from below.

"Will you quit it, Charlie?" whined a voice out of the scrambler unit's slightly tinny voicebox. "I told you to stop fooling around and playing games on this frequency. I'm on duty, you want to get me hung up?"

"This is Phase Ship Mark III!" snarled the voice of Coop—there seemed to be something oddly familiar about that snarl to Ben's ears, but at the moment he could not place it. "Do you read me, Ground One? This is Phase Ship Mark III in stationary orbit—"

"Come on, Charlie—"

"Let me talk to him!" snapped Ben, momentarily roused out of his mood of empty resignation. He punched to connect his phone to the Communications circuit. "This is Brigadier General Benjamin Shore! Who is that down there?"

"T5 Gerald Hopkins, sir, Station—" the voice broke off. "Who?" It had gone up in pitch. "*Who* did you say you were?"

"Take over, Coop," said Ben, and broke the connec-

179

tion. From here to ground, the procedure would be routine.

——But it was not. After some confusion, the ground station informed Coop that the phase ship was not to land at the installation from which it had taken off, but to proceed to a similar matching orbit above Oldroyd Space Base, an entirely new installation unfamiliar to those aboard the ship and located south of Philadelphia. There they would wait for the signal to land.

The signal did not come for another two hours. Evidently Oldroyd Space Base, whatever that was, was in no hurry to get them down, thought Ben. Well, he was in no hurry himself. When they were finally signaled down, Oldroyd Space Base turned out to be a large bare expanse of concrete with buildings off to one side and a good deal of mobile weaponry in place around the edges of the concrete.

As the phase ship settled on the ground, the mobile weaponry closed in on her, visible in the screen on Ben's desk. Ben heard the airlock doors opening and the rush of the crew to the outside, but he himself stayed where he was. He had put back on the same clothes he had worn nine months before when the ship had first lifted——heavy shirt, slacks, and leather jacket. He had the ship's official log ready on his desk to be handed over when they came for him. Now would be the time to don his uniform——if he had a uniform. But he had none, and anyway, back here on earth with the voyage over, a General's stars would look ridiculous on him. He had never really been a General; and only for the months in space had he been a ship's commander.

He had half-hoped that Nora would show up before leaving the ship with the rest. She had not, however; and in his new indifference to his future, he did not know if he was truly sorry she had not come, or not. At best, a last meeting with her could only, in the long run, be uncomfortable for both of them. It was unlikely that they would be seeing each other again, though Nora could not know that. And anything she might say, she would probably remember with distaste and discomfort later on, when the publicity about his trial would leave her in no doubt about his sins and his true character. Ben sat waiting, and after a while the door nearest the airlock corridor was opened and a thickset middle-aged Major in an Air Force blue uniform, but with a golden circle on the jacket's right breast pocket, put his head into the office.

"General Shore?" the Major asked, hesitantly.

"Yes," said Ben. The Major looked relieved and came in, followed by a young Lieutenant and two enlisted men with sidearms and half-guns. The Major and the Lieutenant were also wearing sidearms.

"You're to come with us, sir," said the Major. "I'm Major Green. This is Lieutenant Wheald." Ben stood up behind the desk and the Lieutenant held the door open for Ben to pass through first.

"The ship's log," said Ben, indicating the heavy black-bound volume on the desk.

"Oh, yes—I'll take that," said the Major, scooping it up. "Go ahead, sir."

They went out. Outside, the two enlisted men and the two officers hemmed him in. As they emerged from the airlock, Ben saw that a tarpaulin-like cover was being hastily stretched over the phase ship, and that enough weaponry was in position already around it to fight a small war. The Major led Ben through the tanks and rocket-launchers and across the concrete to a small military plane with strangely massive jets in the trailing edges of the short wings.

"Inside, sir," said the Major. They boarded the plane, leaving the bright April morning outside; and Ben, in spite of his feeling of detachment, felt a slight pang. There was no telling if he would get a chance to breath the open air on Earth, again. There were only six seats in the passenger compartment of the plane and one was occupied. Ben took the window one of a pair of seats on the right and the Major sat down next to him.

Ben had expected the plane to taxi away from the weapon-crowded area to get room to take off. But outside the window next to him, the heavy jet motor set in the wing there rotated solemnly until it hung facing the ground, and began to operate. They went straight up like a balloon. The plane must be one of the newer models of VTOL—Vertical Takeoff and Landing craft.

The Major moved beside him and the Major's sidearm dug into Ben's side. He shifted and the Major muttered something, loosening the belt holding the weapon and hauling the holstered sidearm across his thick waist to his other side.

"No danger up here, of course," the Major said, with a half-apologetic smile to Ben.

"Of course," said Ben, dryly. With two half-guns and three revolvers at his back, there could hardly be any danger of his doing anything contrary to the wishes of the Major and his group.

"Cigarette, sir?" said the Major, proffering an open pack.

"Thanks," said Ben. "I don't smoke."

"Do you mind if I—"

"Go ahead, go ahead," said Ben, almost testily. It was rather overdoing it, catering to the prisoner's wishes this way. Ben wanted to snap out that he had not been condemned, yet.

"Thank you, General. —It's been a scramble," said the Major, lighting up with obvious relief. "With so many private industry satellites up, some company's radar was bound to pick you up before we could get you down and out of sight. But we'll have you safely under wraps, now, before the news hits the streets."

"Yes," said Ben, bleakly. Of course, the news services would have a holiday with a notorious criminal like himself. He wanted to ask the Major if the phase ship's lifting had actually set nuclear bombs to falling around the world, but he could imagine the major staring at him and answering something like—"*You should know!*" The landscape reeling by a few thousand feet below the plane showed no scars of destruction.

"Somebody said—" Ben turned to see the Major looking at him with an incalculable expression that could be either ghoulish horror or hero worship, "you lost a third of your personnel aboard the phase ship?"

"Robert Scott lost all of his party in 1912 trying to

reach the South Pole!" snapped Ben. Snubbed, the Major fell silent.

They slid in over Washington at perhaps five thousand feet, rotated the jets in the wings once more and began to descend vertically toward the five-sided, horizontally layered shape of the Pentagon. They were dropping toward the central courtyard. Amazingly, as they came close, a good-sized area of the courtyard surface sank down and slid aside, revealing a dark opening into which the plane descended. The thunder of the jets, even through the shell of the plane, in the confined space of the shaft below ground level, was deafening. Eventually they touched surface, and the noise ceased.

"This way, sir."

The Major and the rest of the armed escort took Ben off along echoing underground corridors, onto a small railway car for a short tunnel ride and through other corridors into a suite of rooms where three-dimensional photographic murals behind curving glass windows gave an illusion of being above ground. The floors were carpeted and the furniture was solidly comfortable, including a small kitchen area with refrigerator and electric stove. Meals, however, turned out to be sent in, in the more orthodox fashion of keeping prisoners. A tech sergeant wheeled in a table with breakfast almost as soon as Ben was inside the suite.

"There'll be a lot of people coming to see you as soon as things are scheduled," said the Major, leaving Ben alone with the breakfast table and the tech sergeant. But for the first half day, no one came. Ben spent the time reading the magazines on the coffee table in the living room of the suite—he was astonished to find himself literally hungry for the printed word. He read news stories on the concern about overpopulation and the food supply, on something called the Chantry Guild and organizations known as "marching societies"—all new titles to him—with the absorption of someone who has been away for twenty years. However, by midafternoon the Major's prophecy began to come true.

The first visitor was another tech sergeant with an officer's dress uniform, which he proceeded to fit with a tailor's skill to Ben's tall, lean body. They were making him pretty for the trial, thought Ben with distaste. Then came two officers with a stenographer to ask questions about the trip of the phase ship. These had barely gone when a short, slim, young-looking Major with somewhat the same incisive tone and manner Kirk Walish had possessed showed up, identifying himself as Ben's defense counsel. Ben was required to go over the whole story of the voyage again with him. The defense counsel—his name was Jameson, Major Alan Jameson—listened with a hard, incredulous stare that made Ben wonder whether perhaps Jameson would not have been more at home in the prosecutor's role than on the prisoner's side.

"My God!" Jameson interrupted, when Ben got to the part about his decision to go and look at the worlds the Golden People had taken from the Gray-furs. "You mean you decided to go close to those planets, after what you'd learned from the Gray-furs?"

"Inhabitable planets were too scarce not to," said Ben, "But didn't you read all this in the ship's log?"

"Some of it," said Jameson. "Everybody wants to get their hands on that log. But what I read didn't give me a picture anything like it does hearing it from you. The log reads like a statistical report. You must have ice water in your veins!"

Ben felt a small guilty glow of pride at that. It was not true, of course—but he had hoped from the beginning of the voyage that the crew would think of him as someone with ice water in his veins. By this time the crew knew better, but it was something at least to have this Adjutant General's Department officer think of him that way. Ben began to entertain kinder thoughts of Major Jameson. He went on with his story.

Major Jameson heard him through without further comment until the end then proceeded to inform Ben, who had only the smallest notion of such things, how the court-martial would take place. There was a preliminary list of some thirty-seven charges against Ben—

Jameson reeled them off—ranging from Ben's abandonment of the installation in his charge without proper authority, through his taking the phase ship and such diverse charges as those of responsibility for the deaths in the crew and misappropriation and misuse of government equipment. The list might be increased before trial time, but would probably be cut. Jameson went on with matters of court-martial procedure. To Ben, who admittedly was unqualified to judge, it sounded as if his defense counsel was more interested in stage directions than in meeting the charges. The uneasy feeling this gave rise to encouraged Ben when Jameson was done to ask a question he might otherwise not have asked.

"What do you think my chances are?"

Jameson stared at him hard for a moment.

"What do *you* think your chances are?" he retorted.

"Not good," confessed Ben.

"Glad to hear it," said Jameson sharply. "A general court-martial's not a laughing matter—never a laughing matter. As a matter of fact—" his tone softened somewhat, "I think we've got pretty good answers to most of the charges here." He tapped the list on the coffee table between them. "There's just one point that has me really worried—"

"My taking the phase ship and the people on her," said Ben gloomily.

"No, no," said Jameson, impatiently. "That's ancient history. They won't be digging into that again. No, it's the deaths—and particularly the death of Captain Walter Bone. The other deaths are all justifiable under the circumstances, and anyone would expect a few. But after all, Bone was a Nobel Prize winner, and you shot him down with your own hand. Moreover there's nothing in the official log of complaint against him before the day you killed him—"

"He wasn't responsible," said Ben. The words came out rather grimly. The death of Walt still sat heavily on Ben's conscience.

"Are you a psychiatrist?" snapped Jameson.

"Of course not," said Ben.

"Then don't go venturing an opinion like that in the

court-martial or we *will* be in trouble. I'll be going over the most important of the possible questions and your answers with you in the next day or so—there'll be time enough for that." Jameson gathered up his papers and took off.

The next forty-eight hours were a wild flurry of Jameson and of other officers wanting statements, usually under oath and signed, about some incident or part of the phase ship's voyage. Ben's uniform had been finally fitted and delivered and he wore it self-consciously during these interviews, aware of the lone gold star on each shoulder. At the end of this time, Jameson told him that the court-martial was set for 9:00 A.M. of the morning of the next day.

Ben had trouble sleeping that night, dreaming wildly of somehow escaping from a firing squad and stealing the phase ship to take to the stars once more. But after his early breakfast a visitor came who was the last man Ben had expected to see—in fact he had largely forgotten Marsh Otam.

Marsh was still forty pounds overweight, still with his face lined by worry wrinkles, but looking eager and cheerful. He was carrying a light brown-leather briefcase.

"Marsh!" said Ben. Marsh pumped Ben's hand, sat down with the briefcase in his lap, and suggested that Ben pick up the phone in the kitchen area of the suite and order drinks—something Ben had not realized that he could do.

"Well," said Marsh, almost shyly, when they were seated with the briefcase between them on the coffee table. "You did it, Ben. It happened, just the way you said it would."

Ben stared at him sharply. But there was no mistaking the expression of the face before him this time. He knew Marsh too well to misinterpret a gaze of ghoulish interest. It was pure, unadulterated admiration he was observing in the look Marsh was giving him.

"What happened?" said Ben sharply.

"The international tension," said Marsh. "It collapsed—just as soon as word got out you'd gone. Everybody was scared to death at first—but it made them all sort of huddle together and join ranks. Then, when you didn't come back, the scaredness leaked out of them."

"How fast did they expect the phase ship back?" asked Ben, startled.

"Well, when you didn't come by Christmas . . ." said Marsh, almost apologetically.

"They gave us up for dead. Is that it?"

"Well . . . they were starting to rewrite the U.N. charter about that time . . ." said Marsh, "and then the President's death—"

"Death?" Sharp on the shock of hearing this, came the revelation to Ben that he had been unconsciously counting on at least a friendly attitude from the White House to help him with his trial. Now, with the former Vice-President in the executive office . . . a man Ben had had no dealings with and whose name he barely knew . . .

"Heart," Marsh was saying, with a slight uneasy twitch of the fingers toward the heart under his own chest layers of excess fat. He had gone on talking without noticing Ben's sudden thoughtfulness. "Of course there were changes. —But the point is, when you came back like this, everybody went wild. They're still going wild for that matter. Look here—"

Eagerly, he unlatched his briefcase and pulled out editions of the *News* and the *Star* from late yesterday and this morning's *Post*.

"You ought to see the foreign—particularly the English papers," he said, thrusting the pages of newsprint into Ben's hand. "But I didn't have time to pick up anything but the local papers on the way here this morning. Take a look at them."

Ben took the top paper and stared at it. He was rewarded with a three column cut of a picture of his own face—from a photo taken eight years before. It seemed to him he had looked much younger eight years ago.

Below the picture was a "profile" of him—character and personal history. He winced as he read. According

to this he was "enigmatic," a man "of many talents."
How could they expect their readers to swallow such
obvious attempts to talk him up into something larger
than human? The front pages of all three papers were
full of such stuff. There were also news stories reporting
"the scars of alien weapons" on the hull of the phase
ship, and an anonymous but reportedly reliable source
was quoted to the effect that only Ben and one other
member of the crew had returned alive.

On the other hand, there were some sensible speculations quoted in an interview with qualified scientists,
concerning the possible implications of the phase ship's
voyage and return. However, most of it was guess and
nonsense. Ben shoved the papers aside.

"There's some mail here, too, for you," Marsh was
saying eagerly. "Just the cream of the cream of it, so to
speak. You've got half a mailroom full already and
more coming in every hour over at the Pentagon. These
were some of the important letters in the first bunch
that came in."

He deposited two bundles of envelopes, each with a
rubber band holding it together, on the coffee table.
Ben picked up one bundle and saw that the long envelope on top had the name of someone he had never
heard of in the return address top corner, and below it
were the words *Office of the President* above *AdCo
Corporation* and a New York address. He had never
heard of the AdCo Corporation.

"That bunch is business letters," said Marsh. Ben
dropped them back onto the coffee table. "The others
are personal."

Ben removed the rubber band and went through the
stack. To his astonishment, they were all from eminent
people, personally congratulating him on the trip of the
phase ship and the reported fact that he had found habitable worlds. Nearly all were signed by men whose
names Ben recognized, although he had never met their
owners. Most were from people in the scientific fields,
but they included among the exceptions letters from two
ex-Presidents of the United States.

This was an entirely different matter from the overblown and momentary publicity of the newspaper front page. Ben realized with a sudden, guilty start that he was actually well on the way to being famous. He would not believe it—even with these letters in front of his eyes he could not believe it was to him they had been addressed and written. *General Benjamin Shore: Dear General: I must tell you how deeply I . . .* and so forth.

Outside and apparently out of step as he had always been with the people around him, Ben had dreamed of doing something solid for the human race he belonged to, but with which he could not seem to communicate. That was what had been behind the building of the phase ship. It had never occurred to him to foster the wild hope that the something solid he did would be recognized and credit given him for doing it.

Now that it was here before him, he drew back from it in his mind. He distrusted it. There must be a joker in the deck somewhere.

Marsh coughed. Raising his eyes, Ben saw the other man looking literally sly. Marsh was holding one more letter.

"And this," said Marsh, "by special delivery."

Ben took it suspiciously. It had no stamp, although it was sealed, and he did not recognize the handwriting, although it looked vaguely familiar, as if he had seen it once or twice before, and it was the sort of hand written by a woman—his heart gave an unexpected lurch. He tore the envelope open and unfolded the single sheet of paper within.

Dear Ben:
I didn't know you weren't with the rest of us until they had hurried us all away from the ship. Now they say I can't see you because I am supposed to be one of the witnesses at your court-martial. I can't even write you without the risk that my letter will be opened and read by someone. But I thought of

*Marsh Otam and got in touch with him. He says he
will give this letter to you personally when he sees
you.*

*You have to know that everyone who was on the
ship with you feels the same way about what you did.
It was one of the bravest and most wonderful things
that history has ever seen, and no one who was in the
ship could miss knowing this, any more than they
could miss knowing what a great and courageous
leader you were for all of us. They will all be testifying to that fact at your court-martial.*

*Marsh has promised he will help me see you as
soon as it's possible, which he says will probably be
tomorrow, some time after your court-martial is over.
I will be waiting for you, then.*

                                    Nora.

Ben automatically refolded the letter, put it into its
envelope and the envelope into an inside pocket of his
uniform jacket. These words of Nora's, coming on top
of the letters from people of reputation, were having a
profound effect on him. Long, long ago, he had given
up any hope of any escape from his personal loneliness
and his position among men as an outsider. Now, when
he least expected it, acceptance and even love were
being made possible to him.

It was typical of the ironies that had dogged him
since he was old enough to recognize the fact that he
did not think like most people, that these things should
have come to him now, on the eve of his court-martial.

Marsh, apparently raised by the situation to a near-
telepathic ability to interpret the expressions that must
have passed over Ben's face on reading Nora's letter,
plunged into the question of the court-martial, himself.

"You know," he said, lowering his voice evidently
without realizing it, "there was a hearing held right after
you left with the phase ship. So you shouldn't have to
worry about that part at your trial."

"Hearing?" echoed Ben, numbly.

"That's why I was able to visit you, like this," said
Marsh. "The findings of the hearing will be read into

the court-martial record—neither I, nor anybody else will have to testify over again. And the findings cleared you com—"

"Wait a minute," said Ben, coming alert. He remembered now how Jameson had dismissed the charge of taking the phase ship and the people aboard her, as ancient history. "What hearing?"

"Why, there had to be a hearing after the ship and all of you disappeared," said Marsh. He looked Ben almost defiantly in the eye. "The word of the takeoff was bound to leak out. In a world ready to blow, our government couldn't let the mistaken notion get around that you'd taken off under anything less than strict orders to do it. —Particularly since you got away without anyone noticing it on radar. Of course, I couldn't testify to personal knowledge of your orders, but Sven Holmgren—you recognize the name?"

"No," said Ben.

"He'd been—" Marsh's gaze still dared Ben to accuse him of anything, "secretly appointed to a new Cabinet post by the late President. He'd been appointed Secretary of Space, the month before you took off, though no one knew it until the hearing. He was able to testify, and besides that, to show a rough draft in his own handwriting of the order he had coded into the Presidential message I brought you that day—the order that sent you up into space."

Ben stared at him. But Marsh's gaze did not waver.

"What happened," asked Ben, "to the copy of the message I sent back with you?"

"Oh, it was produced at the hearing," said Marsh. "It helped to back up Holmgren's handwritten draft—anybody could see the two were identical." He stopped and sat watching Ben.

"Yes . . ." said Ben, deep in thought.

"I thought you would," said Marsh, smiling with a smile that invited Ben to smile along with him. "That's already taken care of. And all the other charges just deal with things that happened on your trip. So, you see there's no need to worry about the court-martial."

He was so eager, he was so sure that everything was

taken care of, that Ben, sinking back into the bleakness of despair, could not bring himself to break the bubble. He could not make himself tell Marsh now that it was not the matter of taking the phase ship, but the matter of Walt's death that was the charge most likely to condemn him at the trial.

CHAPTER 13

SHORTLY AFTER, THEY were interrupted by the arrival of Jameson, and Marsh had to leave. He left behind the letters, and Ben tucked them absent-mindedly, those he had read and those unread, into a dresser drawer in the bedroom. Jameson barely had time to go over some of the more important points of testimony for the last time.

"I'm hoping not to have to expose you to questioning at all," Jameson said. "We'll see how things go." The armed guard was already at the door—four half-gun-bearing military policemen and a Lieutenant with holstered sidearm. They went back through the same echoing corridors and rode the same underground railcar, then ascended into a corridor where daylight flooded through first-floor windows.

They crossed a narrow courtyard. The morning was cool and bright, but damp-aired from rain that must have fallen recently, to judge by the wet grass alongside the water-darkened sidewalks. They entered a further corridor and went along it to an escalator that took them up three more floors.

It was not yet nine o'clock. They were forced to wait in a large, square-windowed room set up Spartan fashion as a lounge, with ashtrays and straight-backed folding chairs.

"When can we go in?" Jameson demanded of a passing Captain.

"Soon," was the answer. "They're not done setting up all the tables and chairs in there, yet. They cleared it yesterday to wax the floor." Ben felt a strange twinge of indignation that waxing a floor should take precedence over the court-martial of a man facing capital among other charges. Standing, with the sunlight coming hot upon him through the window alongside, he half-dozed from a sort of emotional exhaustion.

He was roused by the approach of a gray-haired bear of a man wearing a Lieutenant General's uniform in Air Force blue. There was the same gold circle on the breast pocket of his jacket that Ben had noticed on the Major who had escorted him off the phase ship.

"Chief of Staff, Space Arm, General Sven Holmgren," Jameson was introducing him, with politeness if no grace.

"I'll see you later," said Holmgren, shook hands and went off.

Eventually they were allowed into the brightly sunlit trial room. Ben took his seat at one of the smaller tables with Jameson and the Captain who was his assistant, facing the long table with the windows behind the eight empty seats where the members of the court would be sitting. Then the members of the court were entering, and they were all rising in the room, except the armed guards back against the wall, behind Ben, who were already on their feet. The court seated itself, the rest of them were seated, and the court-martial commenced.

What took place after that came back to Ben later as a series of flashes—bits of incidents out of the whole proceedings. In the bright room, with the voices droning around him, he drifted into a feeling of unreality, a disembodied feeling. To begin with the charges were read, and after that there was a good deal of reading into the record. For the first time Ben heard the conclusions of the hearing held on the disappearance of the phase ship, but got little more out of it than Marsh had already told him. A number of documents made their appearance, including the log of the phase ship and the personal logs of its crew members.

The testimony of the phase ship's crew members began, and Ben came to life briefly when Nora was being questioned by the prosecuting officer. She answered in a calm, level voice, but did not look at Ben.

"You're a registered nurse?" demanded the prosecuting officer.

"Yes sir," answered Nora. —

Later, they got on to the subject of Polly Neigh's accident.

"You assisted General Shore in this amputation, with the help of Lieutenant Sorenson?"

"Yes, I did."

"In spite of the fact you were aware that General Shore was neither a physician, nor a surgeon, nor to your knowledge had any previous experience with such operations?"

"Yes sir."

That was not good. But later, it was Jameson's turn to question her.

"Now, Captain Taller, you've said that you assisted General Shore in this amputation in spite of the fact that you knew he was not ordinarily qualified to perform such surgery. Can you tell us if there was anyone at all on board who *was* qualified to operate?"

"No sir, there was nobody."

"Including yourself?"

"Including myself."

"In your opinion, then, as a registered nurse—in the absence of anyone qualified to amputate this leg and in face of the absolute necessity for such an operation, who was the best unqualified person aboard to perform the surgery?"

"General Shore."

Later yet, it was Coop testifying that he had tried to pull Hans Clogh physically out of the vine clump and make him run for the phase ship on Old Twenty-nine; but that Hans had fought back and to delay would have meant missing the advantage of the path Ben had blown through the herbivores; without which, testified Coop, he and the others could never have reached the ship alive.

"Then you believe," asked Jameson, "that if General Shore had not planted the two lanes of explosives earlier, none of you would have been able to reach the ship, safely?"

"I do," said Coop.

But a little later they came to the subject of Walt and Ben was asked to testify, after all.

"You say, General," said the prosecuting officer "that this brief conversation you had in Captain Bone's stateroom was the first and only indication you had that Captain Bone did not wish to return to Earth?"

Ben had to admit that it was.

"No questions," said Jameson.

Tessie Sorenson was next to be questioned.

"I have here," said Jameson, opening one of the personal logbooks to a location marked with a slip of paper, "an entry made by you the day the phase ship lifted to return to Earth. I will read a portion of it and you tell me if it's correct . . . *Walt came into the ship carrying one of the alien weapons just now and took it into his stateroom. He didn't see me in the Special Stores room here, writing up my log. The way he carried it gave me the shivers—just like one of the Golden People . . .* is this entry correct?"

"Yes sir."

"You saw Captain Bone then with the alien weapon. Weren't you aware that all alien weapons aboard were supposed to be locked up in the keeping of the ship's commander, General Shore?"

"Yes sir."

"But you told no one about Captain Bone's possession of such a weapon?"

"Well, I thought there must be some good reason for his having it—"

"But you told no one?"

"No sir."

Finally, after several more bits of testimony by other crew members, there was Lee Ruiz.

"General Shore had left you in command of the phase ship, yet when you ordered Captain Bone to stay at the ship, he ignored you and led an armed party against the aliens?"

"Yes sir." Lee's face was pale and his voice monotonous. Ben felt sorry for him.

"That's all, Captain Ruiz."

At the adjournment for lunch, which in Ben's case

meant a tray meal for which he had no appetite, Marsh appeared. Marsh was concerned about something to do with Ben's seeing Sven Holmgren, the bear-like Secretary of Space whom Ben had met briefly before the beginning of the proceedings. But Ben was too occupied with what still lay before him in the trial room to concentrate on what Marsh was saying.

After lunch, Ben was back on the stand again. He answered questions as simply and directly as possible, but he found it hard to give an adequate explanation of his reasons for drawing the revolver from the safe and having it ready when he called Walt to his office. No, he had had no intimation that Walt might be armed. He ended by comparing the impulse that had caused him to arm himself to the impulse that had led him to plant the two lanes of explosives on Old Twenty-nine. For some reason this comparison seemed to impress the court favorably.

Then the officers of the court withdrew to consider their verdict, and Ben was forced to sit uneasily counting the minutes until they returned. All his disembodied feeling of detachment was gone now. His mind flickered with the images of his forebodings. He remembered as a boy overhearing a physician friend of his father's telling about the hanging of a murder-rapist during the last war, when the physician had been in the army and on duty on that occasion—and how the executed man's neck had literally stretched when the weight of his body came against the noose. He found himself sweating.

The members of the court were filing back into the room.

"—you will stand," he was being commanded. He pushed back his chair, which squealed noisily, and got awkwardly to his feet. He was aware of Jameson rising beside him, and felt extraordinarily grateful for the companionship.

The verdict was being read off.

". . . As to Charge Number One—not guilty. As to the specification of the Charge—not guilty. As to Charge Number Two—not guilty. As to the specification of the Charge . . ."

The reading voice continued. Finally it came to the end. Not guilty to all charges. Not guilty to the specification of any of the charges. Ben's knees felt weak. He wanted to sit down, but the president of the court had something more to say.

"It is the unanimous opinion of this court that General Shore, during his command of the Phase Ship Mark III, executed his responsibilities not only properly, but in a fashion indicative of the highest courage, determination, intelligence, and gallantry. His conduct is deserving of the greatest praise this court can express, and in so expressing it, the court recommends General Shore to the deepest gratitude of his country and the world."

Abruptly, there was a sudden upwelling of noise. The orderliness of the room dissolved. Jameson was shaking his hand. Somebody else was pounding on his shoulder. He moved in a crowd of bodies to the door and out into a further crowd where hands were everywhere to shake.

"Come on, come on—" said Marsh, who had appeared out of the press of bodies and was busy dragging Ben clear. "Excuse me, gentlemen—" this to the officers around Ben, "General Shore's due at the White House right away. You can't keep the President waiting."

They broke into the open.

"White House?" said Ben.

"Yes," said Marsh, almost running down the corridor, "it wasn't supposed to be until tomorrow, but the press has the White House practically under siege. Word of your court-martial got out. I knew they couldn't keep that quiet. In here."

He led Ben into a waiting elevator where an enlisted man was holding its door open to immobilize the cage at that floor. The door closed behind them. They descended.

"I'll tell you all about it in the car on the way there," said Marsh.

The elevator stopped at last and let them out into a basement garage. They crossed a stretch of bare concrete floor between thick, low pillars and entered a limousine with gray, four-door sedans parked before and behind it. The moment they were in the limousine all the cars started to move.

"Medal of Honor," Marsh explained to Ben. "Don't you remember?"

Ben vaguely remembered someone speaking to him about this—something to the effect of the Medal being voted him almost immediately after his return had become known, before the trial.

They came up a ramp into the sunlight, rolled down a short distance of walled driveway and out into the street. A roar of voices met them, mounting as they emerged. Ben saw that the sidewalks on both sides of the street were choked with people held back by police.

"Nothing planned about this, either," grunted Marsh. "They've been gathering since word got out you were being court-martialed today." His elbow nudged Ben's ribs, his voice spoke in Ben's ear over the noise of the crowd. "Wave—smile at them. It's you they're cheering!"

Ben managed to get some sort of smile onto his face and lifted his hand woodenly. It was all too fantastic to be real. As they left the Pentagon behind, the crowds thinned out and the policemen were no longer to be seen. Soon the demonstration was left behind, and shortly thereafter they were at the gates of the White House.

But here there were more people, and the cheering, once Ben was recognized, started all over again. Their cars passed through the high gates and followed the curve of the drive up to the White House.

There was a swarm of people, half of them with cameras, and some TV equipment, at the North Portico, but Marsh hauled Ben through them, brushing aside the clamoring questions with the answer that General Shore could not stop to talk, now. Inside the entrance, they were met by a Major General. Marsh introduced him, but so hurriedly that Ben did not hear who the officer was—who escorted them on through the building and finally into an office. A slight, harried-looking man in his fifties rose from behind a large desk and came around it on the plum-colored carpet to face them.

"Mr. President," said the Major General, "this is General Shore." Ben was suddenly horror-stricken. He had forgotten the name of this new President standing before him. It had not occurred to Marsh to remind him, and for some reason the Vice-Presidential name of nine months before refused to come to Ben's mind. He knew it as well as he knew his own . . . almost. But for the life of him he could not remember it now.

Here he was shaking hands with the President of his country and he had not the slightest idea who that was. Luckily the words "Mr. President" could cover the necessities of address—but it was an occasion with the quality of nightmare. The President was talking to him, calling him genially by his own name, revealing an amazing knowledge not only of the phase ship project, but of the names of all those who had been with Ben aboard her. Ben answered awkwardly. He thought he saw a hint of exasperation in the Presidential eye at the lack of a minimum social ability in this White House guest. He found himself in desperation laughing too loudly at a really mild pleasantry by the Chief Executive.

"Well, perhaps we should go meet the press and get the ceremony over with," said the President. "The last few days must have been difficult ones for General Shore."

They returned to the portico, where the President introduced him to several members of Congress and a few more officers of General rank wearing Air Force blue without the golden circle emblem Ben had noticed on Holmgren, who it seemed were there as representatives of both Congress and of the service Ben had belonged to when his medal had been voted. This concluded, the President made a short speech into the microphones and TV cameras before him and then presented the Medal of Honor to Ben. Then the chief executive excused himself and left Ben to the press representatives who crowded around him, clamoring their questions. He answered each one as briefly and straightforwardly as he could. No, he did not know his immediate plans. Yes, he might take a vacation. No, he did not know if he was going to transfer to the Space Arm. No, he did not know where the phase ship had been moved to . . . and so on.

Finally Marsh broke in to make his excuses and strong-arm a way through the still-questioning crowd and into the limousine. They escaped.

Once out in the streets again, they drove around until the limousine was no longer attracting attention—Ben noted that the cars escorting them had disappeared.

"We'll go see Sven, now," said Marsh, leaning forward to give instructions to the driver in the front seat. He leaned back and rolled down the window on his side of the car with a sigh of satisfaction. Ben rolled down the window on his side. The warm, bright air of the spring day blew in his face. It was still hardly more than early afternoon. He glanced at his wristwatch—twenty minutes to three.

Marsh sat without saying anything, and Ben himself felt no urge to talk. The silence after everything that had been said this day was blissful. He inhaled deeply of the warm air flowing at him through the open car window, and like a small explosion the thought erupted in his mind that he was free.

Not only free—but cheered by crowds and honored by the President. Never, at any time from the moment he had first determined to steal the phase ship, had he dreamed of anything like this. Even now, there was an unreal feeling to it all—and, the moment he had admitted that much to himself, a cautious corner of his mind began prophesying woe to come, in compensation for all this current good fortune. There would be that joker in the deck somewhere along the line—perhaps it would be in this coming interview with Sven Holmgren, the bearish Secretary of Space.

The limousine turned at last off the street into a ramp leading down below an old, granite-sided office building. They came to a halt in the damp dimness of a basement garage.

"I'll be about an hour," said Marsh to the driver as they left the limousine. Marsh took Ben by the elbow and steered him toward the yellow-lit interior of an elevator.

"Oh—before I forget it again," Marsh said, as the elevator carried them upward, "I made a reservation for you at the Sheraton under the name of Walter Ben. —The hotel knows it's you, but they're good hands at keeping things quiet. Register under your own name and you'd be mobbed. And I've got your civilian clothes upstairs in Sven's office. You can change into those before you leave. Nobody much knows your face yet— pictures in the paper don't always look like the living man—and in leather jacket and slacks you ought to be able to go anywhere without fuss.

The elevator stopped and opened its doors. They stepped out into shining hallways with frosted glass windows hiding offices on either side.

They went down the corridor, passing a number of officers in the blue of Air Force uniforms but with the golden circle on the breast pocket of their jackets that Ben had noticed on the Major who had escorted him off the phase ship. Some of these spoke to Marsh familiarly, and Marsh answered.

"This way," said Marsh at last, ushering Ben into a large and well-furnished reception room. He spoke to the woman behind the small fence-like barricade. "We can go in?"

"Yes," she smiled past Marsh at Ben. "He's been waiting."

They went through an inner door into an office equally large, but somewhat more business-like than the reception room had indicated. Behind the single enormous desk, Holmgren was at work in shirt sleeves. He had just been acknowledging his receptionist's intercom message of their presence.

"Good, come in!" he said, getting to his feet and prowling around the desk over to a filing cabinet. "How about a drink? You probably need one after all this." He touched the filing cabinet, which opened up to reveal itself as a disguised liquor cabinet with a small refrigerator section from which Holmgren extracted ice cubes for their glasses. "Bourbon? Naturally—"

"—Here's what I want to talk to you about, then." he continued, as soon as they were seated in the comfortable chairs in one corner of the office that served as a small refuge from the efficiency of the rest of it. Ben felt the tall glass cold against his hand. "We're going to have a real, working Space Arm—that's what's behind all this Chief of Staff appointment of mine. Anybody able to think as far ahead as the day after tomorrow can see it's got to come."

Ben drank from his glass and found himself liking this Holmgren. Not so much for what he had said so far as for something about his attitude that was a relief after the complexities of the day.

"The President agrees, naturally. But equally naturally, it's the other services bucking it, and Congress needing to be convinced. On paper, I've got it now— that's the result of the President being head of the Armed Services. But in real life—" Holmgren's heavy arm swept out in a gesture, "You see this retread insurance building we're in. I've got the title, a handful of clerical workers, and a few hundred volunteer transplanted officers from the Air Force. A lot of them, ones who weren't too well-satisfied in the Air Force and were looking for someplace better. Your coming back just at the time when you can help us is a godsend."

Ben's painfully acquired awareness of his own nature as a lone wolf and outsider pricked its ears, and he woke abruptly to self-protective awareness.

"Well, I don't know—" he was beginning, when Holmgren surprised him by nodding understandingly before he could finish phrasing his polite doubt about having to do with the new Space Arm.

"Certainly. Certainly, I understand." said Holmgren. "I've looked at your record. I want you, of course, but if you should turn out not to want us, I can't blame you. The most I could offer you would be a drop in rank, anyway. We'll be using navy-type rank when we get organized, and Captain is probably the best I could do for you—which is down to the equivalent of Colonel. But never mind that now. You think it over and give me your decision in a month or two."

"Glad to," said Ben. He took another drink from his glass. It struck him as very obvious that Holmgren did not really want him in the Space Arm, which of course was Holmgren's own baby. Naturally, the other man would not enjoy having as a subordinate an untouchable hero, someone who could do no wrong in the public's eyes. Ben would not have wanted someone like that as an underling either, if he had been in Holmgren's position. On the other hand, Holmgren was wise enough to realize that the publicity he could reap from associating Ben with the Space Arm was worth almost any cost.

Holmgren was continuing to talk. "The point is, your return with the phase ship is just the sort of publicity I need to blast an appropriation out of Congress, so we can start to grow here. You're going to be in the public eye from now on, and you're going to be talking to reporters and TV audiences. You know how big space is and how big an organization and an armed service we're going to need eventually to deal with it—the day's going to come when it'll be bigger than all the rest. But for now—well, there's hardly anybody but me who realizes how lucky you were to get back at all in your little unarmed ship."

It was true, thought Ben with a sudden, cold feeling inside him. The amazing thing was that Holmgren recognized it.

"The point is you brought back information that's been needed, even if no one understands it yet. —Maybe you don't understand it yourself—" Holmgren stared penetratingly at Ben for a second. "If we try to go charging out there like conquerors, the way your Golden People did, we're just inviting someone to clobber us. And we can't go out there with the idea we can run like your Gray-furs, because for us there's no place to run to. —*That* thought probably hadn't occurred to you."

It was the first sour note Holmgren had struck. Ben opened his mouth to say that it had indeed occurred to him, along with a number of other things. Then the humor of a situation in which Holmgren lectured him about outer space struck through to him. He felt himself grinning inwardly, and sat silent.

"So I wanted to have a word with you," said Holmgren. "If you'll just remember to speak up for the Space Arm when the chance crops up, I'll be deeply grateful. And if you decide to come in with us after all, I'd guess you probably wouldn't need to stay a Captain long. And of course there'll be other things open, once we're set up. Military governorships—that sort of thing—on those new worlds. The Democrats will be back in after the next Presidential election, and they've always been space-minded."

He finished his drink abruptly and rose to his feet. Ben rose too, trying to hide the fact that with his last few words Holmgren had lost him completely. Holmgren understanding the middle course that the human race must pursue to survive in space was one thing. Holmgren hinting at the bribe of high office for him was another.

"Well," Holmgren was saying, "I suppose you'll be glad to sneak off to your hotel and call it a day. Marsh knows where your clothes are. Call me any time you're free."

He shook hands briskly and turned back to his desk. In an empty adjoining office where Marsh took him, Ben changed out of his uniform while Marsh chattered cheerfully.

"Tremendous character, isn't he?" said Marsh. "The kind who moves mountains."

"Um," said Ben, noncommittally, pulling on his slacks.

"Well, you'll be spending the next few months spreading the cash around, I suppose," said Marsh, shaking hands with him in farewell after Ben was dressed. Ben looked his surprise. "Your loot—the offers in those business letters I brought you," explained Marsh.

"I didn't read them," confessed Ben.

"My God!" Marsh stood, marveling at him. "Why there must be a million for you in endorsements alone!"

"Oh?" Somehow the thought of money had not until this moment worked its way into Ben's mind. He laughed, a little self-consciously. This was the final touch—this was all it took.

He turned away from Marsh and opened the door from the office they were in.

"Just down the corridor to my left to the elevator?" he asked.

"That's right. And right from where you get out of the elevator on the ground floor. You'll see the street door just in front of you. Step out of it, turn right again, and walk down to the corner. You'll see a cocktail lounge there called William's Place. Don't let anybody direct you any other way," answered Marsh. He was looking sly.

"Why?" asked Ben, seeing the question was expected of him.

"Nora's waiting inside the cocktail lounge for you," said Marsh. "I told her you'd be coming out that way after leaving Sven."

Ben stared at him, turned on his heel, and went out of the office. The door with its frosted glass pane banged shut behind him.

He strode rapidly down the corridor, but as he went, the reaction started to set in and his pace slowed. By the time he had reached the elevator and rung for it his mood had changed completely. He laughed ironically at himself.

Of course Nora was not waiting for him down at the cocktail lounge. Marsh did not know her well enough to understand that. Ben himself, caught up for the moment in the never-never land of cheering crowds and Medals of Honor and offers of military governorships, had for the moment been ready to believe that Nora, too, was to be found at his feet, just waiting to be picked up.

But Nora was not like that, to throw herself into the arms of the hero of the hour. If she had really wished to see him again, she would have come to his office before

aving the phase ship after they landed. All she had
aid to Marsh—the letter she had written to Ben before
he trial—had been to support him in the face of the
harges against him. She would not abandon him while
e was under the ax—she would not have abandoned
ny of the crew in such a situation. But she would
udge, quite rightly, that he no longer needed her moral
upport now that he stood acquitted and with the world
n his hand.

The world in his hand—Ben laughed again to him-
elf, as the elevator stopped before him and he entered
, punching the button marked *M* on the control panel.
he doors slid smoothly closed and the elevator started
own. It was good—a profound relief in a way—to feel
imself back in his old shell of hard-learned cynicism,
olated and apart from the rest of humanity. Looked at
rom the old, reliable point of view, he could see the
rass shining through the silver plate of everything that
ad been thrown at him in the last few hours.

The cheering of the crowds meant nothing. They
vould cheer the central figure of any recent spectacular
vent. He could no doubt have earned as much noise by
oing over Niagara Falls in a barrel. The Medal of
Honor likewise meant little or nothing. Not that the
medal itself was meaningless, but Sven had mentioned,
hadn't he, that the Democrats would be back in office
fter the next Presidential election? Congress had un-
loubtedly had its hand forced by political conditions
nd the clamor of the press. It had had no choice but to
ward Ben the medal—little as it must have cared to
ut the United States' highest military honor to such
se.

As for Sven Holmgren and the Space Arm, almost
ertainly they were doomed to failure. After a few days,
vhen the public interest about the phase ship's return
ad died down, the chances of the necessary appropria-
ions and the necessary addition of dedicated people to
he Space Arm ranks would become almost nonexistent.
Ben had been wise not to respond to the momentary
ure of an appointment as Captain in those ranks—even
hough he recognized now that working for the ad-

vancement of man into space was the one job he woul
have liked to have done.

The elevator hissed to a stop and the doors rolle
back. Ben stepped out and turned right toward th
patch of still-bright afternoon beyond the glass doo
still some distance away.

No, the thing to do was face reality as he had alway
known it. His place was the place of the Outsider, sol
tary and unable to bridge the gap between himself an
any other person in the world. He must remember thi
keep it firmly in mind, and not be pied-pipered bac
into the chase after that damned elusive will-o'-the-wis
of the future, just because a hardheaded, earthboun
politician had seemed miraculously to have grasped th
almost mystic concept of a middle way among the star
A middle road, lying between the paths of conqueror
and the conquerable—possible to the human people be
cause of their inherent contradiction of character, th
fact that they could go both ways at once with no trou
ble at all.

The middle way and—offer a bribe in the next mo
ment. That was what Walt had not been able to under
stand. Any single individual had a whole universe o
possibilities in him. The brutal one would be suddenl
gentle. The coward would unexpectedly fight. The mos
fearful would turn out a hero. Hans would cling in
vine clump. Kirk would attack a giant barehanded. Al
ways, unexpectedly, when you had given up on them
they did the least likely thing. And the whole tribe wen
forward.

Oh, it was there, it was there, thought Ben sourly
The final reward of success, for whoever could brea
his heart for them, keep his eyes fixed on the promise i
them, and put up with the rest of their characters. Bu
his own bit was done. He had served his tour of har
duty and ought to be able now to quit trying to hel
heave the oxcart out of the mud. He had a right now t
leave it to somebody else for a change, settle down t
keeping a comfortable lighthouse somewhere, awa
from the storms. It was just lucky that exposure to th

tinsel elements of fame and success had helped him realize it in time.

Congratulating himself on having finally peeled away the illusions in him down to the hard core of common sense any man must possess to survive, Ben nodded at the blue-uniformed enlisted rifleman on guard at the door, and pushed through it. Outside, the bright late afternoon sun through the warm, clear air was blinding. The steps before him went down a short way, then turned to his right below a stone balustrade, and ran down a dozen more steps to the street.

He turned, his eyes blinking as they adjusted to the sunlight again. Far ahead, down a full length of block past a green newsstand overflowing with magazines and newspapers, he made out the black and white sign of Marsh's improbable promise: *William's Place.*

He headed toward it. The block was one of those long blocks in a hilly section of Washington, sloping downward toward its far end. Halfway there, Ben came up on the newsstand and slowed to look at the newspapers on display.

Shore Receives Award—a subhead below a picture on one of the front pages caught his eye. Was his face to be spread all over so that everyone would recognize him . . . ? He stopped and took a closer look. But it was a group picture showing the portico of the White House and the gathering there just before he had received the medal. He remembered seeing cameras pointed at him, then.

The vendor at the newsstand was staring meaningfully at him. Hastily, Ben bought the paper he was examining and walked on, looking at it.

No, the picture was a general one and his own image among the others was too small and vague for anyone who did not know him to recognize him from it. The story below it was a standard bit of reporting, wedged between another of the accounts of that occult group that seemed to keep appearing in the papers—the Chantry Guild—and a feature story on more marching societies. The main headlines over all this were concerned with a political matter, some international dis-

pute over conflicting claims to Antarctic territory,
which was evidently heating up amongst the U.S., the
Soviet Union, Britain, and a number of other nations.
The present U.S. Secretary of State, a woman named
Mila Kennington, was quoted as saying that while the
United States sought no conflict in this matter, neither
would this country run from trouble by yielding up portions of the Antarctic continent to which our claim was
historically established . . .

The phrasing of her statement was uncomfortably familiar. Ben had heard much the same words applied to
a number of like international situations since he had
been old enough to read the newspapers himself. Something clicked abruptly in the back of his mind.

Of course! Here he had been giving Holmgren credit
for understanding the Middle Way. But actually all the
Space Arm Chief of Staff had been giving him was the
same shopworn line Ben had just read in the paper he
was carrying; the conditioned response of great powers
that *we aren't interested in conquest; but let no one
misinterpret this stand of ours as weakness. We will not
avoid confrontation if confrontation is forced upon us
. . .*" It was essentially the same line that had led to
military and political involvements Ben could remember
in the past.

—And the Space Arm was, after all, a military outfit, wasn't it? Ben stopped in his tracks, then a second
later, began walking automatically on once more, his
mind seething.

How could he have been so blind? Of course, Holmgren was no different from the people Ben had to struggle against in order to get the phase ship out among the
stars in the first place. The thinking of those people had
been inextricably earthbound. Holmgren's was no different. How could the Space Arm Chief of Staff help it,
when he had never been out in interstellar space, never
experienced the universe at first hand as Ben and the
others with him had?

And it was Holmgren who was going to be in control
of the major thrust of man's adventure into the universe, out among all that might be waiting for us there.

He would muck it up. He could not help but muck it up, because he did not really understand the rules as they operated beyond Earth's warm, familiar atmosphere. Under Holmgren, the whole movement into space was headed for confrontation with disaster—disaster for the Earth and all its people.

But what can I do about it, Ben asked himself uneasily? The man doesn't really want me in his organization. The most he offered me was a small position on his staff; and he as good as said he'd shove me upstairs and out, as soon as he could, once I'd got him his publicity and his appropriations. Even if I took him up on joining, it'd be a case of being up against the same sort of thing I was up against in getting the phase ship loose. I'd have to buck everyone else . . . and maybe it would turn out there'd be nothing I could do, after all. . . .

But on the other hand, maybe something could be done, Ben told himself. There were ways of handling people . . . and he did know space, where Holmgren didn't. Holmgren and the rest of his staff would have to take Ben's word for a great many things. Also, there was the fact that right at the moment Ben had the ear of the Congress, which would be voting the appropriations Holmgren needed. If, in the next six months, Ben could plant in Washington heads the idea that he knew best, that he was the one they should really listen to . . . then Holmgren would have trouble later in opposing him openly on crucial points. If, in addition to achieving that much, he could also manage to talk Holmgren now into giving him some post that seemed innocuous, but which Ben himself knew would have to grow in importance and become pivotal to the work of the Space Arm . . .

Authority in the design and construction end would be the ideal thing. Not forgetting authority for Ben to go into space himself with experimental craft . . . yes, he ought to be able to extract that much from Holmgren, holding out the promise of more headlines in the future, the name of starship-hero Shore and the newest projected spacecraft, coupled together in the most romantic of news story traditions. The time to get Holmgren to promise that sort of thing was now, while Ben's stock was at its highest. Then in the next few months Ben could make such a public display of his position with the Space Arm that Holmgren would be embarrassed by any later attempt to withdraw the authority he had conceded earlier.

He could call Holmgren now—right now. Tell Holmgren that he had thought it over, and Space Arm was acceptable to him. Let the other man think that Ben had recognized the possibility of continued personal glory in an important sounding, but actually nondemanding, job with Holmgren's outfit. Then bargain with him immediately for design and construction authority, as a price for accepting the job.

Yes, by God!

Ben looked around for a phone booth. There was none in sight; but it suddenly occurred to him that there would be a pay phone in the cocktail lounge, which was now only a few steps away. He lengthened his stride and turned in the front door under the sign.

Inside, the sudden gloom after the brilliant daylight outside left him half-blinded. He pushed through a little entryway and stepped into what was evidently the lounge, proper. His eyesight clearing, he saw a large shadowy room filled with tables and, just to his left, a phone in an open acoustical booth against one wall. He crossed to it, dropped coins into it and punched for Information.

"Hello?" he said, when a man's voice answered. "I need the phone number of Space Arm Headquarters. Yes, here in Washington."

There was a little wait, while his vision cleared up further. He could almost make out the faces of the people scattered about the tables of the lounge. Information spoke in his ear.

"Yes?" he answered. "All right, I've got it. Thank you."

He hung up, a steady determination filling him. Not while he was still around to stop them would the Holmgrens of this world destroy human hopes for a place among the stars. Grimly punching out the number that